D1453619

THE PINK ROSARY

by

RICARDO MEANS YBARRA

THE PINK ROSARY

by

RICARDO MEANS YBARRA

LATIN AMERICAN LITERARY REVIEW PRESS
SERIES: DISCOVERIES
PITTSBURGH, PENNSYLVANIA

1993

The Latin American Literary Review Press publishes Latin American creative writing under the series title *Discoveries*, and critical works under the series title *Explorations*.

Library of Congress Cataloging-in-Publication Data

Ybarra, Ricardo Means.
    The pink rosary / by Ricardo Means Ybarra.
        p. cm. -- (Discoveries)
    ISBN 0-935480-59-5
    I. Title. II. Series.
PS3575.B37P56   1993
813' .54--dc20   92-35442
                                   CIP

The Pink Rosary may be ordered directly from the publisher:

    Latin American Literary Review Press
    2300 Palmer Street, Pittsburgh, PA 15218
    Tel (412) 351-1477 Fax (412) 351-6831

This project is supported in part by a grant from the National Endowment for the Arts in Washington, D.C., a federal agency.

Acknowledgments

I wish to thank Dr. Yvette E. Miller for making the publication of this novel possible. *Mil gracias* to Brad McWilliams and Jewell Rhodes for their constant support and criticism during those hard early drafts. My inspirational *padrino y madrina*, Benjamin and Helen Saltman. My father, the one whom I can never thank enough—who not only raised two boys, solo, but gave me my old room back when I needed a place to start over. *Mi hijo*, Rafael, who paid no attention to my closed door. And, *mi corazón, mi vida*, Cynthia, who with her love and faith, gave me the encouragement to write.

For Cynthia,
y para mi abuelita Josefina,
que me cuidaba mucho

One

When did it come?"

"What?"

"The telegram? Phone call?" His voice, as tightly wound as an empty pack of cigarettes, sailed past the old Indian out the window and into the kicked-up dust of the road. Another mystery of the Utah desert, he asked himself, or was it the sacred wisdom of Indians? And why don't I know the answer since the old man does? Beto pushed his boots hard against the floorboard of the pickup and kept them there. He always stiffened up when the old man was driving, his long legs bent at the knees. He didn't wonder how the old man got his license or even if he had one: Robert "Beto" Reynolds came from L.A., Silver Lake, to be exact, the edge of downtown and driving. He figured that like the DMV, Indian pacification under the guise of the Department of the Interior, hands out licenses so we'd all feel like citizens, privileged. But it wasn't this Utah canyon bottom they were in or the hills and valleys of Silver Lake and Echo Park that stiffened his legs; it was the other drivers. He looked at the old man driving, two hands high on the wheel. Beto was sure that he knew all about other drivers; after all, he had survived thirty-one years of life in L.A., although he wouldn't think of it as survival. It was more like getting around, knowing how to react on Glendale Boulevard and the intersection of Effie and Alvarado, what streets to take when the Dodger game let out, which nationality tended not to signal before turning. Silver Lake was full of lousy drivers. It was on the border of Echo Park. Some prof at L.A. City College in a night class he'd once taken had called these places microcosms. That was a laugh. He had, in fact, laughed out loud in class. The guy obviously didn't know nothing. Microcosms. Beto knew other drivers because he knew where they came from. Take the professor, for example. He was a paddy, he'd obey the laws. And he'd shown him, hadn't he, got an A in anthropology and didn't do a thing but take the prof on a cruise. Of course he'd borrowed Ray's ride. Beto smiled, realized he was stiff, that his arms were as locked in place as the old man's hands. Ray had made it happen for him, hadn't he? Ramon Cruz. Ray had lent him his '58, but not just any '58. This '58 was Chevy as art. Impala. And Ray was an artist of the power sprayer and lacquer, an auto body man.

The old Indian eased down a slight grade and over the round rocks of a river bed as dry as everything else in Utah summer. He drove so diligently that Beto felt every rock, every round grumble under the slowness of the truck. He tightened his legs so hard now he could feel the veins in his groin extend. "Oh shit," he muttered under his breath. The old man floored the relic of a Utah ranch Ford as the front wheels hit the opposite bank leading out of the river bottom. Beto felt the front bumper plowing into silt and sand, the rear wheels bouncing. Rocks, stones, even boulders, he imagined, were clanging off the bottom of the pickup. He thought of Ray. Wondered if style would have helped as he wished the truck over the top. Instead, what he felt were wheels, rear wheels, digging in.

"Sweet Jesus, old man, cut it," he yelled. It wasn't a weak shout; he knew the old man could hear him but the Indian, a picture of calmness with both hands on the wheel, gazed forward, laid it on, and the powers of Detroit, those lovers of the hidden V, this man's machine, and the Indian's zen-like application of the accelerator were the combination to sink the differential into a layer of pre-Anazasi silt.

"Jesus, Jesus, Jeezuus," he pounded at the metal dashboard.

"We're stuck," the old man said as he turned the motor off, replacing all the noise with a silence that hammered at the metal cab over Beto's head. Beto looked out his window; he wouldn't look at the old man. He felt that if he just stared out the open window the boring calmness of pink rocks and sandstone would release him. The old man was obviously unconcerned as he reached into his pocket for a tightly crumpled package of Red Man. Beto listened to the deliberate unwrapping, the spreading of foil, the fingers in a tight place, and grabbed the old man by the arm before he could bite off a plug, turning him so they were eye to eye in the dry river bed and asked him, "How do you know it's for me?"

"Buchanan had to go to town."

"It's a telegram, then." He released the arm and sat back. The old man bit off a chunk but didn't start to chew: he'd suck on it awhile 'til the juices got thick and filled his jaw. He didn't suck quietly; he was slurping, the sound a kid makes with a straw in a nearly empty glass. Beto listened to the tick of the cooling engine, the settling of rubber into sand, the old man's tongue warbling over tobacco, and decided he'd try it again since now he might be getting through. He'd try not to rush the old man; naked women couldn't rush him anyway, but Beto was in a hurry. He'd been in a hurry ever since this morning when the old man came out to the Gulch, and now it was more than a hurry; it was a rush, a rush to get somewhere, get out of here, go. He'd ask him anyway because he couldn't stop himself.

"How do you know the telegram's for me, old man?"

"Who else could it be for?"

Beto rolled his eyes skyward in a mock gesture and prayed, knowing that God had his own speed and that it never was the same as his, not when he was in a hurry. "God, please let it be for me," he said to the roof of the cab under his breath slowly, so as not to rush Him. "Please, let it be for me. A novena, no, I promise a novena and the stations of the cross and mass three Sundays of the month if it's for me." He touched his hands together hoping the message was slow enough to get through. He turned to the old man again before he got carried away and promised too much. The Indian was looking at him and smiling, the left side of his face round with Red Man.

"Who were you talking to?"

Beto ignored the question, asking, "why did you wait so long to tell me?"

"You were praying, weren't you?" The Indian was grinning and talking and sucking, all at the same time so that his voice came out warbled and lopsided, the sound a car makes with a flat tire on the side of the road. "I thought you knew," he added, chuckling. The tire flapped against the fender now.

"How could I possibly know? You come out first thing in the morning and tell me there's an important message for me, that's all. How would I know something came for me?"

"Talk to your God."

Beto didn't want to discuss it. Anyway, he was concerned about talking to God since the old man had his own crazy ideas about rocks and birds and everything else and he didn't want God to act slow, to debate his request or wonder about the rocks. "I wasn't praying."

The old man grinned even wider than Beto thought possible with that much chew in his jaw. "That's good, keep your mind open, son," the old man warbled.

He sounds just like my grandmother, Beto thought. Dolores, sweet vicious little Dolores María Bernadette Rivera Reynolds.

That's just like something she would say while slurping at her coffee. It struck him that she was everywhere, but would she send a telegram? Who else would send him a telegram? Ray? And if Dolores had sent it, then it couldn't be good news, could it? The old man's grin extended past his eyes into the soft bill of the Giants baseball cap he never went anywhere without as he continued speaking.

"A telegram is like a dream; it comes from somewhere else, doesn't it? And a dream must have a messenger. I saw the dream, son, and came for you."

Beto wasn't too surprised. The old man openly delivered messages from the universe, read his mind and possibly his soul as well. He'd long ago decided that this was coincidence, or peyote, which he was sure the old man chewed along with his Red Man. And Dolores would use a dream, wouldn't she? The old man and Dolores, what a pair: she dreams and he hears her. Dolores floated past the window, all 4 feet 11 inches of her standing in the kitchen, wrapped in her stained yellow housecoat thinking of messages to give him through the old man. She can follow me anywhere, he thought with horror. And what could he do? He couldn't rid himself of her: she'd find him; she'd found the old man, hadn't she?

If the telegram was from the old lady, then was she the answer to his prayers? It was too much. His eyes glazed and he felt his body go slack, but his legs remained stiff, rigored, tight in his boots.

The old man hopped carefully out of the ridiculously sloping vehicle. He surveyed the truck, squatting to get a better look at it, stood up and spit into the river bed. He grinned and joyfully, if not lustily, shouted into the cab loudly enough to shake Beto, "We're gonna have to dig her out, Slim."

Beto muttered, "of course we have to dig her out," but he continued to look through the windshield. At 7:00 a.m. the Utah sky seen through the dusty windshield of a Ford pickup tilting upward looked as blue as the ice in the bottom of an empty glass. "Dreams, messengers, goddamn right we have to dig." He relaxed his legs and hopped out of the truck.

"Here, give me that." Beto took the shovel roughly, rubbed the handle down, eyed the buried tires, the truck resting backwards, indecently comfortable. "You didn't see the telegram or even talk to Buchanan, did you? There might not be a telegram, old man." He forgot dreams, God and Dolores. The pleasure of smoking the old man out for once made Beto revere the beauty of the curved face filling with sand. "Maybe Buchanan just had to go to town early," he added, exuberantly flinging the full shovel so that sand and pebbles clattered like a rusty tailpipe. The old man smiled all the more and spit out a healthy slug that even the dry rocks couldn't immediately absorb.

"Whatever you say, Slim. I'll get brush for the wheels."

"Yeah, you do that," Beto muttered as he stripped off his t-shirt. "But I'm driving us out of here."

The old man laughed and spit. He watched as Beto dug faster than a pothunter in the middle of the night with the batteries going low. Ol' Slim, skinny and lean, he thought, back and arms and legs as thin as any deer leaping a fence, lean as could be, except for his head. Slim had a head of hair that was thick and curly and dark. A good-looking young man, easily the most handsome man around, a thought which made the old man laugh because they were in one of the least populated areas of Utah. They'd be out in no time, he knew, just as he never doubted the arrival of the telegram, and just as six months earlier he knew that Beto would arrive and it would snow a hailstorm in May, and that Mrs. Halloway, finally fertile after ten years of marriage, would give birth to twins. He didn't wonder about it since there was nothing he could do about the things he saw, not that they were visions exactly; they were more like feelings. It was his hands that could see. Part of old age, he figured. Hands still good for something.

Beto laid down the shovel and surveyed the two paths he had dug like runways leading back and under the rear bumper. He had already dug out the rear bumper which had been partially buried in the river bed like the half-exposed femur of a dinosaur. As he had worked he had thought about the telegram. It had to have come from Dolores. She had tracked him down, but then, he had always known she would find him. He'd been here six months. Of course, he thought, he might be ready to move on; it was getting old playing cowboy and the summer was already over, but he didn't know how to leave. What would he say to the Buchanans, friendly enough to take him in. And then he wasn't sure if he really wanted to leave, but he knew that he was leaving now and she had caused it; he knew that it was Lulu. He called Dolores "Lulu" when he wanted to infuriate her. He used it often. He used it now, but it didn't work any magic; it never worked really. He knew he couldn't win with her, not against that mind, "the reptilian brain," he called it, no guilt, all selective memory. "Lulu," he swore at the bumper; damnit, wasn't it her fault that he was digging this relic out and that he was even in Utah in the first place? He'd shown her: he'd had a job for six months and could have stayed longer except for her.

He thought of dreams and messengers again, but what he needed now was brush. He stuffed the brush and weeds the old man had piled next to him under a jacked-up tire. He let the jack down, hurried over to the other side and jacked up that wheel, loading the hole underneath. I'll bet the telegram was at Buchanan's; the old man heard about it in the morning, he told himself. He stepped back and checked both runways for straightness. He didn't care if his work looked good or was right, just that it was efficient enough. He'd already decided that the bank was too steep to go at it from here, that what they needed was a running start, that their chances were better to reverse out and have a try at it again. That was why he had dug the runways. "Hey you, supervisor, help me load some of these rocks in the back," Beto yelled at the old man.

"You want to get some weight over the wheels, huh?"

"Yeah, that's the idea."

"Right. Good idea, son." The old man either called him "Slim" or "Son," but he couldn't determine if they had any significance. Started with "S" is all he could figure. He'd given up on being called Beto, the name Ray had dropped on him when they were kids, the nickname for Robert that made him feel like a Mex, his L.A. *apodo* that Dolores wouldn't use. The old man had his quirks, and even the Buchanans called him "son" at times, which seemed okay because they were old and married, but they usually called him "Bobby" which reminded him again of Dolores. She'd like that.

"I'll sit on the tailgate, then."

Beto looked at the wiry old man who couldn't weigh more than "one-forty" in his bib overalls and said, "I don't think you should do that."

"Don't worry, Slim, I have excellent balance. Did I ever tell you that I was a champion bronc buster?"

"Many times, old man," Beto said tiredly, looking up into a sky that was starting to spread out under yellow oil.

"I haven't ridden something wild in years, but you know, you never forget." The old man was perched happily on the tailgate, his skinny fingers not yet on the metal, the left side of his jaw quiet for a moment. Calls me Slim, Beto thought, looking carefully at the old man who was dressed in bib overalls and a red cotton lumberjack shirt buttoned to the collar. Loose white long johns the color of sandstone poked out at the wrists, curling back on vein-thin wrists. He always dressed the same, whatever the weather, and sweat the same, no matter if they were down in some oven like this canyon or up on Boulder Mountain where it could get as cold as Christmas in August. He wore the same hat too, not a cowboy hat or a black Navajo hat, but a pulled-down-tight, washed-out San Francisco Giants baseball cap with no definition left past the brim, just round and soft. He imagined the old man had found it in a campground; an Indian could pick up a lot of things Beto'd never expect to find out here. Where had he been? What had he seen? Beto couldn't imagine him out in the world, the real world out past these canyons and mesas. They said he was an Indian. "Half-Indian," they sometimes said, which made him an Indian to Beto because who's half of anything? Just like you can't be half Mexican or half white. Who'd believe that in L.A., he thought; your nationality just depends on who you're talking to. The old man was the only Indian he knew, but then he'd never seen any Indians in Utah, around here at least. The only Indians he'd ever seen were down near the Grand Canyon in that shitty town he'd passed through; and they were mostly heavy and wanted to drink, but the old man never drank; he bit a little chaw, like the ranchers, who never could clean off the sides of their trucks for all the spit they slugged. And of course he had that nose, a nose like that Indian on the nickel, so thin and beaked it could wedge a seasoned round of wood. Thin face, thin all over, but not scrawny. The old man was sinewy, strong; Beto knew he could work all day whatever his age. Half Indian, hell, if he was half Indian then Beto could be half Mexican. It just hinged on who was looking at you. He looked at the old man once more, looking at eyes shaded under the floppy brim, eyes as dark as a burned clay pot. "Ready?" he yelled from the cab, engine running, the flies swarming around the smell of oil on his skin.

"Ready," the old man shouted back, but Beto hopped out of the cab and stood with his hand on the door until the old man turned around. "I don't like it."

The old man smiled. "Son, don't worry so much. If you worry too much when you're young you'll have a back like a curved woman."

"Oh Christ," Beto muttered and got back into the truck. He gunned the engine and turned in the seat so his right arm lay along the back under the window, his head cockeyed so he could look out at the rear of the truck and the old man on the tailgate. He knew the old man was grinning, the old fool. "Calls me an old woman; next thing he'll say I'm like Dolores."

"Here goes," Beto shouted and eased down on the gas. The wheels spun slowly for a second, caught in the brush, and then they were out and on the runways he'd dug, the front wheels bouncing in the holes made by the rear tires, and then they were clear. The old man let out a whoop and Beto grinned.

"You did it, old man, now come on up here in front."

"Go on, give it the horses, I'm riding it over the top," the old Indian shouted back.

Beto was out of the cab, stumbling in the riverbed rocks and sand. "Goddamn it now, get offa there."

"Go on, I can handle it." The old man didn't look at all concerned when Beto rattled the tailgate. He felt the top of his cap, rubbed his jaw once and smiled. Beto kicked at a rock and called him a crazy mother and a crazy fuckin' injun but it didn't change the look on the old man's face.

"See any visions, like landing on your head?" he asked as he got back into the cab, but all the old man did was shout, "Give her the guns!" rather exuberantly. "Fuckim," Beto muttered as he gunned the engine and took off slow and steady so as not to bury the front bumper again. When they had cleared the front, he goosed it, and they were over with a bounce, the rear wheels still spinning. He heard the "yahoo" over the engine noise and the clanging of the beat-up pickup, and he felt excited in spite of himself, but when he looked in the rear-view mirror, the tailgate was empty. He slammed on the brakes and ran. He ran back to the old man flat on the road, flat as spilled milk on asphalt, flat as dust waiting for rain, or a frog that hadn't made it across a highway. He scooped him up, wondered that he didn't weigh much, thought the old man was light as a feather, but told himself to stop it. The old Indian might be dead and what would he tell the Buchanans? Shouldn't have let him sucker me, he thought. I always let people sucker me. He tried to get him into the front seat on the driver's side, saw that it was useless, and started around to the other door. He couldn't see the old man's eyes because of the cap; must be some kind of miracle that it was still on, like water that you spin in a pail. He was having a hard time with the door handle and couldn't decide whether he should put the old man down into the pickup bed or on the road again.

"You gonna carry me over the threshold, handsome?" the old man whispered and then let out a whooping laugh.

"Oh sweet *Madre de Dios*," Beto said, and carried him over to the side of the truck. He propped him up above the wheel-well even though he felt like pitching him in the back where he could ride the rest of the way in.

"What a ride," the old man howled. "You should have seen your face. You were as puckered up as a cow flop. Didn't think I'd make it, did you?" He smiled and spit out a good one. Beto watched it hit the dust, amazed that the old man hadn't swallowed it. At least he could've choked a bit.

"Damn. Smells like brakes burning."

"Your brains," Beto replied. He watched as the old man pulled off his cap and rubbed his head. He looked closer; the old man had plenty of hair left, silver grey, but with a large bump showing.

"We'd better get you home." He realized he was worried for the old man. That was some bump.

"The Giants saved me," the old man said as his hands navigated the soft spot, "but I almost made it. I would have, too, but she kicked up her heels there and me with it." He rubbed his hands slowly. "I could've ridden her 'til the bell, but the hands, the hands ain't what they used to be." He was still rubbing them, then he fisted his Giants cap and put it right, carefully.

"You did all right, old man; you showed 'em." But Beto couldn't stop thinking about the old man. What if he'd broken a leg or arm or worse? He remembered when he and his friends had found a bum in the weeds of their hidden valley where the street-cars used to run. Finding bums had been easy at the tracks. Bums, sleeping off a drunk under the eucalyptus trees. They did what they always did when they were together, a bunch of them, a gang, but too young to be a real gang. Goddamn lazy bum. Sleeping in the daytime in their place, their special place. Wake him up. Kick him in the leg, hit him with a dirt clod. And Beto, crazy Beto wanted his hat, wanted the tired old fedora that maybe once had held a feather. Beto had advanced slowly, but the bum was waiting, he wasn't sleeping; he grabbed Beto by the leg and let out a frightened scream that turned the valley that was their own secret place into a long hallway with no doors. And how could he have known that the dirt clod in his fist held a stone until he saw the blood through the dirt that showered the side of the bum's face. Then he was sprinting for home; they were all running, but he ran past being tired so he couldn't feel the tiredness as he ran more. "You hurt him," Ray had said. "Damn right," Beto had answered, "he would've killed me. You saw him; he had it coming to him." But Beto had seen the blood on the old skin, pouring out of the weathered flesh, blood on old skin; it didn't look right. It didn't look good, blood on old skin, and an hour later when he had snuck back and hidden in the bushes under the eucalyptus, he had heard the bum groaning still.

He touched the side of the truck and then the arm of the old man. "You drive, okay?" Beto said and leaned through the passenger's side to flip the key off. "When you're ready to go," Beto added when he was next to the old man again.

"Hey, I'm okay, feel fine. I'll be a little sore in the morning is all." They were both quiet for a moment in the morning heat. The dust had settled and it was still early enough that the pink and rust of the Gulch hadn't whitened under the press of the sun.

"You know, I almost did a complete flip. I forgot to tuck my chin is all. First thing a horse teaches you, tuck your chin." The old man rambled and Beto only half listened. He was staring at the cliff walls, imagining that he was climbing until he found a cave, a hidden overhang. In this overhang were artifacts left behind by the Anasazi: corn, a *mano* and *metate*, bow and arrow, blankets, drawings on the wall, a earthen jug of clear water, paperbacks by King and Ludlum, an Indian maiden in a doeskin bikini. He shook his head.

"I would've stayed on in the circuit." The old man was still talking.

"What circuit?" Beto asked, but he realized after he said it that he should have known.

"Rodeo, but it wasn't much in those days, not like it is now. The Four Corners was all we knew about." The old man leaped off the side of the truck as if he were a much younger man and rummaged under the seat of the cab. He came back with a rumpled, dust-covered but fresh package of Red Man, the Chief on the package cover looking just as serene and somber as when he was behind the shelf in Hall's store in Boulder.

"There's a bottle of Jack Daniels. You wanta snort?" the old man asked.

"I know where to find it." Buchanan, a Jack Mormon, hid bottles everywhere. He didn't like Mrs. Buchanan to know, but everyone in Boulder knew where Buchanan's bottles were, including the missus. There was one inside the rear tire that lay flat in the back of the bed under a piece of rock, and there was always one under the seat, or in the dash. Every evening Buchanan would check on the horses. He'd make an announcement, but he wasn't asking for help and no one offered.

"Did I ever show you that buckle I won?"

"For what?"

"Rodeo, bronc bustin'."

"No, you never showed it to me." He waited, and the old man

waited. Finally he asked. "Really, when was that?"

"1947, I was All Indian. I never showed you that buckle?"

Beto wasn't interested, but he didn't want to hurt the old man's feelings. Besides, he wasn't in such a hurry anymore, and he was more than relieved that there wasn't any blood showing on the old man. Still, he wasn't sure that he could care less about what the old man was rattling on about and he thought rodeos were boring anyway. "No, what'ya mean All Indian?"

"Well, there was All Cowboy and there was All Indian. That was the way they did it in those days. But that was a ride." The old man chuckled and grinned, but didn't make a move to get inside the truck. Instead, he leaned against the side of the pickup with one foot on the running board and propped his arms on the truck bed just like they do at rodeos, and he chewed and spoke, but not in Beto's particular direction.

"That was a ride. I drew a pinto; they called him Paint, of course. Mean crafty pinto, small like a pinto, too, but I mean to tell you that horse knew his business."

"You mean he didn't like to have his *huevos* cinched up."

"They didn't need to do that with some horses, not the pinto. No, he was a horse made for the rodeo, knew exactly what to do, and that pinto didn't like to lose. Best ride of my life and he knowed it." The old man continued to stare wistfully at the rim of the Gulch and the pinion pines that had latched onto the edge.

"Yah, I'll bet, All Indian. What about Mrs. Buchanan, didn't she say anything?"

"She wasn't there."

"Christ, not in '47. I'm talking about this morning."

"I knew what you were talking about." He was fondling his cheek real good now, ready to spit a healthy one. How could he talk with that stuff, Beto wondered. Maybe that was why he always spoke so slowly. He wondered if the old man chewed when he was talking to all the spirits he said were everywhere.

"Come on, let's get going. Here, you drive. I asked you already."

"I don't want to drive. What's the matter with you? You need a drink."

"I don't need a drink and I don't want to drive. Understand, ol' man?"

"Yeah, but I ain't driving."

"Ohhhh," Beto blew out so hard his lips rumbled. He tilted his head back and rotated it. "All right, hop in. I'm driving," he said finally.

Beto drove fast, in third gear when he could, driving like the old man wouldn't.

"You didn't see her, huh?" Beto asked.

"Too early."

"She was hunting eggs?"

"Maybe."

A covey of quail scuttled across the road, topknots angled high, like Prussian cavalrymen at a gallop. Beto didn't brake or ease off the gas; quail were quick. They heard a thud. The quail exploded into the sagebrush, wings leaving a tattoo of air inside the cab.

"Hit one," Beto shouted, his head out the window, foot off the gas.

"A cicada," the old man said. Beto leaned back in and looked at the windshield, saw juice like tobacco spread on the glass, thin fingers reaching for an edge, the black rubber strip.

"Out already."

"Be a day for deerflies too," the old man added.

"Yeah, one helluva hot beautiful day." He looked over. The old man wasn't chomping or sucking now, but a thin line of dribble was seeping down the side of his chin.

"You tired?" the old man asked.

"I didn't sleep well last night."

"The Gulch is too warm for sleep. Coyotes?"

"Naw, I was just thinking too much."

"The owl came to you."

"It wasn't a dream that kept me up. I haven't gotten any telegrams yet, old man." That set the old man to chuckling.

"You don't like your dreams."

"Don't give me that Indian bullshit, sound just like my. . . ." He stopped. Just saying her name worked up a connection and there were already too many connections going on here. You know what you know and you treat it accordingly, don't you? That was the way to get by. But the old man saw things, said there were these other levels, other lives. Horseshit and premonitions. Dolores had premonitions and guilt. Catholic guilt. Lighting her candles in the alcove to St. Teresa at the church. She could have won the state lottery with all the quarters she spent there. And she sucked it all up, didn't she? St. Teresa, the martyr. Premonitions and connections. Take the old man on the tailgate. Shouldn't he have known, felt it in his hands, like he always said? He drove faster; better to drive than to think. Besides, he'd have to see that telegram to believe anything.

They could see the boundaries of Deer Creek Canyon now, a wide stretch where they would cross. A year-round stream and plenty of cottonwoods and then sandstone behind them. That was what they saw from the road: the tops of cottonwoods and the sandstone.

"We're almost there now."

"You don't remember your dreams much, do you?" the old man asked.

"No. It's because I don't dream much and I don't believe in them. It's called the subconscious, things you've seen before. The owl," he added sarcastically. The old man hopped right in.

"Sure you've seen them, in many lives you've seen them, and not all in the past either."

"Say, you'd better put something on that bump on your head. Rodeo's no place for an old man." He didn't respond, which suited Beto fine. This crazy conversation was getting to him.

They crossed the wooden bridge over Deer Creek which flowed slowly in the summer. Beto downshifted into second gear.

"Any trout left in the pool?" he asked. There was a wide pool where the flat sandstone had lipped up, not worn away yet, downstream from the bridge. The pool was better for floating than fishing, but there were trout hiding in the cattails that ringed one side of the pool. They both saw the family at the same time, camping, breakfast smoke low over the fire, a dull green tent, and the father casting into the pool.

"The old one's in there," the old man said.

"He won't catch him."

"Yeah, but he'll see him."

"That'll drive him crazy, and in two more hours his kids will be splashing."

"He's a wise old trout, that one."

"That's the one whose belly you rub?"

"That's the one."

Madre, he thought, they don't come any crazier than this old man. If he were in Echo Park he'd be sleeping in the weeds at the Lake. Rub his hands and he's got a trout, and owls, and pickup trucks like horses. Connections. He's got a world of them.

Beto asked loudly, "why don't you keep a nice fat old trout like that?"

"No,ooooo." The old man chuckled softly, and then spit out the window. "You don't keep a trout like that one."

"You don't?"

"No. Besides, he tells me where the young sweet ones are hiding."

"Good God," Beto snorted out of his nose. "I got to tell you, old man, where I come from they can tell stories, all bullshit. Good stories, but none of them are as crazy as yours, and I've heard some great ones." He noticed that the old man was looking at him intently, hands folded on his lap, back straight, cap on right, tight, and smiling, a gold-filling smile, his eyes almost closing. Beto wondered if the old man's hands were telling him something now, and then he thought of how he'd like to get his own hands on something nice and warm and suckable in L.A., where he'd be riding in style. He leaned back in the seat, one hand on the wheel. Ray's '58. Cruise the Strip, slow like, hit the clubs and listen to some real music: *salsa*, Los Lobos, a little funk—no more of this cowboy shit—and ride around the Lake and chat up the chavalas. He saw Echo Park Lake floating in the sandstone before him, the fountain shooting straight up, blowing spray on the lovers, the grandfathers with kids in the paddle boats, the pushcart popsicle vendors, the mothers feeding the ducks. He saw cars slowing, young girls hanging out, the Hollywood Freeway crossing the mesa up ahead, trucks blowing smoke as they hit their brakes. Echo Park Lake disappeared and they were between the two long mesas that ran up to Boulder Town and Boulder Mountain. White sandstone now, like a bleached lava flow, the red behind them in the canyons.

"You ever see the ocean, old man?" He spoke out the window at the cooler air that was blowing over his arm. He shifted into third even though the road was rougher from here on into Boulder, a washboard. He lightly touched the top of the door with his left hand, noticed the cicada had dried and sloughed off; only a brown stain remained. He waited for the old man to reply, not wanting to rush him.

"Sure. I was in San Francisco, you know, and I saw the Colorado before the dam." He used some kind of Indian name for the Colorado.

Beto spoke. "Well, the Colorado's not the same; you can't see the other side of the ocean." Beto reflected on the Colorado for a moment. "What I was going to tell you was that this is what the bottom of the oceans must look like. You know those shells we find all the time?"

"Yes, I know."

Beto felt confused; he couldn't remember why he had brought up the subject of the ocean. Something he wanted to tell the old man. "You knew this was an ocean?"

"Sure. Covered with water, filled up bigger than a lake." A lake, something he wanted to tell him, but the old man couldn't see the Lake, could he, sewer pit of Echo Park. What was he thinking of? Pine appeared, wedged in cracked sandstone, roots slithering over the smooth surface. Sugar pines and ponderosas. A big ponderosa was around the next bend. As they climbed to the higher altitude of Boulder and the sandstone broke up there would be stands of them. Which came first, old man, he thought to ask him. The cracks or the seeds?

"Who's gonna bring in the herd now that you picked me up?"

"I am."

"You're gonna have to bring them back from the Henry's and up over Boulder Mountain through the Waterpocket Fold. They won't like it."

"I know the way."

"Yeah, hell, any cow could find her way. Hey, wipe your chin. You want my maps? You're not swallowing that stuff, are you?"

"I don't need any maps."

"Well, I'll go back out if there isn't anything for me. Buchanan'll like that. You and me together. Didn't you talk to Buchanan?"

"Buchanan had to go to town." Right, Beto thought, he didn't dream anything; he saw Buchanan leave for Escalante early; only one reason to go to Escalante that early. A telegram. What a wily old fox. They were near Boulder now, the first ranch coming up on their right. With the ranch came the sudden green fields and the stringed wire and cedar poles every eight feet to hold the desert out.

"Morgan bring his herd in?" Beto asked.

"Too early, he'll wait until fall hits." They looked out at forty to fifty browsing cattle behind the wire.

"Why'd he bring these in?"

"The new fella's rentin' his field."

"What'll Morgan do for winter feed?"

"He mowed his fields twice already."

"Someone better tell the new guy how to run cattle."

"He'll figure it out this winter."

"He won't make it then and you know it." Beto was quiet. Ranchers are strange, he thought, only eight ranches here and yet they'd stand back and let a guy run his ranch into the ground. They were distant, but they'd help out any time you needed, always there in an emergency. "He'll figure it out," the old man had said. So that was the way it was: you either figure it out or get the hell out. Let it run its course. Sounded cold, but nothing he could do about it. "He could run them in the canyons. Deer Creek and the Gulch are warm enough and there's plenty of grazing."

"The ranchers don't like the canyons; they lose cattle and it's too dry in the summer."

"But they're not all dry, for crissakes. You know those cows know where the streams and waterholes are better than we do. Besides, I was talking about the winter not the summer, right? No one in Boulder has ever run a herd down in the canyons in winter, have they? Have they?" Beto didn't wait for a response since he was talking too fast. "No one's tried it, but the new guy should, and no one will tell him not to. Buchanan won't say a word. You know why they don't like the canyons. They're afraid of them." The old man didn't look surprised. Then again, he rarely acted surprised.

"Well?" Beto asked.

"Why would they be afraid of the canyons?"

"I'm not sure." Beto was still talking fast. "But I think they're afraid of those little people down there."

"You mean the Anasazi?"

"Not the Anasazi. I thought they were dead and gone? No, not them, you know—the little people, cause all the mischief."

"The Mokis. I thought you didn't believe in them?"

"Of course I don't. You think I believe in the evil eye too, blessings and all that *bruja* shit. The Church is crazy enough. I don't believe it, but maybe they're superstitious. They're Mormons, aren't they? You don't understand them, do you? Jesus, even my grandmother is superstitious. She covers all the bases." Beto thought that maybe the old man hadn't understood the point he was trying to make. He knew that he wasn't making much sense to himself either.

"Well, I'll tell you, the canyons are better digs than the mountain any day," he said in order to ease himself out of the situation.

"So you're getting ready to leave us?"

Beto was shocked at the old man's question. "I never said that, depends on what I've got back at Buchanans."

"You don't have to leave."

"What are you talking about? You don't know nothing yet, old man, and I was just talking about the canyons and mountains."

"Well, you don't have to leave. If you like it so much, why don't you stay?"

"Where? In the canyons?"

"Yes, for you, the canyons."

"Oh, for chrissakes. What are you talking about? Just because your people used to live in them."

"They still do." Beto turned and looked hard at him. He knew
he was serious and that didn't surprise him, but why did the old
Indian have to figure him out now. Why couldn't the old man just
let him slip away as if it were out of his control, and why all this talk
about the canyons? When he next spoke it came out mocking,
sarcastic. "Old ones. You mean like you. All Indian. You're the only
Indian I've ever seen around here and you're a half breed, old man."

The old man didn't get upset. He could have, but then he
decided that this was not the time for it. Besides, he felt too much
anger in the young man, anger much of the time. He wished that he
could help, but he couldn't ask. Asking would not be the right way.
If Beto would just tell him why he must return, that might be the
source of his anger, the old man thought. Hopefully, time would
work on Slim, run its course, and then there would either be the
anger that would eat him up, or there would be the new man. That
was the way it worked. He looked at his own hands, knobby, the
broken knuckles that hurt in the cold. He remembered when he
would wrap those hands around a bottle, and the fists they would
make, grabbing, prodding, senseless hands once. He felt his hands
grow now as if he were a part of the blood in every vein, as if he were
the very life under the thin covering of dust and stained fingernails.

"Someday, son," he said, facing Beto, "you'll meet them, the
old ones. They're still here, everywhere I look, like the smoke
around a campfire."

Beto snorted through his nose again and, stretching slowly,
touched the old man on the shoulder. "You do that, old man, bring
'em to the Lake too. They'll have a great time, fit right in." He smiled,
but he was still angry, angry that the old man could possibly have
guessed that he might want to leave, that he was driving over this
road in hot dust under a sun that hadn't even gotten hot yet, angry
about the cows and this business with the canyons. He floated on
the hostility like the paddle boats floated on oily water at the edge
of Echo Park Lake with no hull visible under the water, and then
they were at the ranch. He made the left turn hard onto a road
smoothed by long use and yearly applications of crushed rock. He
turned with one hand. The road into the Buchanan ranch was long
and narrow, the house set far off, the driveway bordered by cedar

fencing and corrals. He stopped under a cottonwood that dwarfed the house and the barn. Mrs. Buchanan had started coming out of the house when they turned up the road and she was talking before he shut the engine down.

"Bobby, your grandmother took a fall and broke her hip; she's laid up in a hospital. 'Queen of Angels,' it says." She paused. "I'm sorry to tell you this, son." Beto didn't see her. He heard wind, doors closing in the trees, a horse rubbing its neck over a strand of barbed wire, the rain on the mountain noisy as a spider's web in the birch and aspens. He touched his neck and felt wetness: the ocean? spray from the fountain in the middle of Echo Park Lake?

"What?" he asked stupidly.

Mrs. Buchanan dusted her hands, rounded, work-thick hands. The apron billowed flour dust, filled up the open edge of the sky and the flat fields and the old man in the corner of his eyes, almost to the barn. He wished the old man had stuck around, lean old man in shadows at the barn door. He didn't want to talk about her.

"When did it come, Mrs. Buchanan?"

She answered slowly, like everyone from around here did. Beto wondered if that was because they listened to what each other said or because they didn't say much. He never spoke that slow. "This morning. Bill got a call from Escalante (she said 'Escahlahnt') late last night. He was gonna send Sam for the telegram, but went hisself. Sam was gone anyway, took the ol' red pick-up 'fore the sun rose." Beto imagined that the old man had talked to Buchanan in the dark before morning while Mrs. Buchanan was rising; the old man was always up before the sun anyway. Mrs. Buchanan continued speaking. "Sam took off 'fore we could talk to him."

It was a coincidence, Beto decided. He remembered back to the morning, kicking embers with his toes into the re-kindled fire. He had been awake for a long time, half the night, the last half. Then, when he had heard the pickup from a long way off grinding down the grade into the Gulch, he was so tired that he hadn't been very surprised. He had known it was the old man coming as soon as he heard the unmistakable sound of the truck. Not that it was something he had felt before it happened; he didn't believe in that. Wasn't life like a car drive anyway? Anything could happen, what with all the other drivers.

"The old man must have known something was up."

"Yes, I suppose so." Her voice didn't carry acknowledgement or surprise. She was direct and friendly, not too surprised by anything after sixty-five years on ranches. He looked at her, saw a round face under a coil of grey, no glasses, a long-wearing dress, brown shoes, and immense breasts that didn't curve her back any.

"Bill says to pay you up to the end of the month and tell you to take as much time as you need, of course. We're both concerned." Did she say that knowing what he was thinking, knowing that he might not be back, that he might be glad to leave. He looked down at the ground, at a red and black ant working his way over the boot and up to the tongue. He suddenly wanted to get out from under this huge cottonwood, get away from these people who were supposed to be cold and aloof. There were too many people reading his mind and letting him go. He knew Dolores had caused all of this. She couldn't let him be happy. Dolores had to have him back.

"Bill told me to tell you he'd've been here hisself but they was at that auction over in Tropic, that you've got a job here if you come back. Don't worry none about that. Sam'll take care of things as best he can." She knew, but there were no questions. He began to feel the guilt attacking the corners of his eyes. He brushed at the ant with his other boot, pushing it into the laces.

"Thanks, Mrs. Buchanan. You mind if I make a call?"

"Lord, no." She patted her apron down hard. "And don't thank me. You just holler if there's any thing we can do. Get in that house and call the hospital."

Beto wasn't going to call the hospital. He didn't want to talk to her in a hospital bed, hear her complain about the room, the nurses she called "*negras*," the doctors, and how no one understood the pain she had. He didn't want to hear her voice. He'd call Ray. Ray would talk to her. Ray was patient. He even called her "*abuela*," respectfully. Of course, maybe he should; he'd spent almost as much time at Beto's grandmother's when they were kids as at his own home.

"I'm packing a dinner for you right now. You need it. I don't want your grandmother to think we don't feed you, and son, you're as skinny as Sam."

"You don't have to make anything for me, Mrs. Buchanan." He wasn't hungry, but it wouldn't stop her from wrapping the chicken and sandwiches, the huge slice of homemade pie or cookies that she always packed whenever any trip was made.

"Hush. How old is she?" He wouldn't get away without talking.

"Seventy-nine this February."

"Oh my, and it's her hip. Is she healthy?"

He saw Dolores climbing the long stairs at the front of the house on the hillside, Thanksgiving dinners, planting flowers, picking oranges and complaining. "She's a healthy old goat. I mean, uh, yes, she's healthy alright." And tougher than the venison jerky the old man always brought on round-ups, he thought.

Mrs. Buchanan let his comment pass. She didn't surprise too easily. Besides, she was curious. "Is there anyone who can take care of her besides you?" Funny how they saw things. L.A. was full of people, but there wouldn't be anyone there to watch over her.

"She'll be fine. There's plenty of family to care for her," he lied.

"We're an awfully tight family," he lied again. Mrs. Buchanan looked at him pleasantly as if he'd just told her the sun was up in August.

"Uh huh, she'll be glad to have her grandson back, tho'."

"Right." He was backing up now, moving to the kitchen door of the house. He felt the ant in his pant leg. He stopped and shook his pants and then his leg, but it didn't do any good.

"Let's get you into the house now so you can make that call. I'm holding you up rattling on like this." She started walking briskly to the house, not looking back, expecting him to follow. Beto followed. He passed Mrs. Buchanan in the kitchen, almost kicking one of the sacks of bread she had left in the black garbage bags on the floor, and went into the living room to make his call. He wished then that the old man had never come out for him, that he was back in the canyons. But the old man was in on it. He was as much to blame as she was. Goddamn old lady had to fall and break her hip. It was the old man's fault too. Dolores had found him and he had listened.

An hour later as he stood hunched over, leaning into the short oval door of the trailer he had bunked in, an eight by twelve aluminum teardrop painted bright yellow once, he wanted to talk to the old man. He hadn't seen him since they had pulled into the ranch, and now he could see that the truck was gone, so the old man had already left to go back out to the Gulch. He wanted to remind the old man to take the Waterpocket Fold at night because of the lack of water. He wanted to tell him to take some of Mrs. Buchanan's fresh bread, that there was one calf and mother that liked to lay back behind the rest and then wander off, that you could see the Henry's on the blackest nights. That's what he'd like to tell him. Just tell him because they worked together and he wanted to help. That's what they did, help each other out, even when it really wasn't important or needed, and the other guy would nod and say, "thanks." Hell, he knew he didn't need to give the old man directions to where he was going. He knew the old man could take a pack of winos through the Kalahari if he wanted to. He remembered his first trip, only five months ago, right after he first arrived. It was his first trip across the Fold to the Henry's. The old man had woken him up at three in the morning under a sky as black as a cat's balls. "See the Henry's. Right over there," he had said. "Always keep your eyes on them; head that way and you'll never get lost in the Fold." He hadn't seen them that night, not until he had walked into them, sure that this old man was crazy. But he did on his next trip. Black islands. The fountain in the Lake. How could he not have seen them before? He didn't need to tell the old man a thing, but he wanted to tell him all the same. Crazy old Indian riding tailgates.

He gathered up his two bags and ducked to get out the door. He stood in the heat and thick light of noonday Utah, an inch under six feet tall, in a Laker's championship t-shirt tucked into black Levis, and high-topped leather tennis shoes. He kicked the stick away from the door and shut it solidly, then stopped to look around quickly as if he'd felt a movement in the air like when a swarm of gnats hit, but there weren't any gnats. He picked up the bags and headed over to the shed on the west side of the barn, threw his bags into the back seat of the Camaro and touched the pocket of his Levis to feel the wad he had. Seven hundred bucks he'd saved, not bad, including this month's pay, but then there hadn't been much to spend it on either. He thought about driving out and harvesting the weed patch he'd planted up Deer Creek, up from the bridge, but he dropped the idea as a waste of time. Besides, he had two fat joints in the other pocket and he'd worry about money after he'd blown what he had. It was time to go. He got in the car, saw the key in the ignition, started it up and let it idle. The old man was a stickler about idling engines, so he let it idle. He looked at the grocery bag of food Mrs. Buchanan had packed for him, hungry now already, about to open it and search for a bag of cookies when a dull glint on the seat next to the bag caught his eye. He thought it must be a tool the old man had left behind when he'd tuned the Camaro for him. He picked it up and immediately noticed the heaviness, felt the supple leather. He dangled it in front of him for a second in the direct light coming through the shed doors that made it hard to see the big oval buckle that swung crazy for a moment until the light hit the rearing horse and "Santa Fe 1947." "That sonuvabitch," he swore.

Two

Cecilia McFadden entered St. Teresa's by the front entrance, into the nave with the baptismal font where she had been baptized, past the two holy water bowls and down the center aisle. Cecilia wanted to find the church like this, to walk down the long central aisle, the same entrance she had made for her first holy communion and confirmation, a straight shot up to the altar. Two hundred eighty-eight steps from the street, she affirmed, and then genuflected, her knee resting for a full second on the marble floor. She blessed herself again, touching the warm spots left from holy water. Water that was always warm. Water that she had filled with a jug from the tap in the sacristy. Water that the priests blessed, mumbled into. Water that dried too quickly, requiring this extra effort, a touching up. The church was as empty as she had hoped for. A good sign. The alcoves deep in the sides of the thick plastered walls were silent with candles, seeping the stories of their lighting up to the stained glass windows high near the ceiling and out into the air of Echo Park. She felt the austerity and sacrifice here. Spanish Gothic, heavy, the statues painted lifelike but larger in proportion, the wood dark on the pews and altar, dim light from the stained glass windows. She came here for purification, not to rest, to celebrate the spirit not the flesh, and Cecilia—twenty-four years old, erect, confident, aware of fabric against her skin, thighs touching, the cotton of her panties, sweater sliding over her chest—felt admired in this place. She thought of the walk down Glendale Boulevard to the church, trailing the fingers of her right hand in the chain-link fence of the schoolyard as if it were filled with kids skipping rope, kickballs, the uniforms they wore, and the noise that filled the yard in a pool of amber, viscose and safe. Cecilia had stopped and bent down from the waist to see the wavy lines that curled up from the grey cracked asphalt. She remembered how as a child she had lain down on this warm tar, knees bent, legs swinging. She bent lower when a car horn honked and a voice like hot breath blew past her and parted the heat waving on the playground. "Nice legs, babe." The horn again and she had stood up quickly, rubbing her sensible skirt over the backs of her legs furiously so that she had felt her skin then too.

It was 8:15 on a Saturday morning, humid before the concrete heated up, and two weeks since Robert Reynolds had returned from Utah. Cecilia had seen him twice in the last couple of days, as often as she would see him in a year, and she expected to see him again today, here in attendance. For now she forgot the outside, pleased with her solitude, but she wasn't the only one in the rapturous cool dark. Had she entered the church by the sacristy she would have found an altar boy, eleven or twelve years old, in vestments still, and Converse tennis shoes. The altar boy had been at St. Teresa's since the 7:00 mass which he had served, and instead of walking home to eat breakfast or kill time, he had remained behind, alone, waiting for the next mass. The sacramental water and wine was before him on the formica counter with the large sink. The cruets reminded him of the oil and vinegar servers that they used in the fancy restaurant his older brother worked at. He took a sip of wine straight from the curved mouth of the cruet. The wine was sweet and yellow. A sin? Hopefully only a venial one unless he was caught, he told himself. The boy poured water from an identical cruet into the wine, doing a bad job of it. He stoppered up the wine with his thumb and shook vigorously. Then he bent down and noted scientifically that the two were not level. He liked a balance, preferred baseball to basketball and, suspecting that level water and wine would be less incriminating, he sipped at the wine again. He didn't hear Cecilia, but he sensed her. A presence, electrical currents, boyhood? Whatever it was, he touched the cruets together and, satisfied, began to leave. He stopped and returned to wipe the formica clean. He used the billowing white sleeve of his gown and, working on an alibi, raced out of the sacristy, slowing to a walk only when he had reached the open door to the altar.

"Hi, Ceci."

She turned purposefully, almost indignantly, knowing her solitude was gone. "Jimmy, have you been here alone since the last mass? Not into trouble, I hope?" she asked sharply.

"Hey, no way, Ceci. Are we going to set up now?"

"Yes. Where's Father Reilly?" She listened to her voice, the silence broken. It sounded so high, as if it were skirting the lip of the ceiling, a young girl's voice.

The altar boy twined his fingers behind his back, young face cool, an Echo Park face, and responded. "Father Reilly was in a hurry to leave. He went back to the rectory." He pronounced it "wreck tore ee." Of course he was, she thought. He was at the dining-room table reading the calendar section of the *Times* or *People* magazine, a half-sliced grapefruit in wedged sections and coffee loaded with cream and sugar before him. Father Reilly knew Cecilia would be in the church.

"Do you want me to go get him?"

"No." Her reply was quick and shrill. The boy's face moved slightly as if a breeze had passed over the Lake. She continued, but softer, "Why don't you go home? The funeral isn't until 10:30." She read his face, his eyes. "All right, you can help me." His eyes glistened.

"Bring me the magenta linen." She would have preferred setting up alone, especially today, but now that she had let the boy stay, had made up her mind in the church, she didn't feel any confusion. If he was here he would be made useful.

"The magenta?"

"Yes, in the closet behind the folding doors, against the far back wall. Think. I showed you that closet two weeks ago. Open the doors and you'll see stacks of linens arranged by color. Bring me the reddish purple. It looks like purple with red in it. Purple with red, got it? It's on the right-hand side."

"Red purple?" He pronounced it slowly as if holding each letter.

"Right."

"Why not the black?"

Cecilia started to respond, but stopped, realizing that she didn't have a reason, hadn't thought of an explanation. The choice of color of vestments had come to her when she had thought she was alone. Dolores María Bernadette Rivera Reynolds had flickered in front of her at the altar as hopeful as candles in the alcoves. She could see the tiny, curly-haired woman dusting the candelabra, making adjustments, instructing her sweetly, softly. "Mrs. Reynolds," she had always called her, even when she wanted to call her "Dolores". Mrs. Reynolds had listened to her, a comfort for Cecilia who couldn't talk to her own mother. Dolores had given her a place at the altar and an ear. Was it just that the older woman had been her special friend, one with whom she could relax and tell all her ideas and goals, or was it that Cecilia respected her as the keeper of the altar, some kind of protector like Mary, Margaret, or Mary Magdalene, even? She couldn't speak to the boy until her image of Dolores faded, and then she walked up to him as if she were picking her way through the stones of some high ground, careful not to drag the tips of the imaginary mantle that she could feel on her shoulders. She reached out, her fingers encircling the boy's arm and the white sleeved gown, her eyes and voice direct, and asked him, "Do you have a comb?" He shrugged his shoulders. Perhaps he was nervous in her presence from the wine. He rubbed his head with his free hand.

"Yeah," he said.

"Well, while you're in the sacristy, use it. And change into a new blouse as well."

"Uh, yeah. Okay, Ceci." Then he was walking around the side of the altar to the door of the sacristy, his tennis shoes squeaking on waxed marble. He left the door open, but she didn't hear him; she was alone in St. Teresa of Avila's. So alone she heard waves breaking as if from a long way off. It was the traffic from the overpass built next to the church.

That's where the Glendale Freeway ended. An overpass and an exit on the border of the communities of Echo Park and Silver Lake. The church cupola as exit signal. It wasn't always this way. There had been streetcars. The Pacific Electric Red Cars, and the flattened pennies from their rails that had found their way to the mantles over fireplaces. Parents told unbelievable tales of going anywhere in L.A. for just a nickel. Dolores would fondly reminisce with anyone over the loss of the Red Car. She had told Cecilia how Beto was with her on the last trip it made, a shopping trip to the Central Market. How wonderful it had been: the vegetables and fruits, the Red Car waiting or one coming in another moment, the conductors in sharp-looking hats, the fare. Now she wouldn't even take a taxi. She had told Cecilia that Beto had hung to her skirts, but it wasn't that he was nervous, it was the adventure. His grandfather had told her that the boy pissed ice water. Cecilia had heard her stories, but how could she know that there had once been a natural valley with only two streetcar tracks when all she saw and knew were eight lanes of concrete and the sound of the ocean. Fortunately, not all the memories resided with the elders, and not all the tracks had been pulled or all the valleys filled. One valley was left to the boys. A narrow cut, where a single track, a run had branched off to the zoo and the carousel in Griffith Park. It had rarely been used even then; two trips a day, to the Park and back, so forgotten by the City that a hundred yards of track lay there still. There were a few homes in the valley, shacks really. Shabby, knocked up, thin-sided bungalows in peeling, dingy colors along the steep sides. It had always been called "the tracks," and boys never went alone to inspect the abandoned cars or wake sleeping bums. There they met, as tight as organized gangs—Riverside or the Parque Locos—to protect their forts hidden in the trails of thick underbrush and eucalyptus. There continued the stick wars and dirt clods and the bums, always the bums. Cecilia didn't know of the tracks, but her altar boy did. The tracks was their "place." The tracks as "history" left to boys, as the homes in the winding streets on the hills looking down became childless. The city planners referred to it as gentrification. Dolores said that it was those guys with the identical moustaches who were buying up the homes. The clean, good-looking men of Silver Lake. They remodeled the houses of the old immigrant middle class and it was called chic. But what could they see? They never came down. And the commuters who passed the valley on the freeway wouldn't notice it either because of the trees planted by the men in orange, and also because they were checking their speed and jockeying for position on the exit that came right after the valley. The hidden tracks, tracks as "memory."

The Glendale Freeway was already eighteen years old and still unfinished, but who cared? It wasn't the streetcar rails and there wasn't a Red Car. The valley was hidden and the mayor and the city planners could wring their hands over the exit. Engineers could sharpen rows of lead, and still there were the abrupt wooden barricades painted yellow and black to guide the unknowing away from the graffitied concrete bumpers, linked by cable to hopefully prevent a leap as exciting as The Accident.

This story, too, had been passed down by those with the memory. Cecilia knew about it and she hadn't even been in school then. A car had lost its brakes at the top of Fargo Street and had plunged down the longest and steepest hill in L.A., launching itself over the streetcar tracks at the bottom and landing in the two-pump Flying A gas station at the other side. The flight happened at recess in full view of the uniformed Catholic students across the street at St. Teresa's school. The car, a '49 Dodge, stopped finally at the first gas pump, shearing it off at the base, so that the tall globe-topped pump had spun clattering across the street where it bounced into the curb and lay, the globe broken, the dull red paint along its sides scraped, under the gaze of pupils who were by then pressed cheek and jaw into the horny wires of the Cyclone fence. Gas, rose-colored in those days, was flowing out of the pump and onto Glendale Boulevard. Rose wine, the Dodge at rest. The school had had to be evacuated. The nuns had led the pupils up Baxter

Street in single files until the firemen said it was safe to come back. A few of the boys, Beto included, stayed back, hidden by the baseball backstop to watch the man being pulled from the wreckage of the Dodge. All eyes focused upon the man's head in the light of noon, bright, shining, unlike the gas which had stopped flowing and the dull pump stand carried away from the curb by the gas station attendants. The Accident was imprinted in the record of the hidden tracks: a man's head illuminated from across the street, the body stretched out on the sidewalk on wet concrete, a battered Dodge with one wheel off the ground, so that the shutting off of the ambulance siren went unnoticed. The boys were impressed by color, silent in the shadows of the backstop. Beto had been afraid that the man wouldn't move, so that even after the ambulance had come and the white sheet had been spread over him and he was carried on the stretcher into the ambulance, Beto had waited to see the man wave and smile at him through the windows of the ambulance. He had seen the sheet rise and his spirits had jumped. He had been ready to wave back and smile too, but it was only the attendant adjusting the sheet and the attendant didn't look out. Then the ambulance was gone and Beto had thought of his father whom he couldn't remember.

But Cecilia wasn't thinking about the overpass or The Accident. She was listening to the ocean and studying the stained glass windows that were set so high along the roof line. The only light in the church this morning came from the rows of stained glass, light that sank into the dark wood of the pews. She noticed for the first time that the glass vibrated with the passing cars. She asked herself about the windows. How were they cleaned? Perhaps it didn't matter since they went unnoticed, the gaze of the faithful directed forward. This was unfortunate, Cecilia thought, because the glass was old, authentic and lovely in its twisted lead. The commuters would miss them too, for had they had time to look from the narrow, descending turn of the overpass, instead of seeing beautiful windows depicting saints and angels they would've seen only roof tiles and pigeons shitting.

"Where do you want this linen, Ceci?" The altar boy's voice startled her and then was swallowed by a passing truck.

"Give it to me." She took the bundle and climbed the three steps to the altar, placing the stack of linen on the left-hand corner. She acted busy. "You were at the rosary last night." It wasn't a question.

"Uh huh."

"Who was with Robert?"

"Robert?"

"The grandson of the deceased." He didn't understand. "The lady who died."

"Oh, you mean Beto."

"Yes, Beto. Do you know who was with him?"

"No, I don't."

Cecilia spread out the altar mantlepiece. The boy held the end as she talked, unfolding it sideways. She watched what she was doing, wanting to appear unconcerned. "There was a woman with Robert, I mean Beto. I think she was with him."

"Oh, the girl with Beto. You mean the one in the mini?"

"Yes, that's the one. Do you know her?" Cecilia had reached the end of the altar. She let the end down carefully so it would hang over the edge a good eighteen inches. She had kept her eyes on the mantlepiece, but when she bent down to sight the long edge, she caught the boy's face, grinning.

"No, but I've seen her before. I think I've seen her with Ray." That was all he offered.

She moved the candelabra a fraction. How could Robert bring a woman like that to a rosary, she asked herself. She used both hands this time to move it back. The woman had been dressed in black all right. Black leather mini, French nylons, pumps, and a thin leather jacket. That was all, a thin leather jacket.

"He's strange," she mumbled.

"What?"

"Nothing, nothing." She felt her face redden, and her lips tightened. "I was just saying a little prayer."

"Oh."

Three

Beto drove with his left arm bare and straight, right hand loose on the shifter. The truck was flying over a lumpy two-rut Utah mesa top road, at about thirty miles per hour. So what, he thought. He looked at her and steered at a loose mound clumped with sandstone. Tina was still there.

"Beautiful morning," Beto said, watching the road again. She didn't look at him, but stared straight ahead as if this were a Sunday's drive to mother's house on the Hollywood Freeway, except for her arms. Her arms were crossed tightly over her breasts as if to keep them in place.

"Rough road," he said. She turned from the waist up and gave him a look that stuck him into the sand beyond the window as if he'd been sucked out and left there to watch them pass by. Two heads, an arm, and dust.

"What's up?"

This time she answered. "I don't know. Why don't you tell me; you're the one directing this show." She spoke with the pure sarcastic and confident voice that she had perfected with brothers she was left to watch over too often. But it was the first time she had spoken to him in over two hours and Beto didn't want to let it go. He was hungry, driving alone, tearing up his new truck.

"Why did you come out here?" he asked, "you're making my life miserable."

"You don't need my help."

"I guess I can figure that out, but you haven't even tried to like it yet. Goddamn pain in the ass."

"I have to like your goddamn ideas?" she spat out quickly as soon as he had finished speaking. Her words seemed to stick to the dash under the bug-splattered windshield. He was sure that he was staring at them.

"So whattaya want me to do? Turn around here and drive you back to L.A.?"

"So turn around."

"I knew you'd say that."

"That's because you're a brilliant mindreader. What am I

thinking now? Not too difficult, is it, boy scout?" She had taken one folded arm away from her chest so that she could jab a finger in Beto's direction. Neither noticed the speed.

"Forget it," he said tiredly.

"I'd like to, but I'm not the one driving, running this adventure in exotic lands, am I?"

"Forget it, I said." Tina's tongue could blister marble, he thought.

"What's to forget? Come on, Beto, you're the one who wants to talk. I'm here. I'm listening."

"Look, I told you that this was where we were going. That it'd be like a vacation. You could stay as long as you wanted."

"Oh? Then what? You ship me off?"

"That's not what I meant."

"What did you mean, I could stay as long as I wanted? What's that supposed to mean? You brought me out here just for a ride?"

"I didn't say that, Tina. I mean. . . . I don't know what you want to do."

"And it isn't getting any easier for you, is it? Why shouldn't I be happy with dirt up my crotch? Hell, you are."

"What the fuck are you talking about? I don't really understand a word you're saying." His voice jumped three levels and he pounded on the wheel for emphasis. Tina moved back extravagantly, blinking her eyes as if afraid for her safety. They both sucked in their breath as the truck stretched out at the end of a rise before coming down hard.

"Why'd you come out here, then," he continued after they were on the ground again. "I told you what it was like out here. Huh?" He pounded again. She blinked. "Why didn't you say anything?"

Tina Cisneros leaned into him with an erect back, one hand on the seat top, the other with a finger pointing and moving. "I didn't have a choice, lover boy. You show up in your boots and bandana, "Come on, momma, weeee're goin to youtah. Pack 'em up and roll 'em out." She mimicked perfectly any excited two-bit western actor. Beto couldn't help but look at her for a good five seconds, astonished enough to scree past thirty feet of sagebrush before he pulled the truck back onto the tracks. She was still facing him. She was a striking woman, not sweet-looking or lovely, but dark and piercing. She was the woman he cut his finger opening a can of beer for. She had let him stumble over his witty lines and then had laughed. Before her all men were wounded, their pride left in a paper bag crumpled on the front lawn, waiting for the sprinklers.

She teased herself openly, said she had the Mexican woman's curse: legs like a *guajalote*, skinny as a turkey. Or she would heft her breasts and say, "poor little *chichitas*," and laugh. She had large Columbia roast eyes, full lips, and long straight shining hair pulled back over the full high forehead, but when she would look in the mirror she would call her face a hopeless case, the Maya Indian look. Perhaps what set her apart was the bewildering quality that she lived so comfortably at ease with her body, her looks, herself, so much so that other women always took guarded notice. And what a head. Ray said she was *bien Mexicana*. An indirect compliment that included fiery, hot-blooded, jealous, and wise in the ways of the world. A woman who had known her as a child in the outlying towns of San Diego had told him, "She's got five brothers who are so dense they need help to urinate in the right direction. They must have saved all the brains until she came along." He'd also heard that she was sought after by every university in the country, a smart *Mexicana*, more than a fought over quota-filler. He didn't know what happened with it. He didn't care. She made him nervous. He was as sleepless as a loose faucet around her freedom. He had made up his mind to oppose her every chance he had, as he did with Dolores. If he ignored them he might as well tear his shirt pockets, cigarettes would taste of birthday candles, and the door knobs would become as easy to turn as ripe loquats. He thought of Dolores. She was having a funeral today, and everything he looked at seemed covered with the white scratch marks on an overused 45' of Agustin Lara singing "Veracruz."

Whatta'ya mean you didn't have a choice?" He was shouting at the windshield and the steering wheel and the speedometer that seemed broken at 30. She laughed. It was a laugh like sap between his fingers. A laugh she could make when she didn't want to include anyone else, and it wasn't forced with her. "You came along. You wanted to get away too," he added.

"Don't shout at me." She was bracing herself with both hands.

"I'm not shouting." He was, but he kept both hands on the wheel, and he was leaning forward so that his arms were bent and his jaw jutted forward.

"Slow down, Beto."

"I'm not driving fast. This is the way you drive these roads."

"You're frightening me. Now slow down, please. I'm asking you. I'm not telling you, I'm asking. It's time we had a talk."

Now she wants to talk, he thought. Seven hours from Vegas and he had inspired her. He chewed at his lower lip, feeling the dust with his tongue until it was wet and shiny. She's mad because I brought her along. It's my fault, he mused. Dolores would never let me forget either. Dolores was blessed: she could work slowly; she could rub poison on green figs. He took a quick glance. She was back in the corner of the seat near the door, but she was still facing him and her eyes were like ants crawling under his clothes. He wanted to bring his hand up and wipe the side of his face, but he didn't want to lose the road and the brush swinging by in a blur, the mountains ahead—a wall. He regretted ever saying anything to her. He had wanted some action, a response. Any response was better than sullen quiet on a blurred desert road. He took his foot off the gas.

"Look at me," she said. "What are we doing here? Are we going to sit around a campfire, sing songs on your geetar, look at the stars? What? What?"

"I don't give a damn what you do. I'm taking you back tomorrow," he said with what he thought was a cool level voice, a manly voice that had control. He was hoping this would shut her up.

"Did I ever tell you how blessed intelligently I think you are," she answered back in an identical tone. "What an artistic way you have with words? A *real* man would never have responded with such sensitivity and grace. I'm touched, really touched; in fact, I feel so wonderful that you can just stop right now because I'm getting out." Her tone had never changed: he thought she was joking.

"Stop this truck." Her voice had found a higher level that wasn't dear or precious-sounding anymore.

Beto slowed the truck by downshifting into second. He put his left arm back on the rolled-down window so that he could slouch into the corner and rub his hand through his hair. He noticed an ant mound on his side of the road, the conical mound of built-up sand and debris taken from the hive underground and hauled up to the top so it would roll down the back side giving the mound a pitch, a longer pitch down the backside. He could see ants, some hurrying up the slope, others moving in and out of the entrance on the southeastern side. They always put the entrance hole facing the southeast to catch the morning sun. The old man had told him that. He had also said that they knew what they were doing. He considered driving over the hive. It was almost a foot high. He figured it had to be an old one to be so big. They'd repair it in a week; it'd give them something to do under the September sun. He drove by and looked back. He thought he saw the desiccated mandible of a beetle, the pointed jaws waving high, rocking back and forth before it tumbled down the back slope.

"I'll take you to Vegas in the morning. You can catch a bus or a plane there."

"You can take me back now. Do you hear me? Right now. I don't have to stay out here with you." Tina had sprung across the seat, her lips a scant two inches from his cheek. Out of the corner of his eye he saw her lips move and the glimpse of teeth. He thought of the beetle mandible waving at him from the top of the ant mound. He was calmer now. He didn't shout, his voice low, measured and slow.

"I'm not turning around here. So sorry, Tina. And I'm not taking you to the ranch either."

"Big fucking deal," she exploded. "You and the goddamn ranch." It was silent then for several long minutes.

"So where are we going?" The voice was stinging from full lips.

"Deer Creek."

"Sounds idyllic. One long night at Deer Creek."

Forget it, he told himself, forget it, it was better to taste dust. He looked in the mirror and saw the clay of his mother's face, smelled the sweat of her cheeks. Scotch mist in the pale glass. Who was she? What was he half of? Half of what? His mother? Was he Bobby or Beto, or neither of those two? The old man was All Indian, it even said so on the buckle he was wearing. Ray, good patient Ramon told him to forget about it: "it won't help to wonder about her. She's gone." A tall, get under your skin, auburn-haired, Scotch drinker from the English Empire and the City of Glendale. "Your mother told me she had to pick something up at the store, that she would be right back," Dolores had instructed him. "She picked you up, right here in the kitchen—don't you remember?—kissed you and held you and told me to let you know how much she loved you. I didn't think anything of it until it grew late and your grandfather had come home. I never said anything either because you didn't seem to notice." I was three years old, Dolores, he wanted to shout at her now; what the hell would I know? I was too short for mirrors then, and where'd the pictures of my mother go? You think you knew what was best, always know what's best, just like Tina knows best, but look at where you're at today. I've buried you and you don't even know it. You don't even know you're supposed to be buried today at St. Teresa's. You're gone like the pictures you sliced up and I did it to you. Me and Tina, another woman. A woman you don't trust. But you trusted my mother, didn't you? Or did you hope that she would leave me for you? Did you always know it?

Suddenly he thought of the old Indian. The old man might know about the funeral, and this thought bothered him. Maybe they had communicated again, in dreams, or the old man had felt it in his hands. He'd know she wasn't at home. He'd know because of the rosary, the pink rosary. He'd know that Dolores was now called Santiaga Purisima at some squalid dump named Nuestro Virgen de Guadalupe Rest Home in Lincoln Heights. He would tell him, "she made me do it, old man. She hid my mother, kept her away. Can't you find her, feel around the rocks in the stream with your thin old hand and find her, a good-looking white woman who loves me and wants me." He realized that he was working the wheel real hard, his hands kneading the plastic, the truck moving slowly and Tina slumped in the seat. He saw the beetle mandible tumble again, biting into the sand. He imagined tears beginning in Tina's eyes, without sound. He could feel it the way you can feel air move in a dark room. He wished he had run over the mound, he wanted to hit something. But if she wanted to cry it was Tina's problem not his, and he pressed into the seat to feel the cover, rough and dry through his sweaty shirt. The dusty sweat of a morning in September crushed against the small of his back, dust as thick as the air at the Lake. The windows rolled down and more pouring in, so he kept his tongue away from his lips and breathed through his nose, wishing he had never returned home to Silver Lake, that the telegram had never arrived. He didn't mind the dust, not now. It was different dust. Dust that Tina wouldn't like, but then, she didn't like anything about Utah. He knew then why he had brought her, insisted that she come, because he knew she wouldn't like it and then he could be rid of her. He would be good to her from now on, until tomorrow when he dropped her off, and then she would be gone, like Dolores, gone.

Tina was sitting in the same position, head straight, but the beginning of tears had stopped and she just looked tired and sad. She must be slipping, he thought. He could look at her without fear. She couldn't see him. He felt as confident as a cat on a fence post. She was gone, and then out of the corners of her eyes she caught him. He shouldn't have looked over at her. He should have been thinking about dust.

Four

You know Beto, right?" Cecilia asked.

"I've seen him around, sure. He hangs out at Ray's a lot and I've seen him at the Lake," the altar boy answered.

Cecilia knew Ray's Auto Body Shop was on Glendale Boulevard across from the Hughes Market. "Mixville," is what Dolores had called it. "We used to ride horses on the Tom Mix ranch," she had told Cecilia more than once. Cecilia knew Ray was Beto's best friend. Ray from public school. Ray of Echo Park. She saw him occasionally in the Pioneer Market where she worked as a checker. He bought cat food by the case. He had a serious face, he was serious about cats. She couldn't figure him out. Was he a *pachuco*, a *vato*, or an older homeboy? He was polite, and he was Beto's best friend. She had known Robert as a child too. "Bobby," the sisters had called him. An eighth-grader when she was in the second grade. She remembered that he was in trouble more than once with Sister Mary Catherine, the principal. She and the other little students whispered about him as they filed in lines according to grade to the ritual morning mass. He wouldn't attend, hiding out instead behind the baseball backstop. She hadn't connected him yet with Dolores, the nice lady who cared for the altar and served hot dogs on Thursdays with the other mothers.

Her own mother wouldn't come and serve hot dogs. Margarita from the Philippines waited at home, waited for Jim the railroad man, waited and watered the plants in the yard from an old coffee can, while Jim, smilin' Jim, took the waters at Nicks. Quiet Margarita dressed in black and white, black skirt, white blouse, like a pilgrim at Lourdes in the house of her husband, Smilin' Jim, the big redhead who had swept her away from her island. Margarita watered the red clay and the plants flowered. She cared for the stray cats and kept a parakeet. She didn't like to leave the small backyard pushed up against the hillside. She didn't mind that there was rust in the coffee cans.

Cecilia never would have put Dolores, the sweet hot dog lady and keeper of the altar, together with the Bobby who hid behind the backstop, until the day mass was fifteen minutes late because Dolores and Father Reilly had a talk on the church steps where all the kids with craning necks in the aisle pews could see. Dolores was contrite and respectful. Father Reilly shook his head and smiled. Beto pulled bark from the eucalyptus tree that grew off to the side. Cecilia really loved Mrs. Reynolds that day and hoped Bobby would respect her and come to mass. A week after the incident at mass came the day she remembered so clearly, a memory of wind chimes and cold steel. She was on the merry-go-round that the kids would push. She was sitting on the floor in the middle hanging on to one of the bars above her that radiated out of the center. She always started in the middle, holding on tight with her short fingers. The bar was cold and slippery in the morning after mass before the first class. She would slide slowly forward as the metal floor turned, her butt moving inch by inch to the edge until she could stop herself with feet against the bar where it curved down to meet the floor. But that morning the eighth graders were pushing it and she had never gone that fast, so fast, she remembered, that the dizzy helpless pull to the outer edge wasn't fun. The asphalt looked as smooth as a black mirror from the speed and her hands slipped faster on the wet bar. It had happened fast, in that ten minutes between the end of mass and the first class, the merry-go-round filled with round faces. She had yelled "stop," but her voice was tiny in the wind of running big kids. She had her lunchbox between her knees, a Snow White lunchbox, one side with the beautiful young girl in a deathly sleep on a flat rock and the prince bending over to kiss her, the seven dwarfs watching. And then, as if in a movie when the projector slows down, she felt the lunch box slip out from between her knees and jiggle, the dwarfs dancing, for what seemed an enormous time on the rattling grated steel floor before it slid off the edge, before she could remove her fingers from the bar to catch it as it sailed off in an arc so beautiful she could see it all in her mind even as the merry-go-round was spinning her out of view in slow motion, and then all she could hear was the tinkling sound of wind chimes, the Japanese wind chimes made of glass that her mother had hanging on the back porch. When she came around again there was the lunchbox, the lid popped open, thermos on the asphalt, weeping grey milk. That was when she had let go, because it was slow motion now, and she didn't care about anything except her milk and Snow White. He had caught her as she came off the still rapid grate, and she hadn't realized it was him as he carried her in his arms, which was odd, when she thought about it now, because the big kids never held the little kids. All he had said was, "let's go get your lunch." That was all, not "it's all right," or "you're ok." She realized who he was when he put her down and gathered up her lunch even though she was crying hard, but not about the peanut butter sandwich squashed where someone had stepped on it. He had picked up the thermos and shaken it so that it made the wind chime sound again. He didn't say another word, but took her to the benches where the tears stopped, because she was choking like kids do when they're really upset, pushing her gently from behind because she was having a hard time breathing. He had his thermos; she suspected it was his: a black thermos with a chess horse, and a man with a gun. He poured milk into the black plastic cup and said, "Here, drink it; my grandmother makes me warm milk too." That was when she realized that Dolores wasn't his mother, and then she hadn't seen him much until three days ago.

Five

Beto, I don't want to fight with you any more. I've been thinking on it and I realize I shouldn't have come out here. It's nobody's fault. I wanted to be with you. I just thought it would be different."

He listened to the running of the engine, saw the Henry's clear and magnificent before the thunderclouds reached them, felt a coolness like the spray of the fountain on the Lake. He marveled at how Tina could change the mood so definitely. He was relieved that he could not see his face in the dust of the windshield.

"It's not your fault, Tina." The words came out too fast, but he didn't slow down. "Maybe everything would've been fine if we didn't come out here. I should've stayed."

"I know I should have." She wasn't hard now. She could cry when she wanted and speak what was on her mind.

He breathed though his mouth. No problem, really, with the dust, there every morning in the edges of your eyes when you wake so you wish there was water like anyone would. He thought of it sifting into the tightly rolled sleeping bags in the back and then thought of the funeral today, the dust that would be in the closed casket in the hearse from the Gutierrez and Chan mortuary, readied for the ride to St. Teresa's. He wiped at his mouth to clear the corners.

"It's my fault, really. I wanted to get away. I couldn't stay there."

"You know, I don't understand you." But she said it nicely, there was no sarcasm. "What you should worry about is not being there. I told you to wait until after the funeral; you can't just leave before a funeral. Those people will wonder. What were you thinking of? You don't listen to me."

"I listen to you too much."

"You're stubborn and bull-headed and if you listened to me we wouldn't be in this dump." Tina was always able to reprimand him this way. He couldn't believe he enjoyed it, didn't want her to stop.

"It was your idea," Beto said.

"What, to come out here? Don't make my asshole sweat."

"Dolores?"

"It was about time. If I had waited for you, a *sordo mudo*, to make up your mind, I'd still be sweating under some nee-gro." She emphasized the word, drawing it out because she knew how the vision irritated him.

"Don't start with that," he said, but was amused, pleased with the change in the car.

"Then don't start in on Lulu. She's fine, she's with my people." My people. Tina had said that before. They aren't my people, Beto had realized. Tina had handled it, the whole thing. It had been her people. He tried to imagine telling his people, "I'm gonna stick Dolores in a rest home. Yes, I think it's a good idea. She's an incredible pain in the ass to be around, and besides, she's sitting on a sizable bankroll and the house. Custodianship? No, there is a doctor who will sign a death certificate." Who were his people anyway? Ray and the old man? The Buchanans? He couldn't tell them, although he was sure the old man would know; his hands would be fluttering like quail crossing a road and Ray would be at the church today looking for him. But Tina had her people.

"Baby, don't worry so much. You did fine, fine." She leaned over and rubbed long fingers through his hair. Her lips formed into an interesting half-smile and her eyes went sleepy. He looked at her. He could look as long as he wanted now. He looked at her body, graceful in tight shorts and a tank top that was almost too small for a child. He could look a long time in second gear on Two Horse Mesa.

"Baby?" Honey couldn't have poured slower. "Why did you want me to come out here with you?"

"It seemed like you wanted to be with me." He exaggerated the "you wanted." "You wanted to be with me all the time," he continued.

"That's true, baby." He accepted the change of mood completely. Other than the night in the hotel, in Vegas, the twenty hour trip had been hell. It could be forgotten now, and he could put Dolores out of his mind as well. Tina did want to be with him. He was positive of it. In fact, she had never let him out of her sight since he had returned and started up with her two weeks ago. She must be madly in love with me. She needs me, he thought.

"I don't think I want you to take me back tomorrow."

"That's not what you said," Beto replied, not sure if he wanted to rush things now either.

"I was just angry because I thought you wanted to get rid of me." The truck wiggled under his grasp. "That's why I almost started to cry. See what you do to me?" He wouldn't say a word. She was like the old man and Dolores and he was transparent. Tina didn't stop. She reached over and put those long fingers in his hair again. She stroked his neck through the hair, slow strokes, immaculately passing through any snarls. He could purr, his chest and shoulders relaxing. Even the engine was purring and then he remembered the cat he and Ray had found in the reeds on their island in Echo Park Lake when they were kids. It really was an island, at least it was surrounded by water and connected to land only by an old wooden bridge. He and Ray would bike down there in the early morning on Saturdays and Sundays with peanut butter and grape jelly sandwiches they had made at Dolores's house. They'd duck their heads and shoulders as they rode, fly without pedaling down the hills of Silver Lake from the house. He remembered that the wind pressure was beautiful. He moved his hand out of the window now, flat, letting it rise and fall. Tina was still stroking him. He and Ray would spend whole days at the Lake. Their lake. Once it had been a small reservoir with cement sides. Then the city had built Silver Lake, which was fenced in and patrolled. Now the sides of Echo Park Lake eroded in flagrant patches, there was scum on the water, trash and graffiti, and cart pushers with too little cardboard. Their island was secured by a boarded-up bridge. "No entrance," the sign warned. It should have said "no passage," the planks burned through and covered with graffiti. But the barrier was no problem, nor were the missing planks; they made it special. He remembered that the island was bare in the center. Circling the bald spot and the three palm trees were reeds, pompoms and water lilies so thick you couldn't tell where the edge of the island was and the lake began until you tunneled through. That's where the fort was. Ray carried the sandwiches and the two cans of Hires root beer. Ray always carried them in the army knapsack they had found in the basement. They had crawled through the tunnel almost to the cave they had fashioned when the cat had surprised them, snarling, her back high, ears thrown back. Beto was the first to see her and be confronted. He stopped abruptly, Ray banging into him. "Hey, what gives?" "Lookit," was all he said and Ray, who was crawling over him for a better look, started to back away fast. They had backed off into the reeds as far as they could, but the tunnel was tight and she had them for that one good moment, one long second before they caught themselves, and she had known that too. She sensed her time and flew out of the reeds between them, spitting and splitting them apart as they flattened as best they could. They had remained still in their lopsided places and then they had laughed, the belly-wracking laugh of kids. When they left, more than half a peanut butter sandwich broken into sections remained in the cave. It was gone the next day and so began their project. They named the wiry orange and white cat "Spitfire," and although they fed her and her kittens, she never did let them pet her. He felt like laughing. He did. Tina acted surprised.

"What are you laughing about?" she questioned.

"Nothing, nothin', just something from when I was a kid at the Lake."

"Lake? You mean the toilet. They should get rid of it, cover it up."

"You mean like the casket? Full of secrets?" He shifted his right arm to rest his hand on her leg above the knee. She moved closer, almost leaning against him. He let his hand rest, her skin cool in the heat, only her upper lip sweating tiny beads.

"I know what you're thinking about. It's not kosher to have a closed casket."

"Not if you're Catholic."

"I'll bet you were an altar boy."

"You're Catholic too, Mex." He hooked his hand in slowly to her thigh and pulled it slowly to him. She laughed an almost girlish laugh and said, "Who isn't?"

"You know Catholics. You know that Catholics have traditions." He spoke low and continued his pressure on her thigh. He could tell she was interested.

"Uh hum?"

"They want to kiss the dead."

"Beto!"

"They want to kiss the dead on the lips," he hissed through leering eyes and a grin. "They care about death. They may think she's a Lazarus until they've made certain and kissed her dead lips."

"Will you shut up and stop talking about it? It'll be over today and nobody will be missing those lips."

He continued to rub her thigh. It wasn't cool anymore as he moved his hand smoothly over the fine skin. They were a couple of miles from the turnoff onto the Burr Trail, the road down into the canyons and Deer Creek. It would be hotter below, but they would be near the water, under cottonwoods. He reached higher. Her skin became damp wherever his hand rested too long.

"Fish lips."

"Stop it, fish breath," Tina replied, erupting into gales of laughter.

"Catholics are crazy."

"I'm crazy about you," she said, and smiled so that her face went soft, and the long dark hair fell over his arm. His hand stopped high and he could feel her grow damp again. She leaned in even closer and spoke low, "why don't we stop here for awhile? I'm real tired of driving and I'd love to stretch my legs."

He answered in a voice that sounded like water dripping off a flat rock. "It's too hot here. We're almost into the canyons." They were both whispering as if the air were too hot to conduct words. "It'll be nicer there," he croaked.

"I like it here," she said.

He opened his lips to speak and sucked in dry, crackling air. He drove his hand into the wedge of her tight shorts and rubbed her hard, rubbing his middle finger deep. She came at him with her lips and teeth. The truck stopped in a sandy depression. He flicked off the ignition so there was only the sound of sand settling, the engine ticking as the heat rose, cicadas in a stand of tamaracks, and their breathing. He threw his arm around her, and pulled her mouth to his, sucking on her lower lip, biting into it, his hand sliding under her tank top against the ribs, pulling at a breast to bring her closer still. She used both hands to pull his head away, gripping him roughly by the ears and hair. He wouldn't let go until her lip slipped from between his teeth. Gnats hummed in his ears, the air hot and still, his chest rimmed with sweat. She sat back free now and pulled her tank top off fast and smooth, her nipples like a child's dry thumbs.

"Come here," she said, leaning back. He threw off his shirt and pushed against her, his arms around her, as he crawled up her chest, her head thrown out the window so he could look up her long neck. She brought his head to her breast, pulled him into position by the ears and hair. He couldn't hear the cicadas or gnats, and his lips weren't dry anymore, his tongue lapping, his arms tightening around her back, her hands working his head, her head thrown back. His face left a damp spot and a wet brush stroke down her chest to her belly, his legs curled up and pushing at the door. He got up. Tina looked at him. He opened the door and stepped out, pulling her legs after him. She held onto the steering wheel so he could pull at her shorts and the high-cut panties. He dropped them in the sand as she gripped the steering wheel with a strong right hand.

Six

Approximately forty-five road miles northwest from where Tina and Beto had stopped on Two Horse Mesa, was the bridge that crosses the Escalante River. The Escalante was named after Father Escalante, a padre who had happened into the area in the early 1800's to educate the primitives, scattered families of hunter-gatherers that lived in brush huts and followed the pine nut and seed harvests. No one is sure what kind of luck he had, although they know he never came back. Perhaps that's why they named the sluggish and muddy river for him. This was the route Beto normally would have taken. He would have stopped at the bridge, most likely, and pointed out the Moki huts to Tina. The "huts" are granaries, wattle and mud-covered, built in spots that would, hopefully, protect the contents from rats and squirrels. They are impossible to spot on the face of the canyon wall until you've seen them once. Some people in the Escalante area call the mesa "Miller's Mesa." Miller was one of the last of the Hole in the Wall Gang. They say he hid out there. He was never found either. It's mostly called Moki Mesa, though, in order to give a place name to the Mokis, who are blamed for lost heifers and trucks that won't start. The huts are small, about two and a half feet high at the most, and the Forest Service sign, hopelessly situated on the side of the road, layered with arrows and descriptions about how to find the huts is absolutely no help. Like warts, they blend in. But this is one of those spots that everyone takes their out-of-towners, happy to be able to point out something that isn't in grand scale and, of course, explain where the little problem-causing varmints live. This is the easiest road from Escalante to Boulder; however, Beto had decided to take a BLM road, the back way, because Tina hadn't spoken to him since Vegas. He'd also been nervous about running into Mr. Buchanan who had a general store in Escalante as well as the ranch in Boulder and he hadn't wanted the Buchanans to know he was back.

The old man, recently back from his round-up of Buchanan cattle in the Waterpocket Fold, was relaxing under Molly's Nipple at the bridge that crossed Deer Creek. He had come to fish and there were three of them, pierced through the gills, lying in a slow-moving riffle on a bent willow. It was while fishing that his hands spoke to him, quivering as he read them, and so he waited, relaxed to the point of sleep, his head against one of a clump of four cedars in the scraggly shade they provided. It was a sweet piece of camping ground, the same that the family had been at the last time he and Beto had crossed the creek. The smooth, rounded, immense outcrop of pink sandstone fondly called Molly's Nipple because of the clearly recognizable rounded top and tip which could be seen from a great distance, rose behind him. He was sure that Beto would be along any time as he let his eyes close, pulled the brim of his Giants cap low to shade even the dappled light from the cedars, and listened to the water in Deer Creek flow past the pool and down the canyon. From this spot at Molly's Nipple, Deer Creek canyon tightens into sheer walls with no way out until it meets up with the Escalante. He knew every bronzed wall and turn: the narrows where one had to swim bumping along the walls, the overhangs to spend the night in, the extreme silence and solitude of its deep meanderings, and cliffs rising sharply and smoothly to the high rim.

He also knew of the one route out, past the narrows, up the wall that looked as unlikely as all the others, an Indian trail clearly marked if you knew where to look for the pictographs. He could see the trail now through his heavy-lidded sleepy eyes as he remembered how surprised and pleased he had been when Beto had told him of his discovery. Slim had told him in the cool of the evening as they sat, the old man in the rocking chair, on the back porch of the Buchanan house. He had been relaxed then as well, belly full from supper, the work day behind him. Beto wasn't even mildly excited."Yes," he had replied, "just past the narrows."

"Just past the narrows?" the old man asked, sitting up and reaching into his pocket for the Red Man even though he had put it away for the night.

Beto had then told him about the top of the mesa—as strange as a new moon, the whitest sandstone, lava chunks in broken piles, and an oasis, a pool larger than a pothole with trees at one end, not tamaracks, but two or three big ponderosas, and cattails at the water's edge under the ponderosas, and tiny crabs that he said looked like trilobites. "Horseshoe crabs," the old man had called them. It was a beautiful pool, spring-fed, Beto figured, from the taste of it.

The old man had asked Beto if he had seen anything else there. Beto mentioned frogs and had gone to get a piece of the lava he had brought back, but that wasn't what the old man was looking for. He guessed that Beto hadn't seen everything, but what he had seen was good enough.

"What about the pictographs?" he had asked.

"Well, you see, it was raining like hell," Beto had said, describing a thunderstorm that had stopped and wouldn't move on. "A heavy thunderstorm, old man," he had said, "that stopped right there and didn't move, sat right there."

Of course he had known what Beto was talking about: thunderheads that came out of Arizona and New Mexico, gathering first over Navajo Mountain, and then moving fast and dark and god-awful beautiful, dumping as they rolled over to Boulder Mountain where they'd sit until the old man couldn't believe there'd be anything left from those clouds, they had dumped so much. He asked Beto about the qualities of the rain.

"The rain was pouring off the sides," Beto said, "like you've never seen it, waterfalls everywhere, Deer Creek floating higher at every bend. It was really pouring in," he added, and the old man didn't have to say a thing because he could see the waterfalls and feel the gentle creek change from clear to dark brown, moving faster and uglier and rising. He had rocked slowly, forgetting in his excitement to roll down his sleeves when the wind stopped until he suddenly heard the blind wings of night attracted to his hot blood.

"It was a blue belly that showed me, old man," Beto had said.

Ah, the blue belly, he had thought. There were millions of them, and they were curious too.

Beto said the blue belly had been quick as a thunderclap—that was what he had said—but that it had stopped, planted itself in the middle of a pictograph, had risen on its claw tips, up and down, over and over, watching him.

The old man remembered that he hadn't been able to move when he'd heard it; he couldn't rock, and when a mosquito feasted on the skin that should have been covered, he could feel the slow beat of his blood, the needle pulled clean and the skin re-uniting. Time for all things, he had thought, and blue bellies.

"The pictograph looked like a steering wheel, old man. And there were hands all over the rock," Beto had continued. "There was this volcanic marble in the center, and five, I didn't have to count them, five pecked-out spokes or lines, going straight to the rim.

"You could call it a steering wheel," he told Beto, "a steering wheel of the mesa and the canyons and the rain and blue bellies."

Beto had laughed at him.

"What about the hands?" the old man had asked. "Were they left or right hands?"

"Well it depended on how you looked at them," Beto had answered, "whether you were looking at the top or the palms. They were good-looking hands," he said, "looked like someone had spent time on them."

The old man had been shocked by the idea of hands being viewed from inside out, as palms. As if the hands could not only be left there but be pushing out from inside the stone. Hands pushing from the inside or hands holding it back from the outside. Hands, hands on stone, sleepless tattoos, pumpkin seeds in a bowl of water. He had seen many hands pecked on stone, mutilated hands as well, with fingers missing. The surgery of giving. Hands, important as eyes and ears. He knew that they had left this as a gift. What more could they return? The touch that darkened in stone, their hands. His own quivered then like the wings of the fattened mosquito that had just left him, like the rain on the skin of the cliff wall, like the shade under the Cedars.

"I followed the hands, old man." It had been that simple, so simple that he could've missed it, but he had followed the hands to the handholds. "There were handholds; I should show you some time," Beto had said.

The hands led to handholds, the old man repeated to himself, a ladder in the wall, up and out to the rim and the sun, breaking up the storm. "I'll go with you some time," he had told Beto. "You show me." When the time was right, he had thought. So Slim had followed the hands, but hadn't found the cave. He was lucky, but it wasn't all luck. It would take a guide to lead Beto to the cave that he had missed. The old man would know when the time was right. He realized that now.

Even in the shade it was hot, being afternoon, but he knew that that wasn't what was keeping him from sleep. He scratched himself nonchalantly where the ends of his long-johns covered his forearms, the wool sleeves of his lumberjack shirt rolled back. He looked down at his boots, laced high, the leather smooth and dry, two ants crawling furiously, caught in the welter of laces. He ran both hands under the suspenders of his bib overalls as if to relieve the pressure, and then stretched back until his head rested again on the cedar. As he adjusted the rim of his cap he looked out above the mesas at the Henry's, about forty miles off. He knew he liked the way they rose, out of the flatness, three mountains as if one, and then the sky, serene around the vivid three. His eyes came back to the ground around him. There were cedar berries, the ants and their mound rising under the cedars like the Henry's under the stars. He watched an ant carry one of the desiccated berries to the top of a mound and then discard it, the sides already littered. He imagined their concern about berries. The useless seeds that required excavation, and the one berry they feared, that they searched for endlessly, that would nurture, hidden in the mound, the seed they couldn't find that blossomed because of their work, their nutrients and warmth, in their caves. The seed that would root them out, as it grew, bursting the careful construction, the hogan of sand. Cedars and ants. As he closed his eyes again, he thought he heard a truck door slam, and then the starter grinding, scratching at itself, making the noise of a cicada rubbing its hind legs while looking for a mate. He knew it was Slim on his way off of Two Horse Mesa hungry for trout.

Seven

We're almost to Deer Creek. See those Cottonwoods." Beto drove fast while talking. They were on the Burr Trail. It was smooth, wide and easy in comparison to the road they'd been on.

"What cottonwoods?" She saw trees in the canyon. Tina felt something nag at her as if she were about to feel bored. She pushed at an errant strand of thin hair that wouldn't stay tied in a tail.

"Those trees over there, the real green ones. They only grow near water. You see, you can always tell when there's water nearby if you see one. Aren't they huge? Those have been here forever." Tina could feel his excitement. She grew more nervous. She spoke with the sharp voice.

"So what are we going to do here?"

"Whattaya mean, what're we going to do? We're going to camp here. What do you think we're going to do?"

"That's what I mean."

"Well, what do you want to do?" Beto was in high speed. He was speaking quick and moving fast. He wasn't listening to Tina.

"I want a bath."

"Use the stream."

"I'm not taking a bath in a goddamn stream."

Beto looked at her. He felt his stomach tighten. He hoped that a twelve pack of beer would be enough. He had been feeling playful and wanted to continue. He accelerated anyway. He thought that if he could just make it to the Creek they'd be fine. He knew he should act serious.

"So don't take a goddamn bath, baby, but I am. There's a couple of sweet holes we can snuggle up in. They'll be plenty warm, too. Trust me."

"What about fish? There's fish in this stream, aren't there? I'm not bathing with fish."

"Oh, yeah," he exclaimed. "There's some monsters in that creek. You'll have to stay close to me because those fish love pussy." He laughed, which he shouldn't have done, but he could see the bridge, and they were moving downhill.

"Fuck off, Beto." Her voice was highly tuned. "Look at him," she spoke out the window. "He's so proud of himself." She turned to him now, "I suppose you'll want to scrub my back with pussywillows?" Then she laughed, but not for long.

"Where's the tent? You didn't bring a tent?" Her tone was so annoyed he felt the hair on his arms stiffen.

"We don't need a tent, baby. It's so fuckin' warm here, believe me."

She wasn't listening to him and she wasn't looking at him either. "What if it rains?"

"Oh Christ. Then we'll sleep in an overhang."

"What's that?"

He thought she sounded interested. "It's like a cave."

"It's like a cave. Is it a cave or is it 'like a cave.' I'm not sleeping in a cave. Do you see my knuckles dragging?"

"Forget it." They were so close he could hear the creek.

"I'm not sleeping in a cave. You forgot to bring a tent, didn't you? You didn't remember to bring a fucking tent. What did you bring, anyway?"

"I should've brought a gun."

"So I could use it on you, ha ha ha." It was her laugh again, private and excluding.

"I'd like to put it right between your tits." He wasn't grinning now.

"If you could find them," she ha ha'd again. He was braking hard now, the wheels sliding, the thought of wrapping his hands around her throat a pleasant one, until he saw the old red Ford.

"I'll be damned."

"What is it?" She sounded concerned, as if maybe he'd run over a snake.

"The old man's here. Goddamn."

"What old man?"

"The old Indian."

"I don't want to meet any old Indians."

He skirted around the other truck, dust flying, and turned the motor off before they were stopped. He left it in gear, not bothering to set the brake, and hopped out, leaving the door open. He strode over to the clump of cedars and the old man sitting there.

Tina shouted at him. "I said I don't want to meet any of your strange friends. Do you hear me? I want to be left alone."

He pretended not to hear her. "Hey, what the hell." He stood in front of the old man with a lopsided grin, his hands on his waist.

"You get paid for this?"

"Best pay in all the world."

"Catch any?"

"Three, there in the creek waiting for you."

Beto laughed. A strong laugh that he couldn't stop, like breaking out of the water when you'd been held under for too long. "Some things never change, old man." He spoke while he laughed, "and, yeah, I'll cook those babies up. I could eat all three. You clean them yet?"

"No, I was waiting until you showed up."

Beto rubbed at his face to stop the chuckling and squatted in the shade. They heard the angry slam of a door and both turned to look over at Tina, who stood next to the truck glaring at them.

"You brought your friend?"

"Mother of God, no, she isn't a friend. That's Tina, a girl from L.A. I guess you could call her my woman."

"Isn't she coming over?"

"You know as much about it as I do. Anyway. . . ." He left it at that, knowing the old man would figure it out. He would figure it out and be satisfied. The old man was good that way.

"You got a new truck."

"Yeah, I did."

"You're going to stay?"

"Of course I am. Why'd you think I came back out? I wouldn't want to leave those cows alone with you for too long." He immediately felt uncomfortable, lying to the old man like this when he really didn't know what he was going to do. The shade had shifted; the cedars had dropped their wrinkled shade. Beto stood up and pulled off his shirt, and the bucking horse came on like a searchlight pinned to his navel. The old man had to look away.

"You know," Beto said, trying to recover, "I believed you about being All Indian.

"That wasn't why I gave it to you."

"No?"

"No."

"What is it then? You don't want me to tell anyone about your last ride?"

"Maybe."

"Yeah, well, maybe it's my secret until the time is right. How about that?"

"That's fine, Slim." It suited the old man fine because he had his own secret to tell Beto.

"Come on. Let me introduce you to my girl. And hey, the belt is beautiful, really beautiful, man." He leaned over and extended his hand to pull the old man up. He was surprised at how strong the old man's hand was, the grip so sure he had to replant his feet. Had he forgotten? He looked to see if the moon was shining and he didn't let go until the old man spoke.

"Are you sure you want me to meet her now?" His eyes hadn't moved. Beto twisted his head.

"Umm. Hey, it doesn't matter to her, unless it bothers you. It's just her way, old man, if you know what I mean."

Tina was standing in the full sunshine at the edge of the creek where the water lapped up slow-like, where the shadow of the Nipple hadn't struck. There were no horsetails or ferns there, just the thick moss at the edge and Tina, tall and dark and lovely, as the song goes, and half naked. She looked tall at 5 feet 7 inches, but maybe it was because her legs were so long, or was it the shiny black hair almost to her waist? She didn't have much of a waist either, so that might have made her look longer, her shoulders and back narrow, the points of her shoulder bones sticking out. Of course, it could have been the sun on the water, or maybe they were both just staring for too long, but she looked good standing there. She shook her hair, ran her fingers through and stretched sideways so they could see both of the dark thumbs popping from her breasts. She looked so lazy that neither man wanted to disturb her. Lazily she unbuckled her shorts. Lazily she stretched, and Beto knew what would come next. Without bending, she slid them down, and then kicked them away. He was right, but he was concerned that the old man would be embarrassed, and that she had upstaged him in front of his friend. The old man wasn't embarrassed, and he wasn't surprised that Beto was nervous and jumpy. Slim was usually strung pretty tight. He would act as if this was natural, not commonplace perhaps, but fine with him. Tina was a pretty girl. Besides, he knew it wasn't her near-nakedness that caused Beto to act this way.

They both watched her as if it were perfectly clear that their conversation was over and they should be standing with their arms crossed. After Tina had kicked off her shorts, she used that gesture so common to standing women: she ran her fingers along the lower edges of her panties, pulling them higher at the top so the white lacy cotton stretched tight over her rear. Her towel was ready, placed to catch the full, long exposure of the sun. She adjusted her sunglasses, sat gracefully, and then lay down. Her hair caught so that she had to sit up and throw it to the side before laying down again. She pulled at her panties again, adjusted the sunglasses, and closed her lips tight to the sun. She acted as if she were alone, as if the eyes upon her were no more important than the caps on bottled beer.

Beto remembered they had gone to a cheap hotel in Mexico, two days in Baja California. They had walked out on a deserted beach: he had thought they were alone. But later that night, at dinner in a restaurant with people they had just met, she laughingly told the true story without a hint of restraint. How when she had taken her top off on the beach at the verge of the jungle she could see five pairs of eyes. She hadn't told Beto; instead she had convinced him to take off his shorts. He remembered that she had said those damn Mexicans were always following her, that they were behind every bush, as the dinner party roared with delight. She had led the conversation through the night. Beto had tried to smile, but he was enraged and they had fought later, all night long. "They're my *chi chi's*," she had said, "and if I want to tan them, I will." "It isn't right," he had countered, "you should be thinking of me." She had laughed.

Beto gathered the old man's arm as he stepped towards her towel. He moved in front of her, blocking the sun on her belly and said, "Tina, I want you to meet the old man."

She didn't move, and her voice was low. "Hello."

"My pleasure."

"Do you have a name, or do I have to call you 'the old man'?" She spoke with the low voice and the utter stillness of a body in the sun. Beto stirred a piece of moss with his foot. He could have been ten miles away. Like the eyes in the jungle, she had removed him. He stared at the sweat line on her belly that he was shading, remembered licking her there, and chewed the lining of his cheek.

"Well sure I do," the old man answered good naturedly. "Eziequial Bettencourt, but you can call me Sam. Easier."

"That's a distinctive name. You're Indian, aren't you?"

"My mother is, but we don't watch cowboy and Indian movies when we're naming children." Tina laughed a delighted giggle and sat up on her elbows, looking at the old man over the top of her sunglasses. The old man laughed too, and Beto tried to laugh, but it came out as a snort. She's got him, he thought, and knew he might just as well be a hundred miles away.

"Come on. Tell me you have a name like Running Bear or He Who Dives for Salamanders." They both laughed again and Tina reached out, gesturing.

"Sit down." She didn't look at Beto.

"Yes, I do have an Indian name. We're all given one later by the clan. You are supposed to grow into your name, you know," he said while making himself comfortable on the ground at her side.

"Well, what is it then? You're not going to keep it from me, are you? I don't have to buy jewelry, do I? By the way, I left my Visa card at home." She laughed happily and Beto grimaced. She could say the most embarrassing things and yet make them seem disarming and provocative.

"It's really not that special; it's more like a nickname they give you is all."

"Tell me," she half shouted as she sat up and squeezed his knee. "I won't be struck by lightning if you tell me, will I? My car will start in the morning?"

"No, no," he laughed. "Okay, it's He Who Hunts at Night With Closed Eyes."

"Oh my god," she hugged herself and rocked. "We have those in L.A. too, only you know what we call them?" She didn't wait for his answer. "Men." She was rocking wildly, laughing. She seized the old man's arm. To Beto's horror, the old man was laughing happily too.

"It means a spirit owl, Tina."

"Thank you, Beto," she said sharply and returned to the old man with a quick smile, squeezing his arm.

"It does mean that," the old man added.

"Well, do you grow feathers when the moon is full? Do you feel like moving your arms like this?" She waved her arms like a bird and then immediately touched the old man's arm again, giving him a big smile.

"It doesn't mean he hunts at night. It doesn't mean he needs the moon," Beto said sullenly.

She turned and gave him her look, her sunglasses low on her nose so he could see her blink once, then twice. It meant control yourself; you're acting like a child and embarrassing me. She had explained the signal for him many times and she expected it to be understood. Beto understood that he was really hot and he was going to let her have it in front of the old man. He didn't care who heard him.

The old man spoke. "Actually, I grow horns in the night and feathers in bed." They both laughed together as if they were great friends. "I've got three trout here for us. Will you join me?"

"Oh yes, we'll have a dinner party. Beto, why didn't you tell me about Sam? You know, Sam, he's been doing a great job of hiding his interesting friends from me." She arched her eyebrows as she said "interesting."

"You have to cook, Sam, because I can't cook over an open fire and I don't trust him. I love fresh fish. I have a fantastic recipe for trout at home. My mother showed me, actually. It's not much really, onions, garlic, cilantro and loads of lime, but everybody loves it. Right, Beto?" She didn't look at him, and he didn't need to reply, but he did anyway.

"Yeah, you're great, alright."

"Fresh trout. Well, who's going to build the fire? Beto, go clean the trout since you're the original fish monster, and I'll make a salad. We've got lettuce, tomatoes and onions. Sam, you can relax and talk to me." She stood up suddenly, holding her tank top in one hand. She put it on with one quick motion and pulled on her shorts. Of course Beto couldn't say no. He would have to clean them anyway. She had that way with people, and not just men. It was true that she was good at whatever she tried. Even Dolores had liked her when she made an effort, and the distrust would cool down between them for an hour or two.

Eight

Cecilia put the phone in the cradle slowly. She had let it ring ten times and this was the second time she had called in a half hour. The sacristy seemed large to her as she looked around it. She found herself staring at the wall with the sink, wondering why she was chewing her lower lip. She was worried, working on it, chewing. She contemplated the wall, tried to stop chewing, as she thought of Robert. What is he doing? What is he, a flake? He should have called or been here by now. It's his grandmother, not mine. If he thinks the church is organized. . . . She reached for the phone again, but decided against it. This church is not organized. She was working on it so that Father Reilly could drink his coffee and read the paper. At least this place wasn't as screwed up as the Pioneer Market. The manager there was little better than a boxboy without her. Then there was her mother with her shopping lists, asking her opinion of every item, but too shy to go shopping with her. On top of it all, she carried a full load at Cal State. Why was she so organized? I should loosen up, she told herself. I don't really want all this responsibility. Her boyfriend was the only person she knew who was more regimented than she. He set his clothes out for the week ahead; they dated every Saturday night, movie and dinner, and then back to his place to get it on once before midnight. He called every Wednesday night. He even laid out his socks a week ahead. Once every Saturday night and then he'd take her home. She couldn't imagine Robert acting that way; she couldn't imagine him with matching socks. She had seen him twice during the last four days.

She remembered that the light had been identical four days ago in the morning, late morning; it was the light from the stained glass windows that made it similar. He's changed, she had thought, really changed. He was more hidden than ever. Beto had come in after mass to tell Father Reilly that his grandmother Dolores had died and he wanted a mass this Saturday and a rosary, and that it had to be a closed casket. Just like that and then he had left. He didn't say "hello," although he had looked at her twice, once coming in and once going out, acknowledging her, but not speaking, and now he expected her to handle everything. He hadn't said a word at the rosary, although she knew that she had ignored him—she had been uncomfortable with the girl he had brought. She decided that the best thing to do was not worry. There was an hour and a half remaining before mass, plenty of time for everything to work out, or for it all to be a mess, down the tubes. I can't stop myself, she thought. I worry; that's all. I'll call Ray. Ray's his best friend; Ray would know. He was a business man of sorts. He would know. She would just call Ray; one more call, and then she would feel better.

She picked up the phone. She noticed that her hand had never left it. She called the operator. She hated to call the operator, but there wasn't a phone book in the sacristy. She asked for Ray's Body Shop. "L.A.," she said. She wrote the number down on the clean pad next to where she had written "Ray's Body Shop." She underlined the number after the second recording. She was just starting to tap out the numbers when she heard the voice. She wheeled, slamming the receiver down harder than she wanted. The undertaker was half in the door, as if a man that wide could not be more than half way in a door. He had a fat red face, the collar below buttoned too tight. A sad face with drooping eyes. But it wasn't the droopy eyes or hairless mustache, or even the shiny suit and shoes with liquid black shine that indicated his profession. It was the hat. He held a small black hat in his hands. He held the hat with both hands, the fingers over the brim so she could measure their shortness, thick short nails on blunt fingers. It was also the fingers. She wondered if she looked surprised as she noticed her heart beating quickly. He was stepping into the center of the doorway now, as she brushed her hair back with one hand and touched the pearl earring in her right ear. She kept her other hand on the phone. She looked into his eyes. He wasn't dead yet, close, as his black eyes flicked warily, taking it all in.

"Ceci." His voice was not a funeral director's voice; it belonged to a soprano in the opera; it waltzed through his non-existent moustache.

"Mr. Gutierrez, you're here early."

"Did I surprise you?"

She hesitated. "Yes, actually you did. I—I didn't expect you."

"You were making a call. Should I wait for a moment?" he asked, but he didn't move. He hadn't moved since he'd slipped in past the doorframe. She hesitated again, and he spoke up.

"I'll be out of your hair; I know you have a lot to take care of. I just wanted you to know that I was here. I'm setting up now." He waited, not moving. She noticed that he had combed his hair straight back, like an undertaker, but he didn't have much hair. It was long on the sides, slicked down and combed back artfully. She could see it was thinning on the top. If he turned she would see how long it was in the back. She suspected that he was careful to have it barbered correctly, but it wasn't, the thin hairs looped over his tight collar. She should have known; everyone knew Gutierrez lived at the mortuary. It hadn't always been a mortuary; once it had been a sanitarium, but Ceci had only heard that story. She wondered if he cleaned his hands, scrubbed his fingernails before he ate. Surely he did, but he lived at the mortuary so she didn't offer to shake hands with him. Did he have stuff under his fingernails? Blood, clotting liquid, stuff? She didn't want to think of it, but she did. She noticed that her hand was still on the phone, and that she was rubbing her thumb along the edge of it. She looked at her thumb, half expecting to see black from the phone under the nail. She'd wash her hands later; she'd wash them well. She wondered if Chan, the other partner in Gutierrez and Chan, was the mortician, the embalmer, the one who did all the gutty work. That would explain why Gutierrez didn't need to wash his hands before he ate.

"You know it's a closed casket. I wanted to remind you that the casket was to stay closed. That's all I was told—that it was to stay closed."

Cecilia decided to move. I'll walk over to the linen closet, she told herself. She did and opened it. She pretended to be studying one particular shelf. She forced herself to touch the linens, to finger them.

"Yes. I know that the casket is to remain closed," she said over her shoulder.

"It's a little strange, don't you think?" He hadn't moved. Her fingers stopped for a moment. He continued, "a closed casket. I don't get too many closed caskets, not in this neighborhood. You have any idea why they wanted it closed?"

Her fingers closed on a chalice cover; she decided to pull it out.

"No. Not really, Mr. Gutierrez."

"Yes, strange that it's all closed up. A person shouldn't be all closed up unless they don't look good. Even then we can make them presentable. Babies, now babies are another matter. No one wants to see a baby in a casket, just too hard on the women. But a young woman, nice looking too, shouldn't be closed up."

"You think she was young, Mr. Gutierrez?" She thought of Dolores Reynolds who looked young for her age, but who was at least in her eighties. Gutierrez lived in the mortuary, she thought. Perhaps he drank a little every night, alone in the mortuary, just he and Chan, who wasn't a heavy talker.

"Not a day over twenty-one, rather young to die from diabetes. Like I told you, they don't like to see them when they're too young."

She smelled him. A sour smell like wine left overnight in a metal cup. She realized that he had moved. He was close to her. It was his breath that she smelled. He must drink in the morning too. He should drink vodka, she thought, if he drinks first thing upon waking at the mortuary. She turned to face him. He was too close. His hands were rubbing the brim of the hat, moving it in a circle, one hand at a time, like any other old person turning a car wheel.

"I didn't know you could die from diabetes anymore?"

He left one hand on the hat; the other one moved out and opened palm up. It was a very short thick hand that didn't look capable of embalming work. Chan must have thin hands, she decided.

"To tell you the truth, it's rare, but they do go into shock and all, and if you can't hit them with the insulin they can go. Her arms were marked up good too; she was hitting those shots for a while; in fact, some were still red." He stopped and looked at Cecilia. His eyes, which weren't moving, looked like periods on a page; they were that small.

"Her hip?" Ceci asked.

"What about it?"

"Nothing."

His hand left the brim, left the turning of the wheel for another corner. Then he touched her arm. She didn't want to recoil, but she did. Her eyes widened; his flickered. He squeezed her arm slightly like a man who wanted to feel flesh but couldn't. He would squeeze a doorknob the same way.

"I won't open the casket."

"I appreciate it. I just don't want any problems with her relatives and all. They paid good money and they were adamant, demanding really. The sister, that is, she did all the talking."

"Yes, the sister."

"You met her, of course. She always do all the talking?" He waited. Ceci didn't reply. "Ran the show, did all the talking. The brother didn't say a word. Skinny fella, let the sister do it all, but she wanted it that way, if you know what I mean. Dressed to kill, if you know what I mean."

"Yes." Cecilia remembered the night of the rosary. She had an idea who the sister was.

"I know I've kept you and I've gotta go too, but I have to tell you the darndest thing."

"What's that?"

He paused. She waited. The air was cold in the sacristy. She heard a wave break against the windows; it was a truck on the overpass. "She told me to bury her the way she was. The sister told me that. In nightclub clothes, not a dressing gown or a pretty dress, just the way she was in those nightclub clothes." He paused, not moving, and started to speak again. "Then the darndest thing. Her brother sneaked in the night before last and spent half the night talking to her. Maybe he thought he'd sneak by, but I'm a light sleeper. I'll bet he didn't want his sister to know, the live one, that is."

There was a knock at the door and a young man's face appeared. Gutierrez spoke without looking around. "I'm coming, Ricardo. Wait for me out at the front, will you?" He waited until the footsteps subsided and then he leaned in, his breath covering her. "Anytime I can be of help to you, young lady, let me know." He squeezed her wrist. His face attempted a smile that missed his moustache. His eyes flicked once more, reading every inch of her. He waited.

"I'll keep in touch, Mr. Gutierrez." It seemed as if he would never move. Then he finally turned and walked to the door.

"I'll be seeing you. Call me if you need me." She watched the doorknob turn. She stared at the doorknob for another two minutes, at least two minutes. She wasn't interested in the doorknob; she saw it, but didn't see it; she just couldn't take her eyes off it. She remembered a kitten she had found in the front yard and brought home, her mother staring out the back window, staring at the yard. She thought of Gutierrez cooking his dinner, her boyfriend folding his socks. What made sense anymore? Her mother afraid of leaving the house? Coming to church? Her mother dressed and then refusing to go, calmly wishing her daughter goodbye? Was Gutierrez crazy? Should she go talk to Father Reilly? Who was in the casket and where was Robert? Cecilia moved her eyes to stare up at the stained glass window high in the room. My God, he came here and talked to Father Reilly. I was here. He told the both of us. It had been after mass four days ago, the eight o'clock mass. Father

Reilly was at the counter by the phone, his vestments still on. He was telling her about the beauty, the parables of Peanuts cartoons. She was only half listening, wiping off the gold and silver service used at the mass. Snoopy as Apostle. She remembered that Robert had come in the doorway just like Gutierrez. He had stood there, half in, and had waited. She hadn't noticed then that he had seemed different. He looked the same, tall and too thin, dressed in black levis and a shirt opened to his chest. She hadn't seen him in a long time, but he looked the same, the way people do when they haven't gained weight or changed the color of their hair. She had been surprised. He never came to mass. But he had stood there and she had watched him, and Father Reilly, who hadn't known he was there, had kept talking about Snoopy and the birds on his dog-house roof. Robert hadn't smiled, though she smiled at him. She had felt like giving him a hug and she didn't know why. She didn't really know him at all, except from their school days.

"Robert. Come in. It's nice to see you." She had held on to the chalice with her left hand and walked over to him, guiding him into the room with her right. He followed, her hand an inch away from his arm. Father Reilly, who had finally stopped talking, welcomed him loudly.

"Robert. How goes it, my good man? Come in, come in." He had gestured with both hands. Beto still hadn't spoken. Reilly had a big smile that he used often, but he was all right, a big man, heavy, thick and soft, going bald, but not trying to hide it.

"You know the young lady, don't you? Ceci."

"We know each other, Father," she had answered for Beto.

"Oh you do, huh, another one of your chasers, eh?" He had smiled and winked at her. "She's a tough one to catch, son. There's a list a mile long, but I'll bet you know that?"

"I imagine so." Beto spoke for the first time. His arms were folded across his chest, and he stood facing Reilly. Cecilia felt the barrier, but she didn't leave. He wanted her to leave—she could feel it. He was different. Father Reilly kept on, oblivious; he still hadn't felt anything.

"So tell me, how's everything? I hear you've been working on a ranch out in Utah. Your grandmother, such a sweet woman, fills me in on everything that goes on. We sure do miss her here in the sacristy. You back for vacation or back for good?"

"I'm here because of my grandmother." She had felt his voice, his stance, cold, but with something else; she couldn't figure it out. She wouldn't leave.

"Oh my, yes, what a terrible ordeal. Of course I went to see her as often as I could, but she's strong, strong as a horse, your grandmother, even came to church Sunday with her walker. Can I do anything for you to help out? All you have to do is ask. We hold Dolores in high esteem here, I want you to know. We take care of our pretty girls." Reilly had beamed a smile and folded his arms across his chest. The men faced each other with arms folded.

"She died last night." That was all he had said, and then he had stood there.

Cecilia juggled the chalice. Reilly stood motionless for a full five seconds, and in that full five seconds she had seen the room differently. She had noticed that the lights were off and that the light, the morning light, was coming in through a stained glass window, the only window in the sacristy. She had never noticed the light this way, not in all the years she had worked here. She saw the room as if it were a scene, removed, as if it were behind wrought iron in an alcove. The two men faced each other in the light from the stained glass window, and then Father Reilly had made a move like a jump to comfort Beto. Beto's hands went up, a reflex, half fists. The priest tried to reach out to him, but Beto took a step back. Father Reilly stopped. He had stretched his hands out. Beto's fists came down. The two men were still apart.

"My God, what happened?" There was anguish in his voice; she had heard it.

"Complications."

She couldn't look at him then. It was as if he were not in the room; he was a voice and nothing else. He had seemed far away and this hurt her. She hadn't known why. Her eyes had gone to the stained glass window, light from the morning full on the glass. She had never looked at it before, the only window in the room. She had looked at it then; she couldn't take her eyes away. They were talking, but Robert wasn't really there, and she didn't want to hear his voice. She had looked at John the Baptist, clean-shaven, one foot resting on a mound of skulls, a shepherd's staff sprouting olive leaves in his right hand. John the Baptist without a beard, his teeth perfect and white after years in the desert eating locusts and honey and hiding in the sacristy. She read the inscription below the piled skulls: "In Memory: María Elena Leon, the Leon Family." No "beloved" or "loving" or "forever" for María Elena here in the back with the priests and the altar boys. She saw a young girl brushing her hair in morning sunlight, long hair, thick, a cat rubbing her legs, the cotton nighty too short but comfortable, her body in the child's nighty. She thought of the mother afraid for her, holding fear in her chest as she watered the plants and never left the home. María Elena with the bright eyes.

But that had been four days ago, and she let her eyes leave the doorknob. "María Elena Leon," she read again, afraid to look away, a child with John the Baptist. María Elena, they locked her away, put her here in the sacristy. They wouldn't do it again. She dialed Ray's number.

"Yeah, hello."

"Ray?"

"Yeah." The voice sounded sleepy. It was heavy and dark, but it relaxed her.

"Ray, this is Cecilia McFadden. At the church."

"Yeah."

"You're a friend of Robert's?"

"Yeah."

"Well, there seems to be a problem or a mistake." She felt confused and became angry. Couldn't he say anything more than "yeah"?

"Did you try to reach him?"

"Yes, of course."

"He isn't here. He left yesterday. He didn't tell you, did he? You didn't talk to him? Yeah, he left yesterday."

"It's all a mistake. Robert's made a mistake," was all she could think of to say.

"There's a problem, right?"

"Yes, there is a problem."

"And you think I can help? I'm not positive, but I believe he went back to Utah."

"You are Robert's friend." It wasn't a question.

"Yeah, I'm Beto's friend. Is it about Dolores?"

"Yes."

He replied quickly. "I'll do anything I can for the *abuelita*. Tell me what it is?"

She told him, starting with Gutierrez, and then jumping back and forth between Dolores and her own mother. She told him about María Elena Leon.

"You want me to come over?" he asked after a pause in her speech.

"Yes, come over here, please." There was a long pause.

"I'll be right there." The phone clicked. All she could hear was the dial tone, the electronic snore. She would have listened to it until he got there, but she wanted to wash her hands. She washed her hands for a long time, and then she peeked out at the body of the church. It was empty. She could see past the flowers in the vestibule, flowers stacked up around the holy water bowls and out past the doors into the sunlight. She saw the hearse and Gutierrez talking with his helper, Ricardo, and the altar boy. They were leaning against the hearse, waiting and talking. He'll come in the front entrance, she thought; I should have told him to come in the back. She ran to the phone and dialed Ray's; there was no answer. She was at the side door when he appeared. He walked into the sacristy, and walked right up to her. The door closed automatically behind him.

"Cecilia?"

"Thank you for coming."

He waited, his hands folded below his waist. He was very calm. She hadn't expected him to be dressed like this—she noticed it right off—he wasn't dressed like a mechanic. His hands were clean, his fingernails were clean, there was no black. Only his suit and his hair and his eyes were black. His eyes were very black. She could look down into his eyes; he was shorter. She had expected a goatee, not this face clean down to the collar, smooth, with small ears against shiny black hair. He forced her to look at his face, his eyes not moving or blinking, waiting. He didn't seem like a mechanic. Maybe she would take her car to him from now on. She looked at his hands again. She saw a tattoo—Was it a cross?—above the thumb, in the fat part between the thumb and the first finger.

"Ray, what is Robert doing?"

He didn't move. "Let's check it out," was all he said.

"You mean look in the coffin?"

"Why not? We've got to check it out."

Her eyes flickered. She touched the pearl in her right ear. "We can't do that."

"Yes we can." And then he moved quickly to the door. Quick, she thought, for such a short man.

"Come on, I need your help to wheel it in here."

"What if they see us?"

"What if they do? You're the lady in charge."

She willed herself to move. She didn't want to, her legs didn't want to, but there was the coffin, bronzed wood draped with blue gardenias on a table with wheels. He knew about the locks on the wheels. He lifted the front end up and over the stairs. She wasn't sure if she was pushing. He had to tell her to close the door behind her.

"I don't think we should do this," she heard her voice say. He didn't stop. He threw the mantle to the floor and used his car keys to break the tiny lock over the clasp. She heard a voice that wasn't hers, insistent and calm and loud inside her. "Open it," the voice said inside her. "Open it. We want to see her. We want to see the pressed eyes, the folded hands. We want to see a young girl." It was just as Gutierrez had told her. Cecilia saw a young woman. A young woman with closed eyes, heavy makeup, thick foundation, wide face, dark hair cut and curled, a short neck and bare shoulders. But Gutierrez had been wrong: it wasn't a nightclub dress; it was a negligee, a black negligee. She could see the young girl's breasts through the material. They were not small. They had slid to the sides. A black negligee and folded hands. And in her folded hands was a pink rosary.

Nine

Beto found the trout stuck through the gills. The thin, snappy creek willow bent over from the weight of the fish lay in the water. He pulled one off, still alive, gasping, the colors speckled along the sides of its belly. He figured almost a pound. Sweet, the young ones were sweet. He felt the trout turning in his hand, the mouth opening and closing, the tail flapping his wrist. He held it tighter, brought his hand high and then smacked the head down on a rock sticking up out of the stream. The fish quivered and Beto could feel currents pulsing through the body to the tail. And then when the current shattered, suddenly, in the center of the trout, he could feel this, too, in his hand, as the tail arched into a stiff curve. He saw the once-rich sides of the native, and watched as the colors dulled until they looked as glazed as the sides of the canyons. It annoyed him, the death of color. He picked up his knife with his right hand and slid the blade in near the tail until it just broke through and then ran it up to the neckbone. He dropped the knife onto a patch of miner's lettuce and with one finger scooped the guts from the cavity. At the neckbone he tugged until the membrane snapped and then he threw the guts into the stream. He hadn't pulled hard, and now the guts lay there in the slow-moving stream on flat sandstone. He washed out the insides of the trout, watching the guts the whole time as they flowed away. He placed the trout next to the knife on the miner's lettuce and bent over to slide another fish off the tamarack. This one was fatter. When he opened it up he saw the roe, bright berries encased in transparent jelly. He didn't want to just throw them into the stream, so he placed them into the water at the edge where they lay in a compact pile. He watched them. He was in shade now; the whole creek was in shade, but he could see the roe clearly. He felt the coolness from the stream in contrast to the canyon. The canyons were the first to grow dark, but they also held in the heat so it remained warm long after the sun fell, and even now he could still feel the reflection of heat on his back from Molly's Nipple. Maybe there was more of a current here at the edge, or maybe it was the lightness of the eggs that made them lift off in ones and twos and float away slowly so that they looked like a string of traffic lights or beads. He held the last fish, the third trout, in his hand. He felt himself squeezing it harder than the others, but he couldn't swing it down on the rock, damp now from the previous deaths. He looked at the eggs again and thought of the rosary and Dolores.

She had cried when he had told her about the rest home. They weren't big tears, just a wetness on the skin below her eyes, under the lashes. She said she didn't want to go away, to be with old people, people dying.

"Why can't I stay at home? You don't have to stay here with me, you can leave," she said. "Just let me stay home."

"Dolores," he said. He always called her by her first name unless he was teasing her or angry, and then he called her Lulu. Sometimes, at night, he might call her *"mama"* when she had difficulty sleeping as he rubbed her head, the hair still curly. And sometimes, too, when he was troubled he would call her that, a whisper, and she would hug him. "It's just that you're getting older. They'll cook your meals, clean; you won't have to worry about a thing."

He told her how he couldn't take care of her because he was leaving and he was worried about her. "I'll come back and bring you home as soon as your hip heals up."

Dolores sat in her place, on the bench at the dinner table where they could look out at the garden on the hillside and the goldfish pond, empty now except for the moss and tadpoles squirming in it. She wrung her hands and fretted over him. "Can I fix you something? I made *frijoles*; I'll heat them up with cheese, the way you like them."

"No," he said. "I'm not hungry," and that was true, because his stomach felt heavy. He went to the ancient refrigerator, noisy in its corner, and pulled out a Coors and a 7UP. He had opened the beer and drunk half of it before mixing her a 7UP and gin. She didn't want the drink. She took one sip, then played with the glass, wiping at the moisture with her fingers, thin, brown fingers, arthritic and cold, she said, but he loved their color and the skin which was thin and smooth at the same time. They saw a tom circle the pond.

"Not so many cats come by anymore," she said.

"The goldfish are all gone," he replied. He looked at the BB gun still propped in the corner. The barrel of the BB gun was another tube, the same dimensions as the legs of her walker standing at the corner of the table. He wondered if the walker had "Daisy" stamped on the legs, a drilled hole for the ammo. He imagined picking up the walker and firing off a volley of four shots. The tom would get more than a sting on the flanks, wouldn't he? He could teach Dolores to swing it up on her morning walks in the garden and spray the bushes. The BB gun had been there for years. She'd always hated it, but he wouldn't take it back into his bedroom. "Dolores, the cats eat the goldfish; that's why there aren't any more." She stared at the tom as if she hadn't heard a word.

"I'm gonna get that one, damn cats." But he didn't move. He didn't have the energy to upset her anymore. Besides, he knew she'd sooner hobble over to the stove, pushing her walker, than have him shoot the cat, even if it didn't hurt them much. He decided to forget it. He didn't want a fight with a breakfast he didn't even want. He tapped on the window and made a jumping gesture with his hands. The tom, alerted, bunched up, but didn't run.

Dolores studied a prayer tract she held in both hands. He watched her lips moving, and then her hand adjusting her reading glasses. She didn't look up from her reading when she spoke to him. She probably knew it by heart anyway, he thought. What the hell good is it to read prayers? Wouldn't that be like the old man reading Hemingway before fishing?

"I wish you wouldn't swear, Sonny." She paused. "I'm not going to buy any more goldfish. It's a waste of good money." She waited again, then looked up from her prayers. "Will you take me to mass?"

The tom hadn't moved. He was still watching Beto through the window, his leg muscles bunched tight. Beto figured that if he moved for the gun, the tom would split, wise old tom; the cats had gotten bold since he'd been away. He finished his beer and looked at his grandmother sitting on the other side of the table. She was still reading or praying.

"Oh jeez, yes. How many times did I tell you I'd take you? Any time you want; you want to go now?" He paused, wishing he hadn't gotten so reactive, but then her lips were still moving and he couldn't hear any words. "Dolores. It's the cats. Do you understand? You've got to keep the cats away. These cats are smart suckers; they know the minute I leave. Lookit, I'll buy the damn goldfish."

Her lips were still moving as she read her prayers, but now she was talking to him. "You spend your money foolishly. How are you going to get ahead?" She stopped for a moment. He watched her lips move and realized that she had returned to the prayers. "Your poppa and I saved. We saved our money. We didn't have fun like you." She stopped, her lips not moving now as she looked up at him. "That's how we bought this house and took care of you. What are you going to do? Tell me, *mi'jito.* You don't stick to anything."

Beto got up from his seat at the table. He needed another Coors. He stopped at the edge of the table and looked back through the window. He knew it; the tom had disappeared. Smart tom, he thought. The kitchen and dining room looked smaller than usual. Same room for thirty-one years and now it looked smaller. Why was that? The dining room and kitchen appeared to be in its usual shape, a rectangle, the dining room set off by a curved Spanish-arch. A picnic-style maple table, dark from varnish, filled the narrow dining room. He could look out from anywhere in the kitchen and see the terraced hillside crossed by cement paths. It was a garden that she had planted and cared for, and it had flourished. From his seat at the table he could look up the terraces and see the lemon and lime trees, the loquats that ripened quickly, the grape arbor that covered the patio and kept it in cool shade even during September.

It had been his place at the table forever, a bench covered in red naugahyde under the Rivera print of two peons. He had only discovered it was a Diego Rivera the month before he went to Utah. It hadn't been the discovery that interested him but, rather, why his grandparents had picked this particular picture since the only other pictures in the house were of the Sacred Heart of Jesus, Our Lady of Guadalupe, and two clown faces from a paint-by-numbers kit, painted remarkably well by his grandfather. The print in the dining room was darker than the original, but then it had hung there for over forty years absorbing the cooking and the cigarette smoke of Jack, his grandfather. He had often wondered about the couple in the print: the man, who looked old but wasn't, was bent under an enormous load in a basket, while kneeling on one knee, readying himself to pop an artery when he stood up; the woman, the man's wife, he imagined, because there was this kind of feeling in the painting, was helping him. She probably didn't want to see him pop a nut, and they must have worked at this basket together anyway. The woman looked younger with her braids and all, but upon closer look, her face was old before its time. They weren't old, he reasoned; they just looked that way, but still he could tell that they were both worried about the load. He had never noticed what was in the basket until he had seen the original. He had asked Dolores about it, but she had had to put her glasses on and stare at it for awhile before she had told him they were *tunas,* prickly pears. She told him that Poppa had bought it, years ago, that he had been very artistic. In the original it had looked as if the basket were loaded with cotton, but still, it was a large basket and it was strapped around the man's head. He supposed his grandfather had been artistic. The picture did hang in an odd place; if he leaned his head back he would hit it. But he suspected that old Jack had picked up the print for a more practical reason—the picture hid the fuse box. Round fuses, the old type. Beto had stuck pennies behind them in emergencies, but he had never really looked at the couple until he had seen the exhibit.

He rested both hands on Dolores's walker. She wouldn't need the walker for long, he thought. She hadn't broken her hip; it was just a bad strain. He wanted another beer but held back. He wanted to leave, too, but he had promised Dolores he would take her to church. She would say something about his drinking if he had another one this early in the morning. He opened the door of the refrigerator, staring at the six pack of Coors. Maybe if he pried the tab off slowly . . . but he knew she would be listening to him. Instead he listened to her rifling through her prayer tracts, her embossed cards with invocations, old church missals, throwaways that covered the end of the table.

"Sonny. It's not even ten o'clock yet. You shouldn't drink so early." He could hear her rustling among the papers. She continued, her voice droning, "It's a beautiful day. There's so much you could do. Remember, you have to take me to church." She tried to give an upward lilt to her voice so that it wouldn't seem like a demand.

Beto didn't answer, but he put back the beer he was holding, closed the door and went to the cupboard. At the sink he cleaned a glass, and then wiped it cleaner still with a dishtowel. He always cleaned the glasses before he used them, wondering, even when he was in primary school at St. Teresa of Avila's, why they were never clean when she washed them. He went back to the refrigerator, having decided on orange juice, and took out the carton he had bought the night before. The top had been mangled. It was torn at the crease of the spout, and when he looked closely he could see fingerprints on the inside of the opened carton. He was hidden. He couldn't see her because of the refrigerator, so he spoke a little too loudly, his voice angry and whining.

"Why did you open my orange juice, Dolores? You have your own." He hefted the primeval juice container that had been used for as long as everything else in this house, to make sure. He felt and heard the juice slop against the sides. It disgusted him; he could smell the fermented oranges from an arm's distance. Had it ever been cleaned, he asked himself, or was new orange juice dumped in before the old was finished?

"I don't know why you buy the cartons, Sonny." Her voice sounded hurt. "I made juice yesterday. It's fresh." She sounded accusing. "You spend your money like there's no tomorrow."

"Yeah, well I see you're already into mine. I don't care how much it costs, just let me open the carton. Alright?" He was speaking loudly from behind the fridge in that tone used for very small children. "I'll buy you your own if that's what you want, but keep your grubby paws out of mine. You stuck your fingers inside. Can't you open a carton right? I've showed you a million times how to do it." He pushed the carton under her nose and demonstrated by pulling the two leaves apart.

She didn't watch his fingers, but looked into his face. "Oh my goodness," she said, her voice racked with anguish. "Look at all I've done for you and you're complaining about a little juice?"

"I said I'd get you your own carton if that's what you want. Can't you understand that I don't want you sticking your fingers inside my carton of juice?" He felt like slamming the carton against the far wall where it would splash behind the stove so she could smell rotting oranges for awhile. "Why is it that you complain about what I buy, but you have to try it all the time? I don't get it."

"Wait until you're old, Sonny," she started off, hurt. "You're young now; you don't think ahead, but the doctor says I have the worst kind of arthritis. I can barely say the rosary at times."

Beto heard the high-pitched squealing laughter of Tina and the old man's chuckle as he stared into the creek. They were probably waiting for him to bring the cleaned fish. He noticed that it was growing dark enough to hide the bottom of the stream and that he hadn't taken his eyes off the roe which appeared fluorescent now in the night water. The eggs, which had moved off so slowly at first, had settled in a string so close that he felt he could reach out and touch them. Dolores had complained about her arthritis. He imagined her nervous fingers calming themselves around the roe. He remembered that he didn't want juice anymore as he put the carton back in the fridge, thinking "she'll drink it." How he had opened a can of beer as loudly as he could to disturb her. He felt his own fingers now and realized that the third trout was lifeless in his hand. He hadn't felt the fish stop its gasping. He picked up the knife off of the miner's lettuce, grateful for the night that would hide the death of color on the sides of the trout.

Ten

"That's not Dolores," Ray said as he looked at the dead girl in the coffin.

"I know it's not Dolores. Who is it?" Cecilia asked sharply.

"I don't know what the hell's going on." Ray looked away. Was it just four nights ago that he had called to invite Beto to feed the cats? The cats on the island, his nightly romance, their night man with the paper plates and the cans of 9 Lives. He thought of how Beto was still fond of the cats, but that he always wanted to hold them. "It not their nature," Ray had tried to explain to him that night.

"I gotta go, Ray," Beto had said before they finished the joint. Ray thought he wanted to be with Tina, his ex, but he didn't say it, and he didn't want Beto to leave so quickly when he'd hardly seen him in the last two weeks.

"How's Dolores doing?" Ray had asked. "I went to see her last week, before they let her out of the hospital. She looked good."

"She bitches and moans like always. So she's fine. Complains about the doctors and nurses, says because the nurses are "Negroes" they don't like her. She's fine. You know how she can be."

"She broke her hip, brother; that's tough for an old lady."

"Take more than that to put her down, you know that. Pure venom in those veins."

"Come on, that's your *abuelita*. She's one beautiful lady."

Beto jabbed at Ray's chest with his finger as his voice tightened. "What you know is she's always nice to you. Ray this, Ray that, 'look what he's done with himself. He's a businessman.' I'm sick of that shit. But you know what she says about you? You don't speak Spanish good; you ever hear her say that, Ray? Dig it, you can't talk right and you're dark too, man; that's what she says about you and yet you stick up for her. She's mean and you don't get it."

Ray had backed up a step. He was disturbed that Beto would talk like this, tell him things he already knew. "What the fuck?" he had said, "she's just an old lady. Don't you think they're all like that, a little crazy? Got their fuckin' opinions?"

"No one's like her, man. You don't think she's trying to drive me pure fuckin' insane? She wants me around to fight with and that's it. She took her husband to the mat, every morning and every evening; I saw it. He had to get drunk every night. Only way he could live."

Live to die, Ray thought. A Catholic suicide. A lot of pain in that family. Dolores' husband had been English; that could explain a lot. And Dolores hiding her own culture all those years. A lot of pain, but what family is free of it? "No, man, this may sound crazy to you, but you gotta think of this. Your *vieja* may look tough, but she's got pain too, and she loves you, brother. It's her way of showing it."

"I've got the pain. What the fuck do you know? You're set up; you got a good thing going. Whatta you know?"

Ray saw the cats feeding; they ate too fast, gulping, their eyes fixed anxiously on the men in front of them. He wondered if they were always this nervous.

"You're not going to get me hot at Dolores, or you. What's eating at you?" Ray heard himself speaking, but he was watching the cats. He wondered if they would think he was talking to them, but he saw that when they had finished the food, the plates clean, they disappeared.

"Give it up, Ray."

"No, you come on. She's holding on to you hard because she doesn't know any other way. She's there for you, but you see, she doesn't have any power, not really. What if you were gone, what would she do? You're it, man. She's all alone, but you don't want to see it. I don't think you know how important you are to her."

"I see it every day; you're the one who doesn't see it."

"I do see it; I see you. I see her. I knew your Poppa, too, you know? They were rough on each other. But maybe Dolores felt like he was only there because of you, not for her. You know what I mean?" He felt that he had never spoken so much, tried this hard to make sense of something he had never attempted to put into words. "Beto, look at these cats. We come here and feed them and we can't even touch them; you know what I mean? You remember Spitfire? Never let us pet her, but that didn't stop us from coming here all the time with cat food and peanut butter sandwiches. Hell, there ain't no great reward, 'cept that we care about them. They'd get by without us, but it wouldn't be the same. Not for them and not for us. It's just one of those good things, man, that's a pain in the ass—your old lady needs you."

"You come here. You feed them, not me. If you're so hungry for attention, why don't you reach out and touch someone yourself? Why don't you get laid for a change?"

That's why he hasn't been right, acting strange, Ray thought. He knew he'd have to mention her now. There was no way out of it. "Beto, why didn't you tell me you were running around with Tina? You didn't have to hide it from me."

"I don't want to hear about it, Ray," Beto said as he turned and started to walk away. "I've heard one speech already. You don't have nothing to do with Tina anymore. She's mine now. You're just like Dolores—you don't trust her. Your problem is you don't trust women. That's why I didn't tell you. Now let's go." Beto was waiting in the dark at the bridge. Ray looked at the cleaned plates.

"You go on," he said. And then the anger that had built up spilled. "It's no skin off my fucking back what you do, but your attitude is shit." Ray heard the echoing footsteps on the bridge and then a car starting up and pulling away. He had reached down to pick up the cleaned plates. He realized that they felt heavier than when he had carried them over, and yet they were empty. He carried them across the bridge and tossed them in a trash can like he always did.

The next day Beto had called to tell him that Dolores had died the night before. Beto hadn't wanted to talk. Ray was worried that he had said too much that night on the island. If he had kept his mouth shut, would Beto be here at the church now? He looked at the dead girl. "Maybe Gutierrez made a mistake?"

"Gutierrez knows. That's why he told me so much."

"Yeah, but he lives in the mortuary."

Cecilia remembered Gutierrez's hands and fingernails and how he ate his meals at the mortuary, thinking Ray was half right, but still, this was supposed to be Dolores, and she knew that Gutierrez or Chan couldn't do that good of a makeup job on anybody. "This is supposed to be Dolores Reynolds," she said emphatically.

"Well, it isn't, but that's her rosary."

"Are you sure?"

"Yeah, I'm sure. She never went anywhere without her beads. I must have seen that pink rosary on the dining room table a million times.

"These pink rosary beads?" Cecilia asked. "Then Beto knows what's going on. How could he do this?"

"Wait a minute," Ray answered defensively. "You don't know

that for sure." He held his hand up in front of him as if he were gently holding back a rolling truck.

"Don't get defensive, Ray. Robert went to the mortuary with his sexy number, the sister," she said sarcastically, "who paid cash for a closed casket. You know, the sister who demanded that her sister be buried with these clothes on. Come on, that sounds real normal. Then Robert came here and told Father Reilly and me that his grandmother had died. But he was there. Gutierrez told me that a young skinny guy was with the good looker. Now he's nowhere to be found and you want to defend the jerk." She swallowed hard.

Ray looked at her guardedly. If there was one thing he was afraid of, it was a woman moving quickly. He had come to believe that if they weren't planning something when you met them, they would be soon. He cursed Beto silently. "Don't get emotional, Cecilia." He regretted saying this the second it had slithered out, as Cecilia advanced on him, her finger in his chest.

"I'll give you emotion, since you believe your stupid friend wouldn't actually pull something so stupid. You came over here immediately in your brand new black suit, didn't you? You knew something was up when your bosom buddy left town, didn't you? So you came over here before I dropped the phone, didn't you?" She stopped jabbing. "You cover his back a lot, don't you?"

Ray stopped backing up. He had been stepping slowly backwards as she advanced, worried that this woman was going to tattoo the button of his white dress shirt onto his lungs. Not only did she make him nervous, but she also made him feel foolish, and he hadn't felt foolish in a long time, at least since his ex had left. Ray denied foolishness, but in the face of this woman he had backed up. On top of that, he did feel foolish for standing behind an obvious fool, Beto. It was a moral crisis that he didn't have to intellectualize over. This was neighborhood. Barrio. You back up your friends in the face of the others: the bad guys, good guys, the cops, city, institutions, the world. Your friends were like family, and yet, your blood family, whom you may despise, is the only line your friends cannot cross. The family is always to be protected and it is understood that your friend is a protector of your hearth, your family. Ray understood this too well. Not only was Dolores the family of his best friend, but she was also like blood to him. He saw her at the kitchen table with her beads. He wondered if Beto saw things the same way as he did.

"Cecilia, I want to find Dolores, I want to find her alive and healthy. Or I want to find her . . . and give her a proper burial. I don't know what Beto has done here. It looks like he has done some crazy thing, but I have to talk to him before we do anything about this." He looked at her. She was taller than he; she had green eyes. He tried to explain the matter of family and neighborhood to her. She looked unconvinced.

"I'm awfully positive that your friend Beto has made a great big mistake, probably the stupidest mistake of his sorry life, and now I'm in the middle of it and I don't like it one bit. I don't really care about protecting him and I'm sorry that this has become a family matter for you, but I'm calling the police." As Cecilia walked diligently to the phone, she noticed that she was taller than Ray. He's under five foot five, she thought. He's loyal, but no short lowrider was going to push her around. Ray put his hand over hers on the phone.

"Wait," he said. "Let's talk about this another minute before you call the cops. Please?"

"Hey, I have a dead girl who is supposed to be an eighty-year-old woman who is supposed to be dead and buried in an hour."

"The police will be no good for anybody; believe me. We've got to talk to Beto first. I've known him all my life. I have to protect him and that might protect the old lady too. You've gotta understand me. He thinks Dolores is ruining his life, but he wouldn't hurt her. He doesn't know it, but he is confused by his love for her."

She waited, struck by his passion and tenderness; then she spoke. "I think I understand you, I really do, but this thing still doesn't make sense. Listen to me. If he's in trouble, it may be the best thing to go to the police. They may save her, if she's still alive."

Ray was shocked. She doesn't understand, he thought. He noticed that although her hair was reddish, her skin was light brown. She's too tall, yet there was something oriental-looking about her. "Okay, yeah, yeah," he said, trying to think out loud. "Right. Let's look at the girl again," he said, stalling for time, as he kept his hand on hers on the phone. "Maybe she's got some i.d. on her."

Ceci didn't want to look at the dead girl, but she also didn't want to lose control. She reasoned that another few minutes wouldn't matter, and there was something so unusual about Ray that even if she didn't trust him completely, she didn't want him to leave.

"What do you think you're going to find, a green card?"

"Not funny," Ray said, but he lifted his hand and walked away from her over to the coffin. Cecilia watched him feel around the sides of the coffin and the dead girl. "Jesus, she's heavy. Will you help me? I want to turn her over."

"I will not touch that girl."

Ray succeeded in turning the girl on her side and then laid her back down when he didn't see anything unusual. Cecilia heard the rosary hit.

"Hey look at this." She breathed heavily as she stared at the corpse. She noticed first that the rosary had slipped from the dead girl's hands. The beads felt worn and surprisingly warm when she picked them up. The rosary was very pink, a soft pink, a little girl's pink, a pink you wouldn't see on a rose.

"See these marks on her arm. She's been hitting up. A doper. These are recent. See how red they still are?" She held on to the rosary and followed his fingers with her eyes. She saw that, yes, there were marks, three of them that were puffy and red. "Gutierrez said she was a diabetic."

"Diabetics don't use dirty needles. Get me a washcloth."

"What for?" She sounded annoyed.

"I want to take off her makeup. See what she really looks like. Maybe she was beat up. I think so."

Cecilia looked, but the light wasn't very good. Maybe Ray had a point, but she was suddenly feeling exhausted. If she were at the Pioneer Market and felt this tired she would sneak a *Cosmopolitan* into the ladies room and take one of the sex quizzes. It seemed like a better idea to her than taking off a dead girl's makeup. She spoke at the dead girl who was laying flat on her back again. "Here, I'll get you some Vaseline, that'll take it off better."

Ray expertly cleaned off the foundation, wiping surely with his short fingers. Cecilia wondered if he hadn't applied makeup before? A large family, for his sisters, she rationalized. He cleaned off several layers until he had exposed a sweet-faced young woman. Some mascara remained in streaks along the side of her face, but they could see that she was very young, a teenager possibly, with nice skin, clean olive-colored skin. The bruises made her look younger and sweeter, and Cecilia suddenly felt very sad for this girl, and then for María Leon in the stained glass window. She wanted to cry, but held it in. She looked up at John the Baptist. She had never felt this way towards the Baptist before. My life is terrible, she thought, a lousy job, a boring boyfriend, a frightened mother, a non-existent father, and now this poor dead girl in my church. She found herself reading the inscription on the window over and over again. "María Elena Leon, María, María," until she felt as if she were close to her, hovering over the stained glass window like the white dove over the head of the Baptist. She was concentrating so intensely now that she noticed the errant scratches in the stained glass and how the melted lead wasn't as smooth as it appeared. There was a tiny hole where air leaked in. Above the hole were the eyes of John the Baptist glaring at her as if she were unclean next to the holy man of the desert. It sounded just like wind chimes, she later told Ray, even though he still couldn't understand why she had thrown the jar of Vaseline through the face of John the Baptist. "I did it for the girls," she said.

"You alright?" he asked a little fearfully after staring at the hole in the stained glass window for a long moment.

"I'm fine, fine," she said, never taking her eyes off the window. "Let's get this girl out of here. We need to hide her," she added.

Ray looked visibly stunned, worried that someone had heard the window break. "Are you sure you're okay?" He waited, then said, "let's lock her up and wheel her back out."

"No, not in the casket. I have the perfect place. We're going to hide her in your garage."

"What?"

"We can't leave her in the casket."

"We can't put her in my garage. No way, no way."

"We can't get Dolores back if María's ten feet under. Don't you think?"

"María?"

"The dead girl. Where's your car?"

"It's in the driveway."

"You shouldn't have parked there, but this time you did good. Here, help me dress her."

"In what?" He felt overwhelmed and he couldn't seem to help it.

"Altar boy clothes."

"Isn't that a sin?"

"Yes. Help me."

"I'm not taking her into my garage."

"Right. Just help me." They carried the dead girl dressed in altar boy gowns out to the white Chevy. Cecilia's idea was to put the body in the front seat between them, but it was so stiff it went in at a strange angle.

"That's alright," Cecilia said. "It looks like you have a girl resting on your shoulder. Don't worry so much," she continued. "Two chicks, the talk will be good for you."

Ray backed out of the driveway too quickly, forgetting that the curb was old-fashioned and steep. The front bumper scraped loudly. They both jumped and looked at one another. Ray's eyes were round and he cursed under his breath. In fact, he was so nervous he forgot to put on his shades, and had to drive with his head tilted forward because he didn't like Maria's head on his shoulder. The dead girl was staring at the overhead light. They passed a lowered mini Datsun pickup with low profile fat tires on aluminum wheels, smoked windows, a beautiful aquamarine paint job and violet pinstriping. The bubble backwindow was hand-lettered with the legend, "Just you and me, Babe." He recognized the work. Cecilia looked too. The truck caught up and pulled close. A very cool-looking dude in a hairnet leaned out and spoke across the windows.

"Hey, Ramón, wha's happening, *vato?*"

Ray had to look at the man and then he realized he didn't have on his shades. It was Gil, Flaco, and another homeboy he recognized but didn't know. He was worried. He had already decided that he and Cecilia would stop by the garage. They would pull in and get off the street with the dead girl. He had gone this far, but no way was he leaving the dead girl there, and now these *vatos* would want to stop in and talk about the paint job.

"Hey homeboy." Ray tried to squint as he spoke, to make up for the lack of sunglasses. He could feel the wheel sliding, his hands wet.

"Where you hanging, man?" the hairnet asked. The pickup was so close it seemed as if the *vato* were in the seat with them, two girls and now a homeboy.

"I can't party, homes, I got to drop off the *chavalas.*"

The dude in the pickup smiled wide, showing teeth. "Yeah, man. You need any help?"

"I'm fine, man, fine. It's cool."

"Your chavalas are very quiet, Ramón." Gil was hanging out the window smiling, his friends laughing, Cecilia staring him in the face. "Who's the redhead, man?" He laughed again.

Ray was more than uncomfortable. He was hot, but he couldn't show it. These *cholos* shouldn't be talking to him this way, but he didn't know that it could get hotter as Cecilia leaned out the window and shouted, "Go blow a dead goat, you fuckin' wetback."

Ray veered the Impala across Glendale Boulevard and down a narrow side street which led to Silver Lake. He narrowly missed a Toyota Corolla which he didn't notice at first because he was hauling Ceci back into the car. The last view he caught of the pickup was of the three guys driving past the street, leaning out the windows, shouting. Cecilia saluted them with her middle finger. She was ecstatic.

"Why'd you do that?" he demanded. The dead girl, in the turmoil of the quick turn, had slipped off his shoulder and was laying in his lap. Cecilia didn't answer him as she pulled the corpse back into its almost sitting position. Neither spoke until they pulled into the cool concrete of Ray's Auto Body Shop.

"So your real name is Ramón, huh?" was all she said. He wondered if she were really this crazy.

Eleven

The old man had built a cooking fire in a blackened circle of rocks. It was a small fire, yet the pot balanced between two flat rocks was almost boiling. Young stems of green cattail shoots stuck out a good foot.

"You found some green ones?" Beto asked.

"Up past the bridge, in the shade of the cliffs and the cottonwoods, there were still these young ones. Your girl said she'd try them." He winked at Beto. Beto didn't respond. He squatted at the edge of the fire, balancing the three trout stuck through the mouths and into the tails. He had cut the three thin willows long enough to hold the trout and shove the butt end into the ground. They hung inches over the flames of the small fire, bending against a rock used as a fulcrum. The trout began to sizzle immediately, the cut edges turning up.

Tina spoke up from behind Beto. "God, they smell good, but aren't you gonna cook them in butter? I have some in the cooler. Remember I made you buy some?" He felt her legs against his back. They were bare and it was night and still warm in the canyon; it would be warm until long after the moon rose. He wanted to ignore her, but not the pressure on his back.

"You don't need any butter with these babies. See how they're sizzling? These trout have been fattening up all spring and summer, waiting for the old man to come along."

"Beto, this man tells me he caught these fish with his bare hands. Now I don't know who's the biggest liar, you or him, but I think he's had more practice at it."

Beto turned the sticks so the trout were belly up.

"Only be another second now. Hey, what you got there?" the old man asked Tina.

"I made a salad."

"We don't need a salad," Beto said.

"Listen to him, and he'll eat most of it. I told you I wanted a salad."

Beto watched the fire below the fish. He watched as if they were the only fish he had ever seen and he didn't want them to burn or get soft so they'd fall into the fire. He stared at the fire as if looking at the fish were an omen. He touched each one of the willows; a drop of grease fell and sizzled as he adjusted one.

"So tell me, Sam, since I've never heard of anyone catching fish with their hands except for bears, and I think that's only because they can't string fishing line." The old man laughed easily with her.

"Ask him about the old trout he talks to, that tells him where to catch the young ones," Beto said.

"Now that is a fish story. How big is he, Sam?" She held her arms as wide apart as possible.

"He's not a shark," answered the old man, grinning.

"On two legs you mean," she said, nudging Beto with her knees. Her voice was high and happy. He could feel the alternate pressure of her legs as she spoke. "Does this fish speak in Navajo, or is it Arapaho, or do you just read the bubbles?" The cattails were boiling fast, the water bubbling over the sides. Beto took the fish off the fire; they crackled and sizzled in the hot night air as he held them up and they all looked at the fish silently. As he held them he saw a sliver of red in the sky above Boulder Mountain and then it disappeared as if it had slid into a hole.

"Here you go," was all he said as he handed a stick to Tina and one to the old man. Tina grabbed at the stick, the split wings waving. "Watch what you're doing or you'll lose that fish."

"How am I supposed to eat it?"

"Off the stick," said Sam.

"Hell if I will. Here, hold it for me."

"What?"

"I'm going to get some plates." She shoved the stick into his hands. The trout flapped twice and fell into the sand at the edge of the fire. Beto couldn't take his eyes off the trout in the sand.

"Damnit Tina, I told you to be careful," he said. The fish looked shriveled and tired on the sand.

"Don't swear at me, you jerk. Why didn't you tell me to bring the plates?"

"We don't need plates if you don't jerk around." But she had left, striding back hard to the truck.

It was the old man who bent down and picked the trout up off the sand and walked down to the stream. "It'll be fine," he shouted back to Beto.

"Here, let me have it," said Beto, but the old man had already sunk his teeth into it as he was returning to the fire.

"No, I got it now; it's fine," he said, as water dripped off the meat and glistened on the tail before it ran down his palm and into his long johns. It didn't seem real in the old man's hands, a cooked trout dripping stream water.

"I would have eaten it. Is it cold?"

"Nooooo," he purred, "it's still warm on the inside. You cooked a good fish."

"It could have turned out better," Beto said, but he wasn't speaking to the old man. He was watching Tina's return.

"Here, put my fish on the plate. Put them both on. I don't want another one falling off. Be careful, Beto. How were we going to eat the salad without plates? You can only carry this frontier thing so far. Sit down, baby." She sat on the flattest rock available and although he couldn't see her face, he heard her lips open and close as he continued standing with two empty sticks in his hands.

"Oh my god, this is so delicious. Sam, you should've let Beto eat the one that fell. Come on, honey, sit down next to me. I've got yours on my plate. Do you want me to feed you? Is that what you want? Aren't boys a problem, Sam?" Beto sat down.

"You ready for a cattail, Tina?" the old man asked.

"Load me up."

He put three on her plate next to the trout that Beto hadn't touched.

"Easiest food in the world," the old man said, holding a cattail by the stem and munching. Tina bit into the end of one.

"Tastes just like corn on the cob, only sweeter. It needs butter."

"It doesn't need any butter, Tina."

"How do you know? I'm gonna get some and we'll see." She got up, placing the plate in his lap. "Eat," she told him as she walked over to the cooler. That was her way; she always knew better. It was amazing how no one seemed to mind that she took over. She would wait until they gave her the lead. She sensed perfectly when to accept the responsibility, which she always did. And there was the old man, smiling away, ready to drool, waiting for the butter. Beto looked at the cooled-off trout on the white paper plate in his lap, mouth open and eye as milky as the plate. There was still some color left under the fire-darkened skin where he took his first bite. It was good and he quickly stripped it, but he didn't savor the flavor or pull chunks off with his fingers to press into his mouth. He didn't like the way the butter looked on the cattail greens either, but he didn't say a word.

"Now, doesn't that taste great, Sam? Come on, it's an improvement, isn't it?" She stood next to the old man, watching him intently as if to make sure he was eating every bite.

"Very good," the old man said.

"You bet it is. I know how you boys are. You like things the way you thought of them. The old way's the best way. But sometimes you have to try something new." She came back over to the rock and sat down gracefully. With quick strokes she ran a cattail through the valley of butter. "It's much better. See, now you'll just have to remember to bring butter with you the next time. Mmm, isn't it good, baby? Here, try it." Tina shoved the cattail at Beto's mouth which remained closed. She prodded at his lips roughly, her own lips fascinated and set as if she were trying to turn over a dead cat in the road with a long springy stick. "Chew your food good," she said with that laugh, adding, "Isn't that good?"

"It's fine."

"You wouldn't say it was good anyway, but you ate it all. Want another?" she taunted, as she buttered him one up hot from the kettle still on the rock in the coals. There were no flames, just coals, and it was dark now, but the light of the coals was all he needed to see her eyes. She shoved the cattail at his mouth again, but he grabbed it before she could prod at him. He grabbed it away from her hard. He could see the look in her eyes that reflected the flame that wasn't in the coals. She reacted by turning to the old man.

"I knew he'd eat it, Sam. You shouldn't have eaten the fish Beto dropped in the sand."

"I didn't drop it. You did," Beto said.

"Don't start arguing with me now. He's your friend."

"I told you. . . ."

"But, but, but."

"Hey, you two, my trout was fine, couldn't have been better," the old man said.

But was it?, Beto thought, washed, the meat wet and dripping, his own trout, even, a memory of what it should taste like.

"Well, he just stood there staring at it," Tina said.

"Tina," Beto said, almost shouting.

"Don't get your tailfeathers up. The cattails are much better with butter, aren't they, Sam? Come on; admit it."

"I swear from this day on I will bring butter with me in memory of this occasion," the old man replied. Beto allowed himself a chuckle as he imagined the old man out here with a cube of melted butter and one of Buchanan's half-full bottles of Daniels in the glove box of the old Ford.

"You're a bold-faced liar and a fisherman," she laughed loudly. "And while we're on that subject, you can finish the story, I mean tale, of catching fish with your hands." She was speaking very rapidly. "I wish we had some ice cream to finish off this absolutely fantastic meal. Wouldn't that be great, Beto? Sam, when you come to L.A. to visit us. . . ."

"He's not going to come to L.A., Tina. Why would he want to come to L.A.?"

"Not if you act that way. Well, Sam, you will, won't you? I promise you the best meal, and ice cream afterwards, and you won't have to catch it with your hands." They both laughed. Beto got up. He was tired of the conversation and the meal. He felt that he wouldn't be missed. As he left he felt as if all of his movements were carefully watched, but it was only himself watching and reviewing each move before he made it. The old man and Tina continued talking as he squatted at the creek. He caught bits and pieces of their talk, her exuberant voice carrying over the creek noise. She is so amused, he thought. She sounded theatrical and was talking too quickly. And the old man was enjoying himself, carried away by all the attention. Beto stared into the creek, into the faint reflection that was starting to appear with the moon. He saw them again, a few, still not carried away. Pink beads. He remembered that Dolores had been telling him about her arthritis and how difficult it was to say the rosary, and that he had to stick around for mass.

"When do we have to leave for mass?" he remembered asking her.

"Oh, are you coming, mi'jito? Please, it would make me feel so good to have you there. All my friends ask about you." Her voice was almost girlish. She was speaking towards him, and he could hear her very clearly. "You know what I tell them. He's going to be a professor. He's doing very well in his studies at the university. I tell them how smart you are, but they don't have to hear it from me. I can't understand all the words you use, you know."

He worked at the beer; it made him feel good. Beer before ten o'clock, beer on the countertop. "Dolores," he said, after another swallow, "what do you tell people things like that for? I'm not going to be a professor. I dropped out of school last semester, and I'm not going to a university. I was going to City College. Whatever gave you that idea?"

"Sonny, you can't bounce from thing to thing. You have to settle down." She said "settle down" very slowly, enunciating each letter. "I told you I would help with your schooling. What are you ever going to do? How will you ever find a wife? You think you can depend on your friend Ramón for a job when you don't like to work. Why don't you come to mass and talk to Father Reilly afterwards. He likes you. He asks about you all the time."

"That faggot."

"Oh, how you talk. *Madre mia.*" He heard and watched her make the sign of the cross. She kissed the end of her fingertips. "Why do you speak such nonsense, *mi'jito?* I don't understand you. He's a priest. He has taken a vow of chastity. He wants to help."

He saw her, sitting there, on the bench across the table from his bench, behind her the shuttered window that was never opened. It wasn't her place. Hers was the only chair at the table, the chair at the end, closest to the stove. The bench was Jack's. Squat, bald, ivory-skinned Jack. Until ten years ago he had sat there, and Beto could still see him there every morning. How had this couple ever made it? She was from Pomona. Her family hadn't been wealthy, she said, but they had owned a large ranch. They were Spanish. A dirt floor and a Packard. We are not Mexicans, she would say, but the land grant was Mexican and her great-great-grandparents had been born and baptized in Mazatlan. And she's dark, he thought, eyes dark, black hair still curly and full, the dark skin of her face unlined. He had heard that the Spanish were light-skinned. "People have their ideas," Ray said often, unperturbed when she corrected his Spanish or said, "I bought the *tortillas de maiz* especially for you." And had Jack cared? The English gentleman. "Always turned out," Dolores said. Of course, she had been beautiful, still was, for her age. There were the pictures of her when they had first married and a pastel portrait Beto had hung in his room. Beauty had mattered to his Poppa. Though he had been fat, balding, squat, and incessantly sucking a cigarette, women had laughed with him. They had glowed when he teased them. He had been a hit with beautiful women. "Skirts," she called them. "I put up with a lot from that man," she would say, sitting in his place at the table. What about love? He tried to remember her laughing, his poppa teasing her. "She was too sensitive," Jack had said. What he had wanted was his coffee, black and strong, and his first cigarette in the morning there on the bench, but she had always wanted to know what he wanted for breakfast. He wouldn't talk, instead rubbing his forehead and cleaning his glasses. He had talked late into the night over gin and seltzer when they had played cards and watched t.v., Bobby and Jack. Jack had been happy at night, happy after his first gin. Beto could see the hangover now. A combination of gin and the decision of breakfast. Breakfast was when they talked. Breakfast had been their marriage. He looked past Dolores at the window that never opened. Perhaps it, too, was a picture in a frame. I need another beer, he rationalized. He left the kitchen with the sweating can, walked down the long hall open to the living room, and went into his bedroom, shutting the door behind him. He went to the balcony that faced the street, opened the windowed doors and went out. He looked over the hills of L.A.: tiled roofs, palms, and the freight yards beyond the river across from Frogtown. He saw the secret paths through the yards, the weed-covered lots, the tracks, his friends in single file. This balcony had been his escape route. A skinny pine at the corner that he had used to swing over on, and down or up as needed. The street was empty now, but he saw the streetlamp that Jimmy de la Rosa had busted with a steelie from a slingshot, and Paulie's house, crew-cut Paulie who was so white they'd turn out the lights to see if his skin glowed, and who always had to ask for permission to leave his yard, the only yard with a chain link fence. He remembered the playroom in the basement and Paulie's sister, Mary, who whispered him in and closed the door when Paulie took his nap. They had all left. Only the women remained, old women. Mrs. Josie Van Alden down the street, Mrs. Martinez next door, Mrs. Littlefield and Mrs. Schmitz across the street. And there were the new boys buying the old houses, but he didn't know them or want to. Old women and trouser pilots now; where had his neighborhood gone? He watched Mrs. Schmitz wash and sweep the sidewalk and gutter in front of her house up the street from his balcony. He liked that his balcony had a tile roof, that it was covered and in shade so that he could watch, unexposed. He had found the binoculars on his dresser when he returned. Jack's binoculars, heavy and black, the powers of Zeiss Ikon. And then he had caught her once, Dolores, in the shadows of the balcony peering into the rooms of the boys. But some things hadn't changed. There was Mrs. Schmitz sweeping. Sweeping and calling to her dog Shatzi in the same sing-song voice that had never lost its accent.

"I'll be right there, Shatzi. Quiet boy, I'm right here." Shatzi had been dead for over fifteen years, though Beto was sure that the dog would remain a cause of grief on the street as long as the old women were still alive. The small german shepherd had bit him in the thigh as he was running to the lot next to Paulie's house and the path down to the tracks. Mrs. Schmitz had been sweeping, as usual. She had said it was only a scratch, nothing to worry about; the dog had been excited because he was running. He hadn't thought about it, but later, when he was in the bath and Dolores saw the teeth marks, he had remembered the dog with its ears back tugging at his leg, and he heard his own screaming over the growls, and Mrs. Schmitz calling out again and again: "Shatzi! Shatzi!" It had started to hurt when Dolores became excited. It had started to hurt in the bath water with the pain in her voice. She had called in Jack, but she didn't want to make any trouble because it was Mrs. Schmitz's dog, and because it was the neighborhood. Beto had sat in the kitchen in a towel with Dolores next to him stroking his head and crying. "Don't make waves, Jack," she had said over and over. "Shatzi doesn't have rabies. They're very clean people. The dog doesn't have rabies. Sonny will be alright. It's only a scratch." But Jack had had another gin and yelled at Dolores to shut up, and then he had gone across the street. Beto had made Dolores come with him to the balcony, but she had stayed inside the room where the shadows were. She called to him to come inside when Mrs. Schmitz walked over to the house with his Poppa. It was the only time that she had ever come into their home. They had all looked at his thigh. He had had to lay on the bed with just his jockey shorts on as Mrs. Schmitz and Dolores touched him around the bite and Jack filled the room with smoke. It was only a scratch, Mrs. Schmitz had said. Her Shatzi didn't have rabies. He was a clean dog; he was only playing. Shots she didn't remember. What Beto remembered was Dolores reassuring Mrs. Schmitz that everything was alright, his grandfather's anger, and his own embarrassment with the women poking at his bare thigh. If Dolores hadn't seen the bite, he wouldn't have been embarrassed and there wouldn't have been such a big trouble. It wasn't much, he had thought. Just the embarrassment.

He knew now that if Dolores hadn't ever known, her life might have turned out differently. His life might have been different, too. The next day, the public health officer had come and quarantined the dog. When they took Shatzi away in the dog pound truck, Dolores had cried all that day and the next two. She had watched the house across the street from the balcony, talking to herself, and had finally gone over to Mrs. Schmitz's, returning immediately when Mrs. Schmitz slammed the door in her face. Beto had seen it all from the balcony. Jack rubbed his forehead and wouldn't talk, but went through three bottles of gin in two days. Beto had been happy because he stayed home from school for a week while they tested Shatzi. He was supposed to stay in bed, but he shinnied down the tree next to the balcony and played in the vacant lot next door in the green weeds that were already three feet high. He didn't care about the bite, a scratch, although he hoped that Shatzi wasn't rabid when he heard about the shots he would have to have in the stomach. He remembered that what had worried him the most was that the dog would know it had been he who had caused the public health officer to come. He had decided that he would be very careful when walking by Mrs. Schmitz's house, but he never thought about how Mrs. Schmitz felt, or Dolores either. He didn't understand that Dolores was a nervous wreck, as Jack put it, but he did notice that she was praying all the time and saying the rosary. She still made him breakfast that he didn't eat and he still played whenever he wanted to without telling her. He hadn't known what nerves were, and then they had taken Dolores to the sanitarium on the hill off of Sunset Boulevard in Echo Park. They had visited her there every Wednesday and Saturday, the place where they cut jello into tiny cubes. Just jello, no fruit or bananas like Dolores made it. The first two visits she didn't know who they were, which seemed odd to Beto because she had always hugged and kissed and fussed over him so much. She had sat quietly in a heavy red leather smoker. He hadn't liked seeing her that way. He had tried to give her a hug, but Jack told him to sit, that her head hurt. He had wanted to kiss her eyes because they were black and blue and touch the shaved circles at her temples. Jack had told him it was alright, that she had a treatment was all, like going under a hair dryer. He hadn't understood, but then his poppa wasn't the greatest at explaining until he'd had a belt. He knew it couldn't be a hair dryer, because Dolores came out happy after an hour under the machine and she wasn't happy at all now. After the first week, Dolores had remembered them, but she was still quiet. She hadn't seemed relaxed, which was what his poppa had told him would happen, but she did save the little cups of cubed jello for him.

Shatzi was still here, he thought, as he watched the woman call the dog and sweep the street. Shatzi would always be tugging at his leg with the open eyes and ears thrown back. He heard Dolores calling from the kitchen. He noticed that the can of beer was empty and he couldn't remember taking a drink.

"Sonny, we have to leave in twenty minutes. Are you ready?"

He smelled toast burning. He went into the bathroom and brushed his teeth. She came up behind him as he was rinsing his mouth. He could hear her eating toast. She had waited until it wasn't warm anymore and then had tried to scrape off the burn. There was more black than toast, the bottom all black and the butter clumped and unmelted. She bit and chewed, the burnt crumbs slipping between her fingers and falling to the floor. They stuck to her teeth as well. In her other hand she held a cup; coffee slopped over the side of the cup when she bit the toast. She didn't notice. And she wasn't shy about coming into the bathroom, but then, he never noticed it either.

"Will you cut your hair for me? Please, honey, you are so handsome."

"I think I'm going to grow a beard." He stared at himself in the mirror, but saw her over his shoulder. He watched her dip the toast into her coffee. A clump of unmelted butter slid off and floated in the cup.

"Oh Lord. Don't even kid me. You wouldn't hide your beautiful face, would you? Beards are ugly and dirty. I wouldn't go out with a man with a beard, you know. My mother wouldn't even let them into the house."

"Your family were a bunch of hypocrites; they didn't like anyone."

"My mother liked your poppa, and you know what he was."

"You never had to work a day in your life."

"My God, Sonny." He watched as crumbs fell from her lips as she set them tight. "You don't know. I had to live with that man for forty-nine years. I waited on him hand and foot. He never took me out; we always stayed at home. He was mean to me, you know."

"Yeah, with someone like you, how else could he survive?" He felt bad even before he spoke, but he had said it anyway.

"You can leave right now if you want to talk that way. This is my house, and I don't have to leave it to you."

"Don't get upset, Lulu, I was just kidding. Go get ready. It's nine-thirty. You don't want to be late, do you? Come on, go, move." He pushed her from the back. She was very small, not even five feet tall. She complained as he pushed her out of the room, complaining about all she had done for them, how she had never received, and how her mother had been a saint who had been waited on hand and foot by her sisters and brother, and look, what did she get? He was careful as he pushed her, but the coffee still spilled. Then he noticed she wasn't using her walker; in fact, it wasn't even in the room.

He heard Tina talking loudly, the sound bringing him back to Deer Creek and the present. "You mean you rub their bellies until you find the one you like, and they let you?" Tina's voice was high, almost a scream at the end. He strained to hear the old man's reply but could only hear Tina again.

"Don't get near me then, or I'll be in big trouble." There was that loud laugh again as he walked back up to the fire and over to the cooler.

"Anyone want a beer?" he asked, jumping into the middle of their conversation.

"No. And don't drink them all, Beto. He's just like an *Indio*. Excuse me, a Mexican Indian, when he starts drinking. Once they get started. . . ."

Yeah, he thought, that's what I need, a good drunk. He finished the can and opened another. The mood around the campfire changed. The old man excused himself, said he wanted to take a walk, and Tina was quiet. Beto noticed the change, but he didn't care if he had ruined things. He was thinking about the beer and how he wanted another. He opened the cooler as the old man disappeared into the dark past the edge of the Nipple.

"Another beer, Beto?"

He smiled at Tina and heard himself ask, as if he were whispering in her ear, "you having a good time, sweetheart?"

Her face went blank in the light at the edge of the fire as she stared up at him. "Are you alright?" she asked finally.

He heard his voice again, as if he were a nice young man at a picnic with a sweet young girlfriend. "It's nice out here, isn't it?"

She stood up quickly and, holding him by the chin, stared into his eyes. "Is that what you were doing down at the creek, smoking a joint?" she asked awkwardly as if caught off guard, and then she sniffed at him and let go of his chin. "Why didn't you give me any?"

He sat down heavily in the sand that was warm from the fire or the sun, he didn't know which, but he was glad of the warmth on his bare legs. He raised his can and drained it, sighting over the can top so he could see the long lines of her legs. Her legs were in darkness, the fire behind her wide-open stance, so he couldn't see her skin, smooth as milked coffee, or her white shorts. She was black and naked with the fire behind her. He liked them naked. They were sexier with their clothes off, even if it were in the dark and he couldn't see their eyes, but he could feel their nakedness. He stared at where her legs joined, imagining the hump, the matted mound curving under, the happiness there. He wanted to make her feel good. He wanted to make her feel good so he would feel happiness too, but he knew if he made her feel good, then later he would lose the happiness. It would cost him—her happiness. He didn't see her legs now, only the dark border they made in front of the fire. That was all they were, naked borders. It would be easier to get rid of her and then he wouldn't have to think of what to do with her. That was when he saw her skin again. He would drive her to Vegas. They would leave early after he screwed her once while she was still sleeping. She wouldn't mind; she would think it was a dream. She would still be sleeping. There would be the fight at the bus station or the airport terminal; she would wait until then, sullen on the ride back. She would wait and then hit him hard. He could put her on a plane—that was it—or a bus, whatever was leaving soonest. He'd stop on the outskirts of town and call for the times of departure. There was always a bus or plane leaving for L.A. He'd throw it in her face. She wanted to go back, didn't she? He'd fight with her there at a 7-11 or a Shell gas station, but he didn't want to hang around waiting with her. Flames licked up her legs. He lost sight of her smooth brown legs and saw the white of her shorts, flames on her white shorts so that he wasn't thinking about dark borders; he was thinking about white shorts and how he wanted her and then wanted to be rid of her.

"Beto, what are you thinking about?" She had stood motionless for a long time. Maybe she had read his thoughts.

"Nothing, really. Nothing."

"You're acting strange. What is it?"

"Nothing. I'm fine. Let's go for a walk. I want to show you the sandstone at night."

"I don't want to go for a walk." She still hadn't moved. "I told you and Sam I didn't want to go for any walks. I'm fine. Why do you want to walk at night? There's nothing to see. If I wanted to go on a walk, I'd go. You go take a hike, I don't care. I'm fine, I told you. You don't need me."

How could she confuse him so? He decided then to reach out and grab her and hug her to him. She made him love her. Maybe he was wrong, he thought, and he didn't want her to leave yet. He reached out and wrapped his hands around her butt, caressing it, and pressing his face into the white shorts.

"Tina, I love you," he moaned into the flames licking at her shorts.

"What did you say?" She grabbed his hair and pulled him out from between her legs, but he held on to her ass tightly. "What did you say?" she repeated. "I don't think I heard you right."

His head was flung back, her fingers tight in his hair.

"Don't leave me, Tina."

"What else did you say? There was more. Tell me, baby." She stared into him, but he couldn't see her eyes. He could hear her breathing. He could hear his own breath and the hissing of the logs, and he could hear the sandstone turning white under the rising moon.

"I love you," he said.

Her fingers tightened and then she pulled him back into her, rubbing his head against her sex. "You're a crazy man, baby. What am I going to do with you? You make me crazy. Why do you think I'm so crazy? 'Cause I love you so much. Don't you know? I don't want you to leave me." He pressed hard into her, nuzzling, and she pushed against his face and his lips so she could feel him through the white cotton shorts. He rubbed on her legs, the warm brown skin, and he forgot about the airport as he reached up and unbuttoned her white shorts. She had to push him away to unzip them and close her legs to wiggle out of them as he helped with her shorts.

The old man watched from not more than thirty feet away. He sat on his haunches and casually chewed a plug of Red Man. He was outside of the light of the fire. He would have to wait a respectable amount of time before he could get into the truck and drive back to the Buchanan ranch. Watching reminded him of his childhood, of coupling he wasn't supposed to have seen in hogans and trailers, and of the couple he had once surprised in the willows along the river near where he grew up. He wasn't embarrassed. He was surprised that she hadn't bothered to lay on a blanket and that she had made him take his shorts off. She moaned, he moaned. They were almost finished now. Quick, but not unpleasurable, he thought. Sometimes it's sweetest that way. He remembered a woman he had gone to see in New Mexico. He had gone to her mobile home as often as he could, when her husband, a rodeo cowboy, was on the road or even just in a bar. He watched the way Tina used her hands on Beto's backside, the fingers spread wide, and he saw himself walking through the mobile home, the long narrow hallway from the aluminum door to the single bedroom in the back, the floors creaking, and the walls, too, if he bumped into them. Sometimes he never made it to the bedroom because she wanted him the moment he came in and she didn't care, and it was quick because they wanted it so badly, and then she would send him away just as quickly. He remembered the trailer had been clean, always clean. She had cleaned the place all the time. She was a proper Navajo woman. She had always told him when it was time to leave and he had never argued with her. Once they made love twice, slowly the second time, and then he had left. He didn't think she had liked it slow. He felt himself growing stiff, the memory of it very nice. He would wait a while longer. He remembered his last visit to the mobile home, how it hadn't been quiet and he could hear children playing at the rough wood entry stairs, the house all lit up. He had waited until the new woman of the house had come out to call the children inside, and then he had gone to a window and watched. The house was unkempt; he had noticed it right away, remembering how clean the other woman had kept it. He had watched for a long time. He had watched the new woman cooking, he had watched her put the kids to bed in the living room and get ready for bed herself. He had watched until all the lights were off and then he had tried the door and walked through the mobile home and stood over the woman in her bed and watched her sleep. A woman shouldn't be left alone, he had thought. Yet what was he feeling? A loss? Emptiness? Was it possible that men were more afraid of loneliness than women? That was why they left. He had left his wife, alone, to come here, and he would leave her again and again until finally she would tell him that he wasn't wanted anymore. It had been too late to change anything and now, watching Beto and Tina, he realized that he was still afraid of loneliness. He watched Beto get up and go to the cooler and pull out another Coors. He strutted, his still semi-hard member leading the way. The old man saw himself closing the door of that mobile home, walking off across the desert, walking for half the night. Tina dressed, watching Beto strut. She was beautiful as she dressed, but she kept her eyes on him.

"Where are you going?" she asked as he pulled on his shorts.

"I'm going for that walk." The old man felt loneliness setting in.

"Now?"

"Yeah. Why not now?"

"Stay here with me." The old Indian saw her checking Beto, feeling his currents. She knew what he would do. The old man knew, and he was afraid that Beto would leave anyway. "Baby, don't leave. I want you here with me." Beto turned away from her to tie his shoes. "Damn you. Gotta go, ma'am, but it was nice," she said sharply, and then she turned soft again. "Stay with me for awhile. Will you stay with me, please, Beto, do something for me for a change?"

Beto hesitated for a moment, but his mind was set. The old

man knew. Beto had to get away. The old man felt it as strongly as the night he had stared down at the woman sleeping in the bed and had had to resist the desire to kiss her. Beto knelt down beside Tina and rubbed her head and kissed her forehead.

"Baby, I won't be gone for long. A little walk, maybe I can scare up the old man."

"You're thinking about the old man now? Now? You want to leave? Go ahead. Get out of my sight."

"You're acting like an idiot," Beto said.

"Why don't you just leave?" she said. He hesitated, unsure now.

"Don't leave," the old man whispered in the shadows. "You'll wish you hadn't left. Don't leave."

"Put on your clothes," Beto said. He couldn't leave.

"What? What do you care? You're leaving, and I'm not going on any hikes," she said sharply.

"I said put on your clothes." She jumped in front of him. Beto moved back a foot. She's a strong one, the old man thought. Slim may never understand. Beto stalked off into the brush at the edge of the creek, and the old man could hear her mutter "asshole." The old man slipped away on the sandstone, plotting a course he hoped would allow Beto to find him.

Beto saw the tamaracks and rushes at the creek's edge before he stumbled through them. He didn't care. He had a cold Coors in his hand unopened, and there was plenty of moonlight reflecting off the white sandstone. "Make a lot of noise if you want," and "God, it feels good to be alone," he said out loud. He didn't bother to push branches out of his way. He was drunk and smiling as he walked into the creek. He put one foot in a hole, and then he was sprawling in three inches of water, but laughing. He touched the buckle the old man had given him and then tried to move it so it would catch the reflection of the moon.

"Yahoo," he yelped, and laughed. "Warm night, warm water, it's God's country. Where's the hippies? We could have us a naked moon dance if we could find some hippies." He had heard the story of the hippies living in teepees, up Deer Creek. Ran around naked until they finally just ran off, before the sheriff could haul 'em all in. Hippies in Boulder. Even Buchanan had gotten himself some canvas and a potbelly stove. Beto, sitting in the water looking at the moon, forgot about the hippies and noticed he had lost the can of beer. "Gotta have my beer," he muttered. Stumbling in the creek on his hands and knees, he found it in the reeds and opened it. It tasted warm. He was tired of the taste, but drank it down anyway. "Can't please them," he muttered on. "Can't please the old lady or Tina." He wouldn't say a word anymore. If they wanted him to speak, he'd say one or two words and then shut up. That'd fix 'em.

"I'm not drunk yet. Yes, I'm blotto, but I don't care," he told the trees. He stumbled along through the stream, wondering why she'd come out here anyway. She could be a lot of fun at times, but he had to get rid of her tomorrow, first thing. He remembered his plan, there was the airport and the bus station. She had to get back and make sure Dolores was alright, didn't she? Stealing his friends. Goddamn old man probably thinks Tina's the greatest when she's really a pain in the ass. Never would have put the old lady away without her. He could have been at home right now, watching tv, munching popcorn, Dolores in the kitchen. Maybe he'd walk off a precipice, walk until he found a precipice and just walk right off it. Then they'd all be sorry for treating him so badly. He stopped and tried to take another swallow from the can, but it was empty, so he twisted it and threw it viciously into the bushes. "Dammit," he cursed. Then he felt bad about littering and searched for five minutes in the bushes without finding it. I'll come back in the morning and find it, he told himself, and then he went back into the creek to wash off his face. He breathed deeply, but he didn't feel well. He felt tired and ready for sleep, but he didn't want to go back just yet. It wouldn't be right. He had to wait a bit. Water was running down his legs in irritating streams. He tried to brush the water away, but it was like flies that settle back down again. As he brushed his legs he saw a flicker of movement off to his left where the trees and bushes ran into sandstone. There. He saw it again, movement. He was sure this time as he strained his eyes and became rigid to see what it was. "Just like an Indian warrior," he whispered.

He remembered sneaking through the alleys and backyards of Echo Park, his heart beating, he and Ray silent for so long they would finally scream at the top of their lungs and run for miles, it seemed, to a safe place and then collapse laughing, the sweat sticking the clothes to their skin.

There was the movement again. A man lightfooting it into the brush from the edge of the sandstone. He had been hiding behind a pile of rocks. He caught a glimpse of a baseball cap before it disappeared, and he laughed because he recognized the cap.

"Thinks he can sneak up on me," he chuckled. "I'll show him who the sneaky Indian is." Beto dropped to his hands and scuttled through the stream, quietly this time, with his body so low he was under the tops of the bushes. He was smiling, planning how he would run up the stream and double back quietly along the edge of the mesa and catch the old man from behind. He figured the old man would be moving slowly in the tamaracks to catch him at the stream, but would he ever give the old Indian a surprise. He moved fast, down the stream and up through a break in the brush to the mesa edge. He ran along the sandstone, knowing he was taking a chance, but hoping the old man was studying the spot in the stream where he thought Beto would be. When Beto thought he had circled enough, he stopped and melted into the shadow of a gigantic cottonwood.

From under the cottonwood he could see the whole stream bed reflecting the moon, as bright as if it were under lights, and there, not more than thirty feet away, was the old man on his haunches peering around the edge of a bunch of willows. The old man was staring at the creek, which made Beto snicker so loudly he had to put his hand over his mouth so he wouldn't give himself away. He could see that the entire thirty feet to the old man was in the shadows of the cottonwood. He could walk quietly and then spring himself on the old man. He laughed to himself again, thinking how surprised the old man would be. He snuck up quietly another fifteen feet until he was so close that if the old man turned around he'd be able to count the buttons on his shirt.

He was still in the shadows of the tree and he had to bend over, which he did now, to see under a branch. He was really happy with himself, but something wasn't right. He knew the old man was pretty good at sneaky Indian, so why was he just sitting there, and what was he doing? He could hear a little noise like scraping and a voice. It wasn't the old man, he realized; it was someone else. "Tina," he swore. The more he looked, the more he knew it, and she wasn't wearing a hat. I'll give her a good scare, he decided, teach her to follow me around. He took off at a run, skipping as carefully as he could through the leaves. As he neared the edge of the treeline he could see that Tina still hadn't heard him even though he was moving fast, but it didn't matter anyhow because he was almost there and he'd give her a big scare.

Tina was still bent over, fumbling at something with great intent, but just before he leaped into the moonlight he glanced up into the low branches of the cottonwood. He didn't know why he looked up. He wouldn't ever know. Maybe the old man's eyes had drawn him there. The old man was sitting on a limb and smiling.

Beto didn't have a chance to return the smile. He knew that he was caught and at that moment he sailed into a limb head first. He felt his body go light, then felt it float slowly to the ground. He felt comfortable and warm. He could grin at the old man now. He was wearing the belt buckle and he felt fine, but he wondered how the old man had gotten into the cottonwood and why he had looked up and what Tina was doing. He was sure that if he hadn't have looked up, he wouldn't have hit the branch and he wouldn't have seen Dolores.

He heard the clicking of her beads and the mumbled prayers that reminded him of mosquitoes hovering over water. He wasn't amazed, but he wondered how Dolores had come to be here with her friends and why they were saying the rosary at this time. "Time for the rosary," she always said. "What are you doing here, *mama*?" he asked, but he found he couldn't move his head, and he felt so warm and comfortable it didn't seem to matter. Besides, they weren't paying him any attention. His grandmother was leading the "Our Father." They must have reached a break in the beads; or they were near the end, almost to the cross. He saw the looping beads, his grandmother's pink rosary almost dangling in his face. "See, *mama*," he said, "I told you you'd get your beads back." He felt so happy thinking how everything had turned out alright. She was here with her pink rosary. He smiled at her and tried to tell her he loved her, but he wasn't sure she heard because the clicking of the beads was so loud, and she didn't smile at him or look like she even knew he was there. He saw the old man sitting with Dolores, and Mrs. Schmitz and Josie were behind them. How wonderful, he thought, the old man with Dolores, and then he felt something warm, dripping, splashing on his face. He figured it must be holy water, since it always felt warm, and Dolores liked to sprinkle it around. But the sound of beads had stopped and Dolores was gone and he felt the panic as he tried to move and couldn't as he tried to get away from the dripping which he saw came from a jack rabbit in the claws of a hoot owl perched on the branch in the cottonwood. The owl stared back, ripping into the rabbit, tearing chunks out with his curved beak, the blood splashing down. That was when he tried to sit up, shouting, "*mama, mama.*"

"Relax, baby, it's only water," she said. "Boy you hit yourself good. You were out for over a minute." He saw Tina and the old man. Tina was rubbing his head with a wet cloth and the old man was hunched over on one knee at her side.

"You ran smack dab into this limb here. Knocked you right

out," the old man said.

"That's what you get for playing games, silly boy," she said, trying to make light of it. "Lay back down," she told him. "You were cute enough to kiss when you were out, which I did, didn't I, Sam?" She didn't wait for an answer. "Just like a baby chattering away."

Where was Dolores? He wanted to look around for her. He knew she was here, and he had been forgiven. But Tina had the cloth pressed down on his forehead so hard he couldn't move.

"Put that light up into the tree, on the branch."

"Why?"

"Just shine it up into the tree. There's a hoot owl up there. Shine it up there, willya?"

The old man waved the light in the tree branch. "No owls in this tree."

"I saw one in the tree, picking apart a jack. He was right there on that branch, right over my face." He looked into the old man's face. "Right where you were sitting before I ran into that branch."

"You must be dreaming, Slim. I wasn't sitting in that tree."

"I wasn't dreaming. I saw the biggest hoot owl right there in those branches and he was tearing into a fresh kill. You probably scared him away." Tina moved over and lifted his head onto her lap. She cuddled his head and made soothing sounds. "What about the blood? There was blood sprinkling down on me. I couldn't move to get away from it."

"Calm down, baby, you're getting yourself all excited. Sam's right. You must have been dreaming. You were out and talking a streak. You know, you even called me '*mama*.' I know I should be insulted, but you were so cute." Tina stroked his head.

"There's no blood here, Slim, but I'm surprised you didn't really open yourself up. You must have a thick head." Tina and the old man laughed quietly.

Beto closed his eyes. She had been here. He had called out "*mama*" and Tina had heard it. Dreams. He wouldn't tell them about Dolores. He'd keep that to himself; they wouldn't understand. The old man would think it was important. A sign.

"What were you doing out here sneaking around?" he asked Tina.

"I wasn't sneaking around. I heard you yell, so I got worried and came out with my flashlight. It stopped working and I was trying to fix it when you ran into the tree."

"I couldn't figure out what you were doing. At first I thought you were the old man, and then when I realized it was you, I was going to scare you good."

"Well, that should be a lesson to you, trying to scare me when all I was doing was trying to find you."

"What made you jump into that branch, son?" the old man asked.

"I saw you, right before I was gonna leap on Tina. I saw you perched on that branch, smiling that idiot grin of yours. You were on that branch. Come on, old man, I saw you."

"I wasn't," the old man said, giving him a serious look. "I was with Tina."

"He was, Beto."

"You're lying; the old man was up in the tree." He saw them exchange a look. Caught 'em, he thought, they can't play games with me. And he knew Dolores had been here, but he wouldn't say anything about her. Leave that one alone, he told himself.

"Tina, you think we should take him in to the doctor?"

Tina took the flashlight and shined it on the bump on Beto's forehead. "No, I think he'll live, just a bad bump. Look how the skin's bruised, but there's no bleeding. I think this boy just needs some loving attention."

The attention was nice. It reminded him of the time Shatzi had bitten him and Dolores had worried over him so much, his grandfather smoking in the background.

"I think I'm okay to walk now," he said.

"Are you sure? Sam, help me get him up."

"I'm fine, I'm fine," he said, but as he sat up he felt the wooziness and he let them help him to his feet. The old man and Tina supported him as they stumbled through the brush. Beto started to giggle.

"What's so funny?" Tina asked, straining, his arm slung over her shoulder.

An hour later, after a beer and four Excedrin, the pounding in his head didn't make him laugh at all. He was lying in his sleeping bag, half listening to Tina and the old man. He had never known the old man to stay up so late, but he figured he'd go to sleep when he wanted. Tina, on the other hand, could stay up half the night, then lay down and be out and no one could wake her. There were nights with Tina when she had kept him awake as he was trying to sleep and couldn't; then she'd decide to sleep and was out and he still couldn't. He'd just lie there all night wide awake. He felt fine except for his head. He was close to sleep, but he knew it wouldn't come. Dreams. The old man and Dolores. How'd they get mixed up in this?

Would the old man remember? He'd ask him about Dolores and the beads later. Dolores and her beads, like mosquitoes. He couldn't sleep. There was too much noise here.

It was the cicadas that he heard, cicadas in a stand of tamaracks across the creek, cicadas the size of a roughneck's thumb and the same color in that bunch of dusty half-trees, the trunks no thicker than a child's wrist, eight feet tall and crowded so a man couldn't push his way through unless he had a chainsaw. Cicadas like the clicking of beads and the dust falling from a child's wrist. The old man had told him they did it with their legs, rubbed their legs over wings that were only good for short flights. Hooked their legs over fragile wings, rubbing the shell like a fingernail covering the wings. Is that what they did, rub their legs over the fingernail of a shell? Or was it the wings underneath that, cracking, made the sound? Wings as useless as hairnets, that would load up with dust in the tamaracks.

He remembered hanging out in the toiletries section of the Pioneer Market to see them buy hairnets. They never did come in, not even their women, but he saw them on the corner across the street. Hairnets over short, slicked-back hair. *Cholos* in the late afternoon. Hairnets. There was so much hidden from him. They should make those clicker toys look like cicadas instead of frogs, but then everyone knew how a frog made its noise, and then who would want a cicada? A flying *cucaracha*? They stopped in unison. Why the nets? He would ask Ray. Ray knew about late afternoons.

When the cicadas started up, noisy again, he was reminded of Dolores in the kitchen. It was far into the night, and she was pushing the walker over the linoleum. Thump, then drag, scrape, thump, then drag, scrape, as she went from the refrigerator to the sink to the table, and then back again. In the morning he would find a butter knife stuck to the bottom of the sink with peanut butter, cracker crumbs on the counter, and burned tortilla flakes and scrapings at the stove. She had hated the hospital food and needed to make up for lost time. There had been no salsa, "sarsa," she called it, in some kind of dialect, probably early Californian, but she wouldn't change her pronunciation, wouldn't speak like a Mexican. "How had they expected me to get better," she asked him. "I'm old and I can't taste so well. I have to eat to keep up my strength." He figured that was why she ate so much—she ate at least ten times a day—she could only taste half of what she was eating. Sarsa. He knew they don't make sarsa in Spain, but her sisters made sarsa in Pomona. "I don't sleep enough. Ask Dr.

Hernandez," she told him. Dr. Hernández would tell him how bad she was, how she needed her sleep but stayed awake all night. Dr. Hernández would recommend that she eat more. On her first day back from the hospital Beto had gone out to the drugstore at the corner of Echo Park and Sunset. Upstairs was Hernandez' office. It had been the same office for over thirty years, but Hernandez was just another in a line of renters there. The office was over a drugstore. His grandfather had dressed the windows of the drugstore with Max Factor cosmetic displays every two weeks for Maury, the druggist. Now Maury lived in Encino and the windows were covered in Spanish. Echo Park and Sunset, a blind man at the magazine stand, and hairnets in the late afternoon.

"Your grandmother will recover perfectly. Here's the prescription for her nerves," the young Dr. Hernández had told him.

"She doesn't sleep," Beto had said.

"She is very healthy for her age. The pills will help her sleep."

Beto had walked past the racks of *fotonovellas, La Opinion, Excelsior,* and the nudies. He greeted the blind man who ran the newsstand as he went into the House of Liquors to buy a twelve-pack. When he returned to the house, entering through the front door to the sound of a tv that could be heard across the street, he found her asleep in her chair.

"Dolores, you were sleeping when I came back." He had tried to make her understand.

"No I wasn't, Sonny. I was just resting."

"Your head was back and your mouth was wide open. You were catching flies. I turned off the tv."

"I was resting, *mi'jito.* I was watching Oprah and resting. Besides, you would need rest too if you didn't sleep at night."

"You sleep every night. You're sound asleep whenever I look in at you."

"You think I sleep, but I don't rest."

"If you can't sleep, it's because you eat too much at night."

"I pick. Dr. Hernández told me I was losing weight, that I had to keep up my strength. I pick, Sonny. My goodness, wait until you're old; you don't think about it now. I pick a little bit, but I don't eat enough. It doesn't stay with me what I eat. My body doesn't use it; it goes right through me. You should see what I make; it's this long." Dolores held her hands apart a good twelve inches and looked at each hand. "It's so long it curls up and I'm afraid it won't go down."

"Dolores, I don't want to hear about it. You eat too much,

that's why. You eat more than I do at every meal."

"Sonny, how can you say that? The doctor says I have to eat."

"I just spoke to Hernández and he says you're fine. You're very healthy. You need rest because it's a severe strain. Here, take one of these pills."

"My bones are brittle. You have to remember I'm seventy-nine years old."

"He took an x-ray, Lulu." Beto heard the sound of his voice rising.

"He's a nice man, but he's Mexican."

"He's not Mexican; he's Cuban."

"Worse. Trained on an island. What do they know there?"

"Wisconsin, dammit. He got his diploma from the University of Wisconsin. It's in the United States of America, near the border of Canada. Your husband was born there. If you don't like this guy, why do you go to him?"

"You're so sensitive. You need to relax. Learn to relax. You don't eat right. That's the problem, too much junk food. You should eat at home. You're too thin, *mi'jito*. Sonny?" she said, waiting for him to answer. "Where are you going, Sonny?"

"You're driving me crazy. I'm getting out of here."

Twelve

The Quonset hut didn't shake, and there wasn't a clang as Ray closed the two wooden doors, ten feet high at least, and wide enough for a car apiece. Ray was speaking and Ceci could hear him, but what she was listening for was the sound of unseen trucks. She was amazed at how large the garage seemed without the glare of open doors. He didn't need to switch on the overhead light.

"What are we gonna do now?" Ray asked.

Skylights, three along each side, built out square to the curve, let even the laid-out wrenches, sockets, and grinders glow from their oiled skin. The glass in the skylights was wired, a pattern that she understood, that didn't confuse her, but left her comfortable on Glendale Boulevard.

"What're we gonna do now?" he repeated.

She ignored him again, searching for a floor covered with engine parts and grease, walls of bimbos on tacked-up calendars holding tools in their hands. At the sink she hit the soap dispenser and let her hands fill with pink grains, smelling the soap, but not too deeply because the quality of the place was immediate. She washed quickly, watching her hands the entire time as if to stop herself from making the sign of the cross, and then she followed the pink sand as it was carried away into the drain. She pulled out two immaculate sheets, water blotting the coarse brown paper. She didn't speak as she crossed the clean concrete floor between the counter of tools laid out in perfect array, the acetylene tubes and torches, and the '58 Chevy Impala with the dead girl still propped against the driver's door. She opened the door of the room in the opposite corner of the sink. Inside there was a metal high school teacher's desk against the partition of painted white plywood and exposed 2 by 4's. There was a closet filled with carefully folded pants and laundered work shirts hanging from a metal pole, an open shower stall that was still wet, and over the desk as clean as the spotted concrete floors hung the calendar she had been looking for. St. Teresa of Avila, but she wasn't holding a Snap On impact wrench against her bare belly. Ceci almost genuflected, caught herself, and sat on the unmade bed. Ray, who had followed her in, lit up a cigarette from the pack he had pulled out of the inner pocket of the suit coat he was still wearing. She watched the smoke drift up into the rafters, up to the ventilator that was turning slower than the merry-go-round ever could in the school yard. He didn't take the cigarette from his lips, but she knew that when he did it would be between his thumb and first two fingers. She realized that the only thing she had forgotten to do was count the steps. Ray squinted at her through the smoke, speaking without moving the cigarette.

"What am I gonna do with the corpse?"

"She's a dead girl, Ray."

"You know what I'm talking about." Then he pulled the cigarette from between his lips, holding it like she knew he would. Cecilia tried to smile tough, but she grinned so hard she could feel teeth rubbing against the back of her head. Ray debated whether or not to stub his cigarette out. He made a motion to the ashtray on the desk, but was unsure, and instead looked around and at himself for that something that seemed out of place. Unsatisfied and uncomfortable, he stuck the smoke back into his mouth but didn't pull on it. Cecilia, still sitting not more than five feet away, kept her eyes full upon him. He could see her without looking at her, realizing that he only now saw her. She was a red-headed girl, dark red hair, burgundy-colored, with green eyes whose shape and color contrasted with the red hair. She was pretty, nice-looking, different, taller than he and she was wearing flats. She wasn't heavy, but she was big. He tried to remember her lips—were they wide or thin? He didn't have to remember her legs; he had noticed them enough, and her ears under the shoulder-length red held pearls.

Cecilia didn't move; she wanted to figure him out at her leisure. He acted like a gentleman with a tattoo on his left hand. She stared at the *Pachuco* cross in the soft part of his hand between the thumb and finger, noticed for the first time that it was a cross with four short lines surrounding it like exclamation points. She imagined him with a head band, a white grandfather undershirt, and pressed pants. She would wait. He was either very proper or nervous. Ray would wait too, but she didn't know it. He could be more quiet than anyone. He finished his smoke and couldn't decide on another. When he realized he was tapping the pack on his desk rapidly, he stopped himself by lighting another.

"Cecilia?" he started, but lost himself staring at her face.

She returned his look with a wry smile. "You know, Ray, this shop is awfully clean. You really do any work here?"

"It's an auto body shop, lady. I don't work on engines." What a face she has, he thought. Really some kind of different face. "It has to be clean to do my kind of work."

"Is that so? Specialized work, huh?"

"It's an auto body shop; there's a million of them."

She crossed her legs, put her elbows on her knees and leaned in. "Then, you see, I had you all wrong. I thought you were a mechanic." She waited.

His eyes never left her. Her lips had stopped moving over her teeth. He willed them to begin again. He'd forgotten about the cigarette, felt the ash drop to the floor, and then he hoped he had caught his mind, finally, and could start to reel it in before it went under the fountain again in the middle of Echo Park Lake. "Yeah, I ain't no mechanic." He held up his hands, palms outward as if to prove it to her. "I'm the spray man. But what about this thing going on now? We've got a problem here."

"I know we do," Cecilia answered back.

"A serious problem." Perhaps he hadn't come back to shore. He wished he could hammer it out alone. If he were alone he could think better, but then, he didn't want to see her leave.

"I know we do," she repeated, her voice not girlish, but thick and slow.

"Well, let's figure this business out." He wanted to wipe at the sweat on his brow, take off his coat. It was hot in here. He wasn't making sense, and she was—in his garage. He realized that he had never had women in his garage, at least not in his back room.

"Let's do that," she said comfortably. "Where do we start?" She had lovely hands, he noticed, not vein-piercing like his ex, but lovely. He took off his coat and tie, walked slowly to the closet and carefully hung up the coat. He wrapped the tie around the collar. "Did you meet Tina?" he asked as he unbuttoned the cuffs of the sheer white shirt.

She waited a moment. "I met the bitch at the rosary."

He unbuttoned his shirt, pulling it out of his pants and then reached for a hanger, never taking his eyes off her, off her shining eyes. "Yes, uhm."

Her eyes flashed; he saw it as he reached into the closet again. "Something you want to tell me about, Ray?"

He let it slide.

"You're shocked. You think because I'm a good Catholic girl I shouldn't react like this. That I shouldn't call someone a bitch. Well, we've changed a bit, buddy. We're not all packed off in black anymore, but you wouldn't know since you never come to church, would you?"

He ignored her and found the shirt he wanted, the tan gabardine with the fake pearl buttons. He rubbed his hand across the front, soaking up the smooth material. It was a shirt Dolores had made for Beto's father. Beto never talked about his father. Beto had given the shirt to him when they were in their senior year at Marshall High. It would never wear out, smooth and soft, sharp-looking like Cary Grant. He put it on over his undershirt, carefully buttoning the front and then rolling the sleeves up halfway to his elbow.

"No, I do know." He thought of his mother and sisters, how they dressed in black still, for church, but they weren't shy. They were outspoken; they said what was on their minds. Maybe it was the almost-red hair. "You didn't like her then," he added.

"No, I didn't. I didn't like the way she dressed for the rosary. It was inappropriate, and I didn't like the way she acted. I felt sorry for Beto then, but I think he's gotten what he deserves."

"You think she had anything to do with this?"

"What do you think?" Her answer was sharp, the voice still husky, the sharpness held at the center. She continued. "What do you want? A good Catholic girl's point of view? She didn't bring her own rosary." Ceci waited a moment. "She's got him, and she's a smart alley cat. I don't doubt for a second that she's at the center of this."

Cats. Yes, he knew. He reached for the black Levis hanging ironed. He turned to her and was surprised to see that she was standing and smoking one of his unfiltered cigarettes.

"Excuse me," he said. She leaned against the desk. "But I'm going to change my pants."

"Go ahead. I won't look."

He continued to stare at her without moving.

"Alright. You got anything to drink?" she asked, standing now, her hands on her hips, the cigarette in her left hand.

"There's a cooler in the shop. It's red, says Coke on it. You like beer?"

"Sometimes," she said, turning away from him.

He heard her tap across the concrete floor, past the work-bench, quickly, no shuffling, and then the squeak of the old horizontal coke machine lid. He untied his shoes, placed them below the hanging jacket, and hung up the pants carefully to extend the creases flat against the plastic hanger. He was wearing boxers; he could have changed in front of her. He heard the pop of a can of beer and then he was in his Levis and tennis shoes. He left the gabardine hanging outside the pants. It was made to wear that way, but he still tugged at the front as he came into the shop. She was standing at the car door looking in at the girl. He winced. The can of Miller's was sitting on the roof of his Chevy.

"What now?"

"I think we find Tina and we've got the answer," she said, and then drank from the can. She drank quickly. Nice shirt, she thought. It looks good on him; he looks leaner than he is. She noticed that he was staring at the can of beer. She should have known he wasn't careless. She waited for his reply, watching him lift the heavy lid of the amusing Coke machine that was big as a freezer, and cold, too. She lifted the can off the roof of the Impala as he came over to her and wiped at the wet ring of condensation. But he didn't say anything, and she knew that he was either being polite, or he hadn't expected her to figure it out, to understand. She placed the can on the blue rag he had carefully laid out.

"You're right, Cecilia, but I'm not sure how to find her. She hangs out in another part of town." He had moved to the counter, leaning against the pounded and dented covering of sheet metal, the dull shine wiped smooth of grease. Maybe it's aluminum, she thought. She noticed again that his face was smooth, hairless, with no attempt at chin whiskers or a moustache so that he would look the part. But then it would only be an appearance that she had come to expect. He came from another part of town. L.A. as town, she laughed to herself. If you crossed Glendale Boulevard, or the freeway from Silver Lake into Echo Park, you knew you were in a different land. She lived in Silver Lake and worked in Echo Park. He worked in Silver Lake but lived in the Park. Looking at him, she realized that she'd never even been to East L.A. and it was only five minutes away, the other side of Olvera Street, Chinatown, and the river. But she knew enough to know that L.A. wasn't a town, wasn't even a city; it was territories.

"I don't think Tina's still here, Ray. She'll want to keep a close eye on Beto. If he's left, she's with him. We need them both anyway, don't you think?

"I don't think she'd go to Utah."

"I think she did, but I'll bet you can find out about her. I know you've got to have pull across borders." She noticed that he almost blushed, but pulled himself up quickly enough to suck in a long one, his eyes off her and into the ceiling.

"What if we do find her?" Ray asked.

"We blow the game. Find out where Dolores is and then have Tina pulled in. My father's best friend is a Captain with the Sheriff's; he'll help us. And then there's Gutierrez. He knows what's going on and he'll talk; he's already drank up the money she paid him anyway." She was excited, but she wasn't speaking quickly.

"I don't want to go to the dogs, Cecilia."

She shot back at him, "The dogs, the *perros*, come on. Wake up! This isn't a game of cops and gangbangers. What about Dolores? I know you care about her. And then there's this girl. Who is she? Someone is looking for her somewhere. And I know what you're thinking, but screw Beto; he's a fool, and you know it."

Ray brushed his hand slowly over the gabardine. Such fine material, he thought. He went back to the cooler, found another cold one and returned. He gave Cecilia a half smile.

"Could you move over, please?" he asked her pleasantly. Then he wiped at the non-existent Miller's ring on the deep shine of the roof of the Chevy before he moved back to the counter.

"You don't understand, Cecilia, but I want you to understand because I don't want you to fight it all the time. You see, Tina has her family; they have ways to hide out. The badges'll never find her. Or Dolores. Tina doesn't live in *gringo* town."

"Ray, don't lecture me."

He heard her anger and he didn't want that. "No, no, wait a minute. Don't get me wrong. This isn't a lecture, believe me. But maybe you don't understand the situation."

"You don't have to explain this." Her voice was louder and sharper.

"I think I do. You see, it's important. You have to know where a person lives, where they're from. And the place, the history of the place is important because it's where they do more than just live. It's your pride. You see, it's all there. You can't reach out beyond your corner, your barrio, where your *mama* and *papa* come from. That's all we have and that's why we protect it, and why we cherish it." Ray waited a moment. "Take yourself, for example. You live in Silver Lake. It's a nice place to live and go to church. Sure, you got your friends and family, but let me ask you something. Do you know your *mama's* history, like where is she from, really?"

Cecilia was silent. His voice hadn't risen. It was so smooth and wonderfully modulated that the impact of his question had jarred her. She didn't answer. She had to think. Mama never talked about where she had met the big red railroad engineer. It was in the Philippines, but was it her hometown? What was the name of her hometown? "She's from the Philippines," she said finally.

"OK. Your mother is a Filipina. Do you know if she's from one of the outer islands? Or is she from Manilla?" He waited, and then continued. "I think you don't know and you should. We all should know where we come from and the place we live. You don't have family in Silver Lake. That's gotta be tough on your *mama.* There's no Filipinos in Silver Lake. She's just living there."

Cecilia thought about her mother watering plants in the small back yard out of the rusted coffee can. She watered anything and it would grow.

"And your father?"

"He's Irish."

"Irish. He hangs at Nick's."

"What the hell does that have to do with it?"

"You don't dig his community. He's a homeboy, but you don't know it."

She wasn't angry now. It had left her as suddenly as a group of pigeons rise up in one motion and leave a schoolyard. She realized that she didn't know Silver Lake, the history of her corner, but she wasn't going to be embarrassed by it.

"Okay, tell me all about Tina. I'm listening." She took another drink. "But don't talk down to me," she shot at him, filling his face with her eyes.

He held up both hands. "No way. Look, it comes with the territory. We're marked forever, and it's in here too," he said, patting his heart. "This is why I gotta explain it to you. Tina's East L.A. But that deserves a distinction too. You see, I know that she moved into Lincoln Heights. Hell, she's educated, she didn't have to move there; that's a tough neighborhood. She could have moved uptown to Montebello or Whittier with all the other middle-class *hermanos.* Why does she live there? Protection? Cover? Right. If Tina's got the *abuelita* hidden away, the badges won't find her until someone squeals. But there's no way the barrio's gonna talk. That's the way it is. That's the first thing you learn: never spill. You don't ever be a *Malinche.* The dogs won't find her. I truly believe it. One thing about *vatos.*" He rubbed his hands and looked at the ballpoint ink tattoo in the soft spot between thumb and index finger. "They don't rat, they don't talk. It's been beat into us. You see, the worst thing you can do is talk. There's no one to protect you here 'cept your corner, your barrio. Your community is your home. You know about Chavez Ravine?"

Ceci shrugged her shoulders. "Just that it's the home of the Dodgers," she said.

"The city forced out the whole barrio to make way for Dodger Stadium. They called it eminent domain. A baseball park. Police came in the morning with shotguns and bulldozers to clean out the taco benders. You think we trust police? Not even when they're our kind. I guess you could say I bleed Dodger blue fucking blood. My parents grew up in the Ravine. And I was born there. I know you heard about Sleepy Lagoon, or the Navy and the zoot suiters. The cops watching from their cars, watching the service guys swinging baseball bats, killing a few greasers. Hey, it was during the War. They called it a domestic problem. Had to clear the air. And this kind of thing isn't ancient history, believe me. It happened again in '68, only this time they went after families at a parade in an East L.A. park and killed a reporter whose only mistake was that he was a Chicano and trying to protect himself." Ray stopped, tapped the pack of Camels, and finally pulled one out and lit it. He continued talking when the blue smoke had reached the ventilator turning slowly in the roof.

"Cecilia, I want to find Dolores in the worst way. I'll do my best, you gotta believe it, but not the dogs. The thing is, Red, the big problem is that Tina's in the Heights and we got our own borders, as you put it, and you're right. They're borders, and sometimes even I can't cross them." He stopped then, and stuck the still burning cigarette into an empty beer can. She could hear it sizzle before he crushed the can. He didn't throw it, just crushed it and placed it on the sheet metal counter top where it rocked back and forth.

Cecilia walked over, walking slower than she would have normally walked even in such a short space. She thought that he looked tired. No, he looked sad. Tired goes with sad. She reached out and stopped the rocking.

"So let's cross the river."

"The river," he laughed, a tired snort of air. "How convenient. East L.A.'s on the other side of the L.A. River. Let's see, where do we begin: Boyle Heights, First Street, Lincoln Heights, Hollenbeck, Terrace, Monterey Park, Mission Street, Happy Valley, Whittier, Ramona Gardens, *La Raza*? We'll get the Riverside *vatos* to carry us over from Frogtown."

"I know who Riverside is. Don't try to make me feel completely ignorant. What is it with you? Okay, I'm not cool like you. I'm impressed with your knowledge, but don't let it go to your head."

He wasn't surprised. He'd said a mouthful, but he didn't want to push her away, and he stumbled over his next words. "Hey, I'm sorry, really, if I made you feel, uhh, uneasy. That wasn't what I wanted to do."

"Forget it. You know you're. . . ." She hesitated, searched the ceiling fan for help. "We're different, but not so different when you get down to it. Maybe that sounds silly. I'm sure of what I mean, but I can't put it into words. You know?"

"Yeah, I think I know." He wanted to add something else, but he had already sounded it in his head and was afraid to say it. It didn't sound right. It would be better to wait. "Well you know about Riverside," he said instead.

"Yeah, I know. I live here too, Mr. *Cholo*," she laughed nicely.

He felt better. "And the Parque Locos."

"Hairnets at the Pioneer."

He laughed a tired laugh. "Ragheads, Country Club Malt, right, the *faldas* buy." She didn't answer. She moved in front of him and he leaned back. She took his face in both hands, rubbing his chin. She didn't know why she wanted to be close to him. She remembered Beto at St. Teresa's. He had been distant, trying to hide. Her hands had shook in the linen pile. And now she'd washed her hands, hadn't she, with pink mechanic's soap, next to the counter at the back of the shop laid out carefully with tools under the skylights, and there was a St. Teresa of Avila missing an impact wrench in the plywood sacristy. The only thing she'd forgotten was to count the steps. She rubbed his cheek. "It's time to get busy."

"What first?"

"Hide María."

"María?"

"The girl in your car." They were staring into each other's eyes. His were dark brown.

"Take her back to Gutierrez."

"No," she sniffed. "Stick her in the Coke machine."

"I don't know about that." His eyes searched hers.

"Yes, and then, then," she said, leaning over, trying to stop herself from kissing him—it was a very soft kiss; she knew that she would like his lips—"don't you ever call me 'Red' again."

Thirteen

Sleep. They were sleeping, Tina and the old man, while Beto was up at the bush and then back to the cooler. What was difficult about sleeping under the stars was getting out of the bag every twenty minutes and waiting for the cowboy dawn, that seeping light that could last for what seemed like hours. He hadn't been trying to stay awake or drink all the beer as he guzzled at the last can. He couldn't remember when beer had tasted this terrible, that he could be this tired or dry inside forcing the taste down. He didn't care about sleep anymore, didn't care if the sun caught him stumbling to the bush. He just didn't want to think about it anymore. "Best thing for Dolores," he told himself. But that owl, and that goddamn old Indian; dream carriers, owls. He had hit the branch and had then seen the owl with the rabbit. Maybe he'd just screwed up the time sequence, seen the owl before he hit the branch, imagined the old man. That owl: big ol' hooked talons casually dangling the jack; the jack still thumping, still running, pink eyes open, still running with a pain in his gut, so sharp he can't taste it yet, pink eyes on the branch and yellow eyes above, then the old man and Dolores. I should have brought the rosary back to her. That's what's caused all this, Beto thought.

He finished the can, tossed it among the others, and fought his way out of the sleeping bag and over to the friendly bush at the edge of the stream. He swayed, watching himself in the moonlight, the creek washing over sandstone, one hand on his hip and finally letting go, his hands behind his head now, legs spread, grunting, so that the sound of urine in the sand was louder than the creek. He strode out into the water and washed his left leg. He heard the cicadas start up their chant again. "I should have brought it back. Shouldn't have gone back to the mortuary. Should have returned that damned rosary to her in the rest home," he answered them. The rest home. He had put Dolores in a rest home, but it was right, what with her hip and all. He had to get on with his life, didn't he? She'd have to make friends with the other old ladies is what she'd have to do; stop being so contrary and difficult, make friends, go to Sea World and Olvera Street in a nice white van with the other old ladies. Someone had to get rid of them, too, didn't they? Someone had to pull it up and do it. "Can't wait around forever," is what Tina had said. That was Tina, so confident and sure of herself; she had put it all together. He worked at his teeth and stretched his head back hard and slow, jutting his lower jaw out to relieve the pressure. No, he told himself, he hadn't done it to please Tina. No, he was sure it was a good idea. Dolores had to get out of his way and Tina had taken care of it all. The funeral, the rest home, and $10,000. "Refugees," she had called them. They had had to hide out, bury their little girl secretly. Refugees from El Salvador with $10,000. A funeral and a rest home. That Tina was bright. She could take care of the old lady and do a favor for these refugees. But where was Tina that night? She hadn't had to pack a grandmother's bags, take a drive with an old lady who wouldn't take her eyes off him.

"You're no better than your mother," Dolores had said finally in the truck on the way over to the rest home. It was late; the neighbors were sleeping. He had driven to the address in Lincoln Heights. It wasn't a great address. There were no good addresses in Lincoln Heights, only wood bungalows and stucco apartments from the 30's and 40's. It was the only thing she'd said on the ride over. He'd done all the talking, and she had never taken her eyes off him. The doctor who had admitted them, if he really was a doctor, smelled of cigarettes and looked as if he'd just gotten off work waiting tables. He spoke English with an accent, but not like Dr. Hernandez. He needed a shave. Dolores wouldn't speak to him. Before Beto let the screen door bang closed, he looked back at the front yard, a pink narrow concrete path cutting in half two sides of crab grass, ending at the waist-high chain link fence and gate. He brushed his hand over the masonite sign under the front porch light, "*Nuestra Virgen de Guadalupe* Rest Home." There were no trees or bushes, and the two lawn chairs on the covered front porch needed new webbing.

The doctor, he had introduced himself as Dr. Felipe Bettencourt, was nervous and overly attentive. The other patients, "*sus amigas*," he called them, were sleeping. It was late; he would take them to her room.

Beto had almost backed out of the whole thing when he saw her room. He had been that close, and the memory made him grind his back teeth now. The door hadn't opened until it was lifted, the carpet was the color of rat fur, the paint on the walls had powdered, and the bathroom. . . . It wasn't only that it was tiny or that the linoleum was chipping away; it was the tub that hit him most. It looked as if someone had just wiped at it with a dirty rag or a shirt. He had looked at the doctor, and then at the rust stain down the front of the tub under the leaking faucet. Dolores had stared at him as she sat on the bed, a bed heaped with blankets. The doctor had told them everything would be fine. He called her "Señora" as he wrestled with the door. "She will be fine," he said later, as Beto walked out the front door. Beto had tried to kiss her good-bye, but she wouldn't let him. She sat with her head bowed on the edge of the bed, a tiny plastic black and white TV on the dresser, one picture of Our Lady of Guadalupe, and one window covered by a metal guard.

"I will pray for you," she had said as his hand touched the door knob.

It is always like this, he had thought; she would wait until the last minute, the last second, when the time to leave was most important.

"Grandma"—he called her grandma for the first time in a long time— "everything will be fine, believe me. It's not forever; as soon as I'm finished out there, I'll be back to bring you home." He blinked. He didn't know if he was even going back to Utah, and he surely didn't know when he would be back for her. He just said it, and she wouldn't take her eyes off him.

"I will pray for you."

"Don't worry about me," he had said quickly. "Let me worry this time."

"Someone has to watch over you."

"No, I don't need this, Dolores. You're the one who needs care, always have. You broke your hip, remember?" His voice was mean; he couldn't pull the edge off it. He remembered her walker in the back of the truck. He tried to kiss her good-bye again.

"I will pray that He watches over you." She looked up when she said "He." "I am worried that you have lost your soul."

He called her "grandma" again.

"Bring me my rosary, please, mi'jito." She had stopped looking at him.

He went to her purse. "It's not here, Dolores." He had spread out the contents: a compact, a coin purse, bobby pins, lipstick, a missal, twenty or so religious tracts, a pen, her wallet, more lipstick. The pile looked enormous next to the TV on the painted dresser. He turned the purse upside down.

"It must be at the house. Look in the kitchen on the table. Please bring it to me, my son. Will you do that for me?"

He was sure she had done this on purpose. How could she have forgotten that rosary, the life of her fingers?

"Bring it to me," she said quietly.

He stood by her bed then and she took his hand, rubbing it against her lips. She rubbed it hard; he could feel the driving pressure on his hand.

"I love you, *mi'jito*," she had said as he left.

The drive across the L.A. River to Silver Lake was not usually a lonely one, but he hit every light, the streets too bright. The house was dark when he pulled up to the curb and set his wheels. The bougainvillea that grew up along the stairs and over the front door porch leered at him like a killer, silent and threatening. It was the first night that Tina was not there waiting for him. He saw the blinking light on the machine. "Meet me at Barragan's at 11:30," her voice said. It was 12:30. He went into his grandmother's room, a beautiful room from which one could admire the flagstone patio that his grandfather and father had built, and the garden that Dolores had planted. The windows were open. The air, L.A. midnight air, smelled as fragrant as newly turned dirt. The rosary wasn't in her room. He shut the windows. He remembered that she had told him it was in the kitchen. Why had he come in here? He stopped at her dresser. It was covered with pictures of him growing up, photos propped against the statues of Jesus and The Blessed Virgin, curling in the dry heat. The boy who looked at him was smiling awkwardly out of First Communion, Confirmation, and Graduation pictures. There were more under the glass top of the dresser, between the white lace doily and the glass. He looked at them all. A few minutes later he turned off the light and turned down the corridor that was open on one side to the living room, but highlighted with ornamental iron and curved arches. He had to wait in the dark of the kitchen for a half minute until the ballast in the fluorescent light kicked in. It blinked several times before it went on for good. The rosary was in her corner of the kitchen table. He reached for it, not wanting to look at it. It was a cheap pink plastic rosary that might be given to a girl on her First Holy Communion. Beto could imagine her as a girl. She acted like a child all the time anyway as far as he was concerned. She had better rosaries, gifts from others. They were stored in her dresser. He didn't want to think of the reason she liked the cheap rosary so much. It had only cost him ten subscriptions to the Tidings, and his grandfather had given him the money for five of them. The pink rosary was the last prize the sister had had; the black ones were all gone. He had won it, thrown it in her lap, and now he didn't want to look at it. He'd take it right back to the rest home, stop by Barragan's to see if Tina was still there, and then get some sleep.

He drove over to Sunset and Alvarado. At the corner he stopped at the Salvadorean take-out for a *pupusa*. They were closed since it was after one a.m. He would have bought two even though he wasn't hungry. He made a left on Sunset and drove across the bridge over Glendale Blvd. Off to his right he could see the Echo Park Lake boathouse, its phony lighthouse lit. Past Alvarado, Sunset climbs a hill out of Echo Park in the direction of downtown. He passed bars, Barragan's, and beauty salons. Tina's car wasn't parked on Sunset. He saw one taco pushcart under the piercing light of its Coleman lantern, and three men in *ranchero* outfits eating. A *conjunto* done for the night. There was another man leaning on his elbows into the side of a building, but he wasn't a member of the band. Halfway up the hill he saw the store signs change from Spanish to Chinese or Korean. Who would be here in ten years, he wondered? Everything was changing. Would there be a Dr. Ngong or Kim Yung instead of Dr. Hernández? Would he be able to buy a *taquito*? He told himself he wouldn't be here to see it. Near the crest of the hill, before Sunset drops down into Chinatown and Olvera Street, he saw the painted sign in the bushes off to his left with one light shining on it: The Gutierrez and Chan Mortuary. He and Tina had been there yesterday. He had tried to forget the cubed jello and the shaved circles on Dolores' temples, but it was still the sanitarium to him. Tina and Gutierrez had done all the talking. He had never seen the body. He was almost past the entrance when he turned hard up the street to the driveway. He had to use the curved end of a crowbar to break the lock on the gate. He drove up the long driveway past the front entrance to the back where he knew there was a service entrance. The limo was parked under the solitary light. The service door led into the kitchen. He assumed that's what it was, but there were no hanging pots and pans. He opened an industrial-sized refrigerator. The light illuminated large clear jars of pickled pigs' feet and beer. The pigs' feet were pink and jammed against the sides of the glass. He took two Budweisers, wiping the mouth of a bottle carefully before opening it. The bottle smelled like cat food. He left the refrigerator door open so he could see. He knew which way he should be heading, but he couldn't find any light switches. He knew he should be bumping into things, but the rooms were empty. He headed in the right direction until he saw the blue light under the door at the end of a hall. He opened this door slowly into a room with Gutierrez sleeping in the blue glow of a TV. He knew he hadn't been in this room with Tina. They had been shown to the parlor, not to the room where Gutierrez lived. There was a bed, a hot plate, a small fridge, the TV, the recliner chair with Gutierrez in it, and the TV tray with the pickled pigs' feet. A quarter bottle of Cutty's had been placed on the floor; no ice or booze remained in the glass on the TV tray. "He's pickled," Beto said to himself, but he didn't laugh at his joke. Gutierrez had his mouth open, snoring. He'd kicked off his shoes and loosened his tie. Beto walked around his chair to the room past the parlor where he found the caskets. He had thought that maybe they would have put them in slide-out coolers like he saw in the cop shows, but there were only the caskets. She was young. He touched her negligee, saw bruises on her face and neck. He knew no one would dress their little girl like this, but he couldn't imagine how Tina had gotten involved. He drank the other beer slowly. Touched her face. He didn't want to leave. It was peaceful here. He took out the pink rosary and wrapped it around her hands. He carefully folded her hands, making sure the cross was nestled between her thumbs. He didn't know if he felt sorry for her; he wasn't sure who he felt sorry for. He knew that he felt better being here with her, that he was tired of the way his chest rose and fell, and how he blinked his eyes, and the way his hair grew loudly out of his scalp. He knew that he couldn't give this rosary to Dolores because she didn't deserve it. Not that she wasn't worthy of the rosary, but if he gave it to her she'd think that maybe he wasn't so bad after all, that maybe he would be back soon to get her out. He leaned over the coffin for another two hours; then he left the rosary wrapped around her hands and went home.

Beto realized that he was still standing in the water at the edge of the creek. He couldn't see the moon anymore, but he could feel light seeping into the pores of the sandstone. The old man would be up in another minute. He walked back to his sleeping bag intending to crawl in, but decided instead to re-kindle last night's fire. There wouldn't be any sleep for him. As he blew on the fire he remembered that he hadn't called the Rest Home or Dr. Hernández. And that after leaving the sanitarium that night he had packed and left for Utah in the morning with Tina.

Fourteen

Tina sat up and stuck the heels of her hands into her eyes. Her fingers crawled through her hair. She knew instinctively that her brush was gone.

"Where's Beto, Sam?"

The old man was leaning over the fire stirring a pot. "Well, since you said you liked trout so much, he's out catching a few. He's got two already, so it shouldn't be much longer." He took the pot off the flames and set it on a flat rock close to the heat. "Slept good, huh?" he asked her.

"Fine. What time is it anyway?"

"Oh, it's about seven, seven-thirty."

"Seven o'clock," she groaned. "Is it always this bright at seven? I can't believe it."

"Wait until we get out of this shadow, when the sun hits."

She could see they were still in the shadow of the Nipple. The shadow lay out in the middle of the stream. She rubbed her arms and thanked God for Molly's huge tit. She didn't make a move to get up, just sat in the sleeping bag with her arms around her knees, hugging her back into a shell. She thought of snuggling back down into the warm cocoon of the bag or going for a sweatshirt. It felt cool under the Nipple with the other side of the creek glaring at her. This was the wide section of Deer Creek Canyon which was open to cedars and tamaracks, willows at the stream's edge. The mesa that ran along the other side was soft, no sharp angles there. It appeared dull to Tina. She felt like sitting in the truck with the tape deck going. She could think better with music going, but then she didn't want to see herself in the mirror. She wondered what she should do now. Would Beto stay here if she left? If he would, then there wouldn't be any reason for her to remain here babysitting him. Besides, she was needed back in L.A.: the old lady was safely put away in the rest home, she had to make sure the funeral had gone without a hitch, that Gutierrez hadn't talked, and she was tired of this camping bullshit. She'd had enough of it with her family, and it hadn't been for fun. Crossing the border, sleeping in ravines. She'd had enough of it, and Beto too, but she was surprised that she was so attracted to him. What was it, she wondered, that attracted her to such strange men? She'd have to check herself, watch herself the next time. She thought of Ray, what a good man he really was, but boring. Watch out, sister, she told herself again, you had a good thing going with Ray, but you couldn't take it, had to have excitement. Don't let it bite you and don't do anything crazy now, she thought; everything's in place. She touched her hair, told herself to keep it cool, and then laughed a little, knowing she had this tendency to fly off and not care where the pieces fell. Tina looked at the old man.

"How about coffee, Sam? You make any coffee?"

"I sure did. Here, let me get you a cup. I know how you youngsters like coffee." They heard a whoop from upstream, past the bridge.

"He's got his catch. We'll have that breakfast now."

"How can you think about eating?" She took the cup with both hands. The old man had to lean over so Tina could keep her elbows at her sides.

"Thanks, Sam."

"You're not hungry?"

"I never eat in the morning," she said seriously.

He chuckled. He could see that Tina wasn't a morning girl, or a ranch hand either. Some were and some weren't, but he knew that if you lived out here long enough, there wasn't anything to do at night to keep you from being a morning person.

"You want more coffee?" he asked.

"No. I haven't even tasted it yet. Thanks anyway."

He went back to the fire and poked at the coals. It was a perfect fire for trout.

They heard Beto before they saw him, and then there he was, pushing water in the middle of the creek, the sunny side across his face. They watched him splash into a hole and almost fall. He was wet to the crotch. Tina laughed so hard she spilled coffee on the sleeping bag. She swore. Beto yelled, grinning, "Hey, look at these! That fire ready?"

"You bet," the old man replied. "You need a knife?"

"No, I got mine. Only be a minute."

"Where's my hairbrush, you oaf?" Tina yelled.

"In the truck."

"Dammit." There was no reply. "I said, can't a girl even brush her hair around here?"

"You're a sack. Get out of bed."

"Fuck you," she muttered.

"In a minute," Beto said. He had heard her.

"You're not listening to me. I don't want fish for breakfast. I don't want breakfast."

"More for the rest of us," he shouted on his way to clean fish. Tina leaped out of her bag and stalked to the truck. Beto, cleaning the trout, didn't notice her. The old man was equally busy with the precious fire.

"You don't goddamn care what I want. I hope you choke on your goddamn fish bones. If I wanted to be with a bunch of goddamn lowbrow, knuckle-dragging okies. . . ."

They looked when she started up the truck. They heard the grinding of gears, saw the belch of smoke from the newly awakened engine, the swerving onto the bridge, the grind again, her voice and the truck disappearing up the hill on the road to Boulder.

"What'd she say?" Beto asked the old man, three cleaned trout hanging from his fingers.

"She called us 'okies'." They were both staring at the cut in the mesa where the road passed through.

"I'll be damned," Beto said.

"Good thing it's tuned up," the old man replied.

"She doesn't know where she's going."

"Only one road."

"No croissants in Boulder."

"What's that?"

"Nothing. Forget it."

They spent the next two hours waiting for her return. The old man ate all the trout and Beto watched the top of the hill. The sleeping bags, Molly, the fire, the two men, and the empty Coors cans gathered heat.

"I got some work. You coming?"

Beto rubbed at his chin, but didn't answer.

"Come on up to the ranch. The Buchanans'll be happy to see you," the old man continued. "Now look, she won't be back 'til you take your eyes off that road." The old man lifted his cap and rubbed at his hair with the other hand. He looked up at the road once again, and back at Beto. "You need anything, son? I'll be going now," he said finally, but he didn't move.

"Yeah," Beto answered. It was more an exhalation than a word. "Buchanan leave a bottle?"

"Maybe." The old man knew there was one wrapped up in a greasy rag under the spare tire in the bed of the truck.

"And bring me some beer and ice on your way back out?" There was no reply. "Willya old man?"

Beto waited until the old man had returned with the bottle and left in the old Ford. He had to watt a long time because the old man liked to warm up the engine before he took off. He waved back from his place on the sleeping bag as the old man finally drove over the bridge and yelled, "see you tonight," and then he walked over to the creek and snugged himself down in the slimy mud in the far bank under the tamaracks. There weren't any rocks there, just ooze and shade. The water was cool, and the bottle of Jim Beam that smelled of tractor grease was on the bank in reach of his right hand.

Fifteen

It wasn't that he didn't know what to do. Ray had seen the movies, but he had never been on a trip with a girl. There had been no time with Tina; he had just opened up the shop. They had been married on a Saturday, drunk for two days at the reception in his parents' backyard, and then it was back to the buffing of metal. There had been no honeymoon, not even a trip to the Queen Mary in Long Beach. She had been young, and maybe if she had gotten pregnant, the back room at his folks wouldn't have been so boring. Maybe if he had spent more time with her, had taken her to the Santa Monica Pier, pinball machines, miniature golf. He didn't know. He had loved being with her. She had been so exciting that he hadn't needed to go anywhere. Now he was petrified, glad that he had something to do, glad that he was driving the Impala, so that he could put his two hands on the wheel, watch the road, the speed, the gas gauge, the mirror. And he was thankful that, unlike his ex who only seemed to worry about herself, Cecilia had organized things so that he could drive. She had the maps, told him where to turn, the freeways, changed the radio. She would have packed his bag, he was sure, if he had asked her. Would she suggest a motel now? They had come close in the garage, but if it had happened, would they have left to come out here? It would have been too quick; he didn't know her well enough. And how could they be attracted to each other under these circumstances? Or, really, what did she see in him? It would be better to wait a while longer. He touched the gabardine and planned his next conversation. He thought of Mel Gibson and Cary Grant. What would Cary say? He looked at the gas again and the two bags of trash from Jack in the Box. Was she hungry again? Thirsty? Would she tell him or should he ask? He'd get gas and then they would decide.

"Barstow's coming up, Ray. Let's pull in. We need gas, and I'm dying of thirst." She rubbed the back of his neck.

"Yeah, that sounds good. How much farther?"

"Over this hill, but I think we're gonna have to stop in Vegas too. That's still a couple of hours away."

"Vegas?"

"You must be getting tired, and as far as I can tell from the maps, it's another eight hours into Boulder. Don't you think we ought to get a room in Vegas? There's no reason to kill ourselves." She made it sound like a question.

He waited a moment. "Yeah. I think that's a good idea. I was thinking the same."

"Ray, tell me, where have you been?" she asked slyly. "You've let me do all the talking."

"Nowhere. Nothing, just driving is all." He looked at her in the rear view mirror; it was the only way he could see her face. He would look at her as she moved or when she changed the radio, look at her lovely face or her legs tucked under her on the seat. She was a lovely woman, soft eyes green in the glow of the dash lights, hair violet in the oncoming lights. She lit a cigarette for him, put it to his lips with her lovely hands. Lovely hands, not too thin.

"Why did he say there weren't any hallways? What does that really mean?"

"Oh, Chuy?" Ray groaned silently. She wanted to talk about it again. "He means there is no way in."

"Just because they're Cubans?"

"Well, they're *Marielitos*. They're a different story. They're boat people, let out of Mariel prison in Cuba. Castro let them go at Jimmy Carter's invitation." He looked in the mirror. The road was black behind them, the road so dark he couldn't see her face, but he caught her eyes in the mirror, and then he continued. "Some of them are real gangsters, and some were just thrown in for thinking the wrong way. But, baby, the bad guys just took up where they left off, and this ain't Cuba. L.A.'s fresh, wide-open territory to them."

"But I thought you said Boyle Heights was our territory?"

"Lincoln Heights, and it's wide open. They may be running with any number of corners there. Like I told you, the homeboys are loose in the Heights, fighting for a piece of the turf, and we don't know for sure who the Cubans are with."

"And this guy, Chuy, says Tina is involved? How do you know this Chuy guy?"

"Chuy and me and Beto go back a long way." To the tracks, Frogtown, and the hidden valley, he thought. "He said it, so I believe it." Chuy had confirmed it. Said it was ugly. That Riverside had been approached but wanted nothing of it. "Ray," he had said. "We're a family, Ray. You know, brother, no way we go in for that shit."

"But slaves, come on."

"Slaves, hookers. Good money in young girls." Ray saw the exit sign for Barstow, three miles.

"You know a lot about this, don't you?" Cecilia spoke casually, but her interest was clear. The night rolled past the windows.

"It's my home; they're my brothers. You learn as you grow up."

"I live there too, and I know so little. Well, I've heard of Riverside."

"Yeah, well, it would have been different for you if you had brothers or if you had gone to Logan Street School. You would have known." He felt talkative; he continued, "You see, they're families. My folks still say they're from the Ravine, Chavez Ravine, and they got kicked out years ago. And Frogtown has been a family as long, or longer, than any barrio in town." He noticed that he was dropping into a slang style of speech. He cooled off for her. "Chuy's probably fifth or sixth generation. His kids are homeboys, and he was a *vato*, you know. They know Frogtown's tight; Riverside guys are tight. They have connections. That's a lot of history there, Cecilia; believe me, he knows. But what worries me is that even Riverside can't get in. They don't know for sure where Dolores is. They know it's this bad business and Tina is in it. But Tina is still cool on the street; I can't figure it, but I know that if they don't want to talk, they won't."

"You've known Tina for a long time?"

He was silent. He knew he shouldn't let the question pass, that it would come up again too soon. He wanted to tell Cecilia about his ex, but instead he checked the speedometer and looked into the lights of oncoming cars.

She noticed his silence and wished that Barstow was behind them, that the windows would continue clear and black, and that they could stay here in the Impala. She knew there was something that Ray was hiding from her, and she wondered when it would come up. Well, hopefully they could clear up this thing with Dolores, and then they'd be back and her life would return to its normal state—the market, church, her boyfriend. She saw the lights in the valley, the sign marking the Barstow exit. "All services, 1 mile," appeared.

"That's where we get off," she said sadly.

"Right," he answered.

Ray drove steadily at 60 after they had gassed up and were back on the highway. He let the trucks pass as he brushed the head of the big curl asleep on his leg. She stretched. Cecilia had curled up and fallen asleep instantly after they had left Barstow, instantly as they hit sixty m.p.h. as if the engine had hummed her a lullaby, as if the Chevy wasn't heavy at 60, and tires on asphalt were just more fingers brushing her forehead. His right leg felt as if it were gone, as if it were connected to the seat and her head and the gas pedal. She sat up, instantly awake.

"We're almost there, aren't we?"

"Ohhh, yes, we are," he said, leaning back with both hands and stretching, the Chevy guided by his left knee.

She grabbed the wheel with both hands so that the car lurched out of the lane and into the sand at the edge, spraying the sides like hard rain.

"Hey," he snorted. "Give me that."

"Scared you, didn't I? You're half asleep."

"My right leg's asleep, paralyzed in this position."

She moaned, "Ohh," and leaned into him, rubbing his thigh. "Is it waking up now," she asked and smiled, "or should we stop so you can stretch your legs?"

He wanted to put his arm around her and hug her to him so he could smell her better and kiss her hair and stick his nose and lips into her neck, but "no, I'll be alright," was what he said.

"Do you like Chinese food?" Cecilia asked, bending her head back but not moving away from him.

"I love it." He could see Vegas as they came down the grade. He had forgotten his work, the Impala was racing at 80, and she was still leaning against him.

"Ray, did you ever do anything really dangerous, so dangerous you thought you might lose your life?"

He tried to think. Finally, he answered, "No, I haven't done too much. I ran a few red lights is all."

"You're hilarious. Come on, tell me; I won't laugh. Something really scary."

He tried to think of something, but his mind was like the corner of a garden shed with one hopeful brown spider weaving on a rusty shovel. He couldn't remember the time in lock-up at the Angeles Crest Camp, or his tour in 'Nam. He did think of his ex-wife, but he wasn't frightened now.

Cecilia answered for him. "No, well does this scare you? You're driving ninety miles an hour and concentrating on my chest."

He slowed down immediately, as if there were a line through his body connected to the gas pedal. He saw the overhead sign for Zzyyxx Road and swerved off onto the exit.

"Do you need to catch your breath?" she asked.

"I think so." He chased the road into darkness and killed the engine, letting the car drift into the gravel before it stopped and he shut the lights off. They were cutouts propped in front of the Hoover Dam wattage of Vegas. "You're not tired?" he asked her.

"No, but how's your leg?" she answered, leaning into him.

"I think I better stretch it," he said, and got out of the Chevy to stare at the lights of Vegas.

It was another half hour before he pulled into Vegas and rolled under the canopy of the Stardust Hotel.

"What's this?" she asked, surprised. A casino valet opened the door.

"Well, you wanted Chinese. It says 'Mandarin'."

Cecilia groaned pleasantly. "Yeah, but this looks real expensive. I'll pay half. We'll go dutch. I insist." The valet looked bored as he waited for her to get out and let him close the door. A line of cars was forming behind them.

"No. I'm treating. I insist," Ray said.

"Come on. You've paid for all the gas. I'm paying my half." Another valet opened his door. "Sir," he said.

"Yeah, yeah," Ray replied without looking.

Cecilia got out and bent into the car. She didn't care if her rear end was sticking out, which it was. The valet patted her on the arm. "I don't care, Ramón." She dragged out his name. "I've got money. I want to treat."

The valet coughed before speaking. "You gonna stay or what? This the right place?" They ignored him as he made an exaggerated gesture with his hand, as if he were bowing a lady into the entrance. Someone honked.

"No, no. Really. I want to, Cecilia. Another time. This is special. You get the next one."

"You're very sweet, Ray, believe me, but I'm not going to let you get away with it."

The valet touched her on the arm again. "Lady," he said. "Please?"

Cecilia leaned in and put her hands around Ray's face. She wouldn't let go, and neither would he. Two horns honked and the manager walked over. The manager tapped on the roof. They heard what sounded like rain falling from light bulbs.

"Say, friend. You planning to get married or something?"

"Let's go, eh?" Ray said. They split apart and Cecilia acted as if it were her first time out of the car.

"Thank you," she told the valet sweetly. The valet smiled and looked up into the light bulbs. Ray straightened up, adjusted his pants, combed back his hair, and walked past the manager. He turned back to put his face into the round moon in the tuxedo and said slowly, "take it easy with my ride." Ceci never cracked a smile, although she wanted to laugh.

"The restaurant's closed."

"Ask about room service," Cecilia replied.

"Room service?"

"Yeah, they'll bring it to our room."

"We don't have a room."

"Get one. I'm bushed. We'll order room service. It'll be fun." She didn't see him turn to look at her, a moment later, from the front desk.

"Cecilia, I don't know," he told her when he returned. The noise from the casino surrounded them; dice, people shouting, Buddy and Vicky working on a Neil Diamond number in the lounge to their right, but they felt as if they were alone in the empty lobby.

"What, they don't have room service?"

Ray was silent for a moment and then answered seriously. "Yes, they do. But the guy asked me if I wanted queen-sized."

"That's right," she said. Ray was somber. "What's the matter, Ray?"

"Should I tell him we're married?"

She didn't laugh. That was twice tonight that she had held it in. She didn't know if she could keep it up. "They don't care. You are a sweet, but old-fashioned man. Do you want me to get the room?"

He looked shocked. "No," he replied quickly. "No, I don't want that at all."

"You were in the Army or the Marines, weren't you? What about TJ?"

"Cecilia, that's not funny. Besides, you're a nice girl."

She looked sideways at him. She decided that if he weren't for real, he was, at least, convincing. She spoke earnestly. "Tell him we're married."

"Room 1343," he told her a few minutes later, wagging the key back and forth in front of her face. He was still very serious. The light-heartedness of the carport scene had completely left him.

Cecilia was concerned. She tried to make it less serious by speaking lightly. "Great, let's go."

"Cecilia, he knows we're not married."

"Oh Christ, Ray." She felt the hour, the empty room, the desk clerk looking over at them. "It doesn't matter. Hell, there's hookers in all of these hotels. He doesn't care; he's only a desk clerk making five bucks an hour. For all he knows, you've got a young one who looks like she's going to fall asleep on you in the elevator."

He was silent for a moment. When he spoke his voice was still very serious, but his mouth had turned up into a wry smile. "Let's get married."

She knew that she had heard him because he was standing in front of her waiting, but she was thinking of her hands, what to do with them, and why the lights in the ceiling suddenly felt hot on the backs of her arms. She heard a thump on a table behind her, a microphone popping, and then she asked him, knowing it didn't sound right even as she asked, "did I hear you correctly?"

"Yes. I would like to marry you." He stood erect.

She noticed that he was a good four inches shorter than she.

"Oh." She paused. Ray waited. "Don't you think it's a little quick?" she asked.

"Yes, I do, but it doesn't matter," Ray answered quickly.

She looked past him at the desk clerk, wondered what the room service menu would offer, saw her mother watering plants from a rusted coffee can, and the hole in the face of John the Baptist over the inscription to María Elena Leon. She imagined the young María combing her hair and walking onto a porch, a covered porch that she was never able to leave, but which was filled with the sound of wind chimes. Cecilia smiled slightly at Ray and touched her fingertips together. "I have one request, a condition," she said.

"A condition?" he asked solemnly.

"The Chapel of the Little Pines."

"The Little Pines?"

"Yes, it's two miles back up the Boulevard." Then she laughed and continued laughing, making up for the two times she had held back, until she had to lean against his shoulder to hold herself up. He blinked his eyes several times. "Come on, Ramón." She grabbed his hand. "Go get the car."

Sixteen

Beto sat in the mud, in the silt against the bank of slow water, the still water under his eyes, water to his chin. He sat there as a rancher's truck that he recognized passed over the bridge, close enough that the tamarack branches bent a little from the wind of the passing truck, close enough that had the ranchers stopped, they would have seen his entire body in the clear water and the empty bottle on the bank, close enough that if they had spit a little chaw, they might have hit him. When the sun had fallen over Wild Horse Mesa, he got up, but only when the sun had left the ground, remaining only on the tops of the rock and volcanic plugs and Molly's Nipple. Only then did Beto walk up out of the water and begin to gather a large pile of wood for the fire.

He gathered all the reachable wood, and then searched for more. It was mostly cedar from a dead tree that he toppled from an embankment, and cottonwood branches that collected in the eddies. He carried two armloads up a hideously steep trail to the low overhang halfway up Molly's, leaving the rest in a large pile under the cottonwood. The overhang was hidden behind clumps of cedar so that it was invisible from the ground below, although one had only to follow the narrow trail to find it. He stopped on the trail before coming down for the sleeping bags. This was the beautiful time, the sunlight moving up the canyon walls, moving so fast he could see the shadow creep up and over the top, leaving rust and orange and dark cold spots. He imagined himself pinned on a wall, feeling the sun and shadow cross his chest, his face, and then when he felt the cold, the breeze, he would hug himself against the cliff wall and the heat that was still there. He liked the way it seemed to quiet down with the rush of shadow, a breeze barely moving the wide leaves of the cottonwood. He reached over and felt the pitted surface of a volcanic rock. He carefully rubbed the entire rock until he settled on the shady side, lingering on the lichen, the velvet smoothness, and then he thought of L.A. He saw his grandmother's house, the rough exterior walls painted a creamy white, damp in the setting sun. He thought of the goldfish that for some crazy reason he had stocked in the pond before he left, the cats waiting patiently on the wide flagstones, the BB gun in the corner of the kitchen. Deer Creek was almost dark now, but Beto left his hand on the lichen as he continued his walk through the house. He looked up into the darkening blue desert sky to see blinding edges as sharp as envelopes on the trailing wisps of high clouds, but it didn't calm him. He could hear the stream; it reminded him of the fountain, the Mexican boy his grandfather painted every spring peeing in the pond, and then he could hear leaves collide, water spiders in the slow parts. It was still very warm, the warmth of rocks filling the canyon. Soon there would be the rush of wide wings, night, flapping slowly. He would wait for the moon to cover the mesas, as jarring as a sheet of negatives, a miner, his searchlight drunk among the trees and canyon walls. The night would be noisy, movement in the grasses and bushes, hungry noises, safe in the black hiding spots, safe from the moon. He sniffed the air, but it didn't carry the scent of warm blood to him. He heard the truck then, and decided he would build his fire. He pulled off a strip of cedar bark and set to rubbing it into a soft downy ball. Only a bird's nest was better. He placed the fire ball in the middle of a blackened circle of rocks. He haphazardly tossed the thin strips of wood he had gathered onto the top and sides of the cedar ball. He felt in his back pocket for the matches, a thin, crumpled book from a 7-11. "1,000 stamps worth over $100 for only $2.95," it read. The matches were damp with sweat and the pressure of his butt. He tried one, and then another. The heads crumbled, but he continued to scratch at the striker until there was a groove. He wasn't concerned; he could hear the truck, louder now, and see the occasional flash of headlights. Another match sputtered. It was the first of the last three that caught. He cupped it until the flame was strong, and then he let it go to the cedar bark. The cedar seemed to gather the flame in, smothering it, and then there was the blossom, small and weak at first, too small to blow on. He bent down, careful not to breathe. He whispered. It grew, wanted to die, then came back, fond of the caresses he applied. Now he blew hard, oblivious to the truck that had pulled in below. With every fresh blow his blossom seemed to hide, burrow and rest in the soft cedar, and then the red lick would come, the leaves of his blossom. He kept up this rhythm until the entire ball was seething and all he could hear was the kindling popping, blue appearing at the edges. He sat back and threw in the book of matches. The last two matchheads burst into flame like weak fireworks. He was ready to face Tina.

As he stood up he felt the effects of blowing on the fire and the half bottle of Beam. He thought it was excitement. "What the hell," he muttered, and touched the edge of the overhang for a second before he moved. The canyon was roaring, crackling, sending up huge noxious roars of thick dark smoke. The truck was hidden by a wall of fire. Even the far canyon walls were visible, glowing. He tried to recognize the smell and then started to run down the hill, not concerned with loose rocks on the path. Tina was standing on the other side of the pickup. There was a five-gallon can of gas on its side at her feet, and wads of paper floated up into the cottonwood whose leaves curled and flapped.

"What the fuck are you doing?" he shouted at her. The breeze was blowing flames against the truck. He jumped in the passenger side, scooted across the seat, touched the glass once. He knew it would be hot because the inside of the truck was an oven and he couldn't lean against the back of the seat. He backed it up furiously and ran back to the fire. Flames were shooting into the lower branches of the cottonwood as he shouted "help me" to Tina. Beto crabbed in low and pulled out one log at a time. When he could reach no more, he kicked bootfuls of sand until the fire was centered and four feet high. Sweat ran in dirty rivulets of black down his chest and back. His face was covered with soot and there was a long dark smudge where he had wiped at his cheek. Tina hadn't moved; she had watched the fire contentedly. He couldn't believe that she was so calm. They were on opposite sides of the fire.

"You knew what you were doing, didn't you?" She didn't reply, and her eyes remained on the fire. "You waited until the wind had blown most of the fumes away, but not long enough, huh? It even scared you a little, didn't it? It jumped at you." He could see soot on her face, and he thought he saw a singed eyebrow.

"I had to have a fire too," she replied calmly.

Beto screamed back at her.

"You don't have to shout. It's okay now."

"Shout," he hollered back. "I should wring your goddamn neck. I'm surprised the Forest Service isn't here, or all of Las Vegas." They were still on opposite sides of the fire. He could see her occasionally among the high flames, and then she would disappear. He suddenly felt tired, as if the tiredness had snuck up on him like a kid with a BB gun when all he'd been doing was watching the pretty fish swimming in the water lilies. And he felt like a mess. This was a mess. He looked around stupidly. He would pack up their equipment, go to the overhang and put out the fire, scatter the ashes, and then they would leave, drive to Vegas and get a room.

Tina could feel the change in him. She suddenly wanted to walk over to his side, to hold him, to make him forgive her. She knew that she was hard on her friends and lovers. She tested them. It had something to do with her family; as the oldest daughter, she was expected to care for her older brothers. She hadn't seen them for years. She heard Beto's tired voice, but she couldn't make herself move to him.

"Why didn't you wait for me? I was coming down to get you. I had a perfect spot and a small fire for us in that overhang," Beto said, dragging it out. She didn't say a word. He looked for some movement. He started to walk to her side and then stopped after three feet. "Why didn't you wait? You knew I would come down."

Tina could feel the words chipping at her tongue like flint as she spoke. She tried to stop them, but they were already working under her tongue. "How did I know you would come down? Tell me." She could feel the heat on her cheekbones. "You were just thinking about yourself. I thought you were going to drive me back to Vegas and leave me. When do you ever think of me?" Tears floated out of her eyes, rolled down her cheeks and onto her neck. The soot couldn't hold them back, and now Beto could see them across the fire. He realized he had forgotten about dropping her off in Vegas. He had forgotten that was why he had started a fire. He had been waiting for her to return. He had waited for the entire day, hadn't he? She wasn't moving, and her shoulders weren't shaking, because when she cried it was like a quiet drip from a skylight that sneaks up on you, that had waited until after the storm, and it seemed like the rain had stopped, but there was this surprise, wet and trickling steadily. She turned from him. She didn't want anyone else to know; maybe she didn't want to know herself. Beto didn't feel like saying anything. He wanted a cold beer, or any beer. He was relieved that no one had witnessed this, and then inside him the tiredness broke a little and he knew he didn't want to leave it like this; he didn't want to ignore what she had done. He gathered himself together and walked around to her. On the way he battled with himself: he should just make up with her, forget about it, and pack her in the truck and get the hell out of here, be over with it. But his eyes were frowning as he came up to her and he felt helpless as the anger continued to grow. He wanted to be cruel and shout at her, to show her the wetness on her cheeks that proved she wasn't so tough. He reached out to her and she came into his arms, putting her head against his chest, but his hands became cats bitten by the BB gun, snarling, rigid humped backs, and his hands grabbed her hard.

"You had to leave," he accused.

"Yes I did." Her voice was alarmed. He shook her. "I know that's why you're so angry, Beto, because I wouldn't stick around."

"You ran off." He shook her again.

"That's why you're angry, isn't it? I wouldn't eat your fish and camp out all day. I did what I wanted to. Grow up. I don't need you."

His hand moved; one cat jumped and her head twisted at the blow. She hit him back, more than once. Beto moved backwards, his arms over his face, and then he was on her and they were twisting on the ground.

"Let go of me," he heard her shout, and then he felt the heavy blow of stone to his head. He listened to the night grow quiet, quiet enough that he could hear his head turn in the sand and watch her move in shadows to the truck.

She saw herself walking away calmly, noticed the sweat running freely down her sides from under her arms. She heard herself carefully enunciating the words as if she were learning English or speaking to a child that had just woken up. "Come, we're going now, Tina. Get into the truck. I'll drive."

She opened the door and left it open. The keys were there, as if they were waiting for her. She stared at them for what seemed like minutes and then glanced across the fire at him. He hadn't moved; she had hit him hard in the same bruised spot on his head, but she didn't see blood. She didn't hesitate anymore; she started the engine and turned to look once more. His eyes were glued to hers. She turned to shift, and out of the corner of her eyes she could see him leap over the fire and run toward the truck. She screamed "leave me alone," and tried to reach back with her left hand to lock the door, but the door lock was too far over her shoulder, and she realized she had wasted time. Beto was on the hood of the Dodge now. Tina shoved the shifter into first and pure reaction made her floor the accelerator. Why had she waited, she cursed to herself as Beto leered in at her with his right hand cocked. He's going to bash in the window and get me, she thought, and then the truck lurched; the wheels spun. Sand and rocks spewed out the back, and Beto flew up and over the cab and into the metal bed. She heard another grunt as his body pounded into one side of the bed as she turned the wheel hard left to miss the cottonwood. She thought that the tailgate must be down when she heard the remaining camping equipment and a cooler slide out the back. She couldn't turn around, and she couldn't see him in the mirror, but she hoped that he had slid out too. The truck swerved wildly; there was too much torque, her foot still firmly planted on the pedal. The right side of the truck and the cottonwood met, crumpling sheet metal and tearing at bark. She heard him bounce against the side again and groan. Determination tightened her already-stiff body as the pickup straightened, spinning out of the clearing. The moon had broached the edge of the canyon and it lit up the creek like a neon tube. She could see the road in front of her; she didn't need the lights, but she reached over and yanked them on, and then there was too much white to see. The air in front of the windshield was white and flapping, crashing in at her. "Get away," she shouted, wrenching the wheel hard, blinded by the wings and the round eyes of an owl staring in at her. She heard a crash behind her, felt the splinters of glass, but it didn't register; she saw only wings and beak and eyes. It's here to keep me from leaving, she screamed to herself, and then she felt his hand from behind grab her by the chin and wrench her head back. She realized where the glass had come from; she hadn't shaken Beto loose. He had broken through the sliding back window. Her hands clamped tightly on the wheel and she swerved it back and forth, but he was pounding her head against the window again and again. She felt that her head would open, the hair dampen and mat. If she hadn't hesitated to lock the door, if she had only left instead of looking back. . . . She looked up once more, expecting to see white wings, but the window was clear now so she could see the man, the old man, trying to move out of the way. She pulled against Beto, hands at the wheel, but she heard the thud, and then the truck ran into an island of sand and sandstone. Tina flew forward into the steering wheel and Beto crashed into the cab, his body ridiculously stuffed under the dashboard. Tina had not taken her foot off the accelerator as the engine roared, making the rear wheels spin, and digging the back of the truck deeper into the sand. "Sam," she choked out. She saw Beto grappling from under the dashboard. She yanked at the door handle and started to leap out, but her body stopped. Beto had reached out and grabbed her by the end of her long beautiful tail of hair. He pulled her face next to his, his face hard against her cheek. "Where you going?" he whispered, the sound like stones, dry granite. "Where you going?" he repeated. She tried to scratch, but he couldn't feel pain. "I've got you," he gurgled, and he squeezed her until she stopped fighting.

When she awoke, the sun was full on her face, hot on the blue sleeping bag on the hot sand near the coals of last night's fire. She was alone.

"Beto," she called out in a raspy voice, but she knew he was gone. She got up, stretched a body she didn't know, felt the bruises on her neck and face. Her fingers came away with a little dried blood. She looked around her. The truck was still there, rear wheels deep in the sand. Equipment was strewn out in a line from the cottonwood, the gash in the tree raw in sunlight. The truck bed was littered with diamonds, the rear window a jagged hole. She opened the door, afraid to look, yet hoping. She reached over the column, feeling with her fingers. The keys were gone.

Tina opened the door and sat in the truck. She sat for a long time, long enough to watch dust settle on the hood. There was no breeze. She sat until her palms were wet on the steering wheel. Then she returned to the cottonwood and fell asleep in the shade as she planned how she would walk out at sundown.

Beto watched Tina fall asleep under the cottonwood, and then he came down from the overhang. He thought of the girl with the pink rosary as he tied a rope around Tina's hands and flipped the other end around a branch several times. He was surprised that she didn't wake, but he didn't feel tight in his stomach now like he had last night when he ran across the mesa, in back of Molly's, with the image of the dead girl in front of him and the dying body of the old man in his arms. He had remembered the dead girl's bruises, the body of a purple sunset, and he had fallen twice, coming down hard on his elbows, cushioning the blows from the old man. He had run across the sandstone under the moon, the old man light in his arms, the old man's hands fluttering like quail. What do your hands tell you now?, he had wanted to shout. And why did you come? Why did you come back? "Please, old man," he had whispered, "we're almost there. Please make yourself well." He had wanted to take him to Escalante, to the hospital or Buchanans', but the old man had said, "no, take me to the cave," and Beto, not knowing where or how, had run across the mesa as if the old man's hands were guiding him. "Leap, here, that way," the old man had seemed to say with the pressure of his hands, always the pressure. Beto had found the opening behind bushes in the bare valley at the top of the mesa. He remembered this pond, the frogs, the crabs, ponderosa pines, cattails, the moon full on them, the hands weak as tadpoles around his neck. He lit a small fire in the cave, the entrance so tight he had to pull the old man through by his hands, his hands over his head. He tasted the salt of his sweat and thought of birth, pictures of birth, but he was pulling the old man in, pulling him into the cave. With the fire lit, the cave widened. It was an Anasazi cave.

There were pecked-out drawings of deer, a mountain lion, men with spears and bows and arrows, a frog, a snake, and another wheel that covered the walls. His eyes flashed over the figures, but they would remain with him in their exact order and shape. Handrolled clay pots, a *mano* and *metate*, a reed basket, flint, obsidian flakes and chunks were all placed below the drawings. There was also a woven reed rug and blankets. He moved the old man to the rug and pulled blankets around him. There was no smoke. He wondered how the smoke left and where the hidden hole was. Was death like this—smoke that can't be seen leaving? He went outside, scrabbling through the small opening on his hands and knees, not caring about the rocks, or the bushes that whipped his face. He ran around the mound looking for the hole, the smoke, crying out for smoke. If he could find the hole and stop it up, the smoke couldn't leave, could it? He went back in to the old man whose eyes were still open.

"Sam, old man," he whispered, grabbing the hands of the old man and kissing them. "Sam," he said again.

"I'm still here, son." He tightened his fingers and Beto could feel all the broken bones of his body.

"What should I do?"

"Stay here with me."

"Of course."

"When I die, take my hat off, but leave it with me. Take my shoes and throw them from a high cliff, and fill a gourd with water from the pond outside."

The words wrenched Beto. He rubbed the hands, felt smoothness and warmth, remembered the lichen on the rock. "You're going to be fine. You can do it, Sam," he heard himself say.

"I always wanted to die here, you know. I love this cave, the canyons, the air, the pond outside. It's a sacred cave. The cave of the Ancient Ones. This is the first time I have entered it. You were outside, you know. Do you remember?"

"Yes."

"Funny, I knew that I would bring you here. And I knew that I would introduce you to Them."

"Oh God, no," Beto cried out.

The old man squeezed Beto's hands hard, let go, and folded them over his chest. He smiled and said quietly, "When you leave, remember, son, she needs her beads."

Beto didn't prepare to leave until morning. He remembered the cap and slid it off the old man's head and onto the hands he had folded. He took off the boots and went outside for water.

He had to dig the truck out to get it unstuck. Of course, he could have used the old man's red truck, but he knew that if he took it, he wouldn't be able to stop himself from remembering his last ride out of the Gulch with the old man. How they had been stuck in the riverbed and the old man had ridden them out of there. Tina woke up as he was driving away; he heard her scream at him, but he was sure the rope would hold. On the trip into Escalante he tried to figure out what the old man had meant by beads. Beto had known intuitively that the old man meant the rosary, but he was confused. How could the old man have known? Had he really been there with Dolores under the tree? Beto had even searched the cave in the vain hope of finding a string.

In Escalante, he stopped at the Phillips 66. He filled up the truck and then parked it in front of Whitey's and ordered a root beer float. The root beer smelled of oil and the ice cream had the consistency of old cottage cheese, but he finished it all, threw the cup into the trash, and went into Weaver's General Store.

"Hello, Mrs. Weaver," he said in a close imitation of an old boy's voice. Don't rush, he told himself. "You remember me? Robert, from the Buchanans' ranch."

Mrs. Weaver looked at him. "Why, sure I do. You've come back, huh?" She put down her darning.

"Yeah, couldn't stay away. God's country, had to come back." She smiled at him through tiny glasses. "Brought my boy along," he lied.

"Oh you got a youngin? How old is he?"

"Six. He's a tomcat. I thought I'd do a little hunting and fishing with him."

"Well," she answered, "you know it's not hunting season unless you wanted to pot some jacks." She looked pleased to see him, not worried, just passing time.

He slouched against the counter just like he'd seen all the cowboys do, and hooked his thumbs around the Santa Fe '47 buckle as he explained his situation to her. "You see, I forgot to bring my guns with me, Ma'am. But once I got out here I thought it'd be a good time to show him how to respect a gun."

"You could borry Jimmy's 22. He's in the navy now, stationed in Hawayah. He just loves it. But he'll be back, I hope. You know, none of the young folks stay around anymore. Can't say as how I blame them none, what with no jobs and the environmentalists telling us what to do with our own land. That Redford from

Hollywood is the worst."

He agreed. It was better to agree, even if he didn't care whose land it was, or if the coal strip mines and uranium people wanted to bulldoze the whole area away. He wouldn't be here. "Yeah," he replied. "Those city folks think they know how to run everything. Let me tell you, they should learn to run their own places before they meddle in and ruin somewheres else."

"Isn't that the truth," she agreed. She went on about local troubles and newcomers, but he didn't stop her. He wanted her to feel comfortable, and her talking calmed him.

"Well, what I think I want, Mrs. Weaver," he said, finally, when she had come close to talking herself out, "is a single barrel pump action. That is a 12 gauge, isn't it?"

She perked up. "It sure is, and a beauty too. We sold two last spring. It'll run you $212.00," she said anxiously.

"That's okay, I'm loaded for bear. Whatever's good for my boy. Let's see, why don't you give me ten boxes of shot?"

"My land, Bobby," she exclaimed. "You aiming to clean out the Burr of all its jacks?"

He smiled as he watched her unlock the case, pull the heavy shotgun out of its holder and lay it down on the counter. He didn't want her to close up the case, so he picked up the gun and swung it around to the back of the shop. He aimed it, and checked the chamber like he'd seen Buchanan do. It was as clean as he expected. He pumped it and fired the action. It was smooth and oily, and it smelled good.

"Say, let me look at that revolver, the 38 Colt. Is that an automatic?" he asked casually.

"Well, it's a semi-automatic, and the clip holds ten rounds. Everyone loves it for plinking, but you know I can't let you have it for a week. I have to send paperwork up to the Sheriff, and you know how he is with paperwork. They've gotten stingy around here and hard-headed, as if we didn't know anyone we sold our guns to."

He knew she was thinking about the sale as she handed the pistol over to him. Guns were handed down around here. There weren't many sales to be made, and he had over $400.00 laid out on the counter top.

"Oh, I understand Ma'am, but you know me. You can find me out at Buchanans', and if I have to wait a week I'll already be back to L.A. with my boy 'cause I have to return him home. How about if I fill out all the papers, and then come back in a week as if I never had the gun? No one but you and me would know the difference."

She looked at him, looked at the counter, didn't have to do any figuring. Her eyes grew tight, her brow crinkled, and she looked around as if hoping her husband would walk in and take this whole problem away from her.

"I don't know, Bobby. Well, I wonder what Mr. Buchanan would say. Heck, he trusts you. I know. He says you aren't like the other hired hands he's had before. Okay, but you have to promise me that you won't tell a soul and that you'll be back in a week, you hear me?"

"Don't you worry a bit," he said, smiling. She worked quickly. He bought 250 rounds of ammo and a roll of duct tape on his way out. The pistol was in a box. She put it in a paper bag with the tape. He carried the shotgun under his arm. He was almost out the door when she called out.

"By the way, where is your boy? I'd sure like to see him."

He stopped, his hand on the knob, and for a minute he couldn't think. "Oh, he's down at the creek with Sam. They're waiting for me."

"Well, you better hurry along." She waved, and then dived back to her work.

As he drove out of town, Beto made up a plan to help him get by. He knew that he would have to take Tina, of course. They would return to L.A., and if there were any problems, he would use the gun. It would be that easy. He didn't think about what he would tell Dolores or Father Reilly. He was more worried about what Tina would think.

The paved road coming back from Escalante went through high desert. When he dropped down into the canyonlands he sucked in his breath. It was beautiful, as always, the deep canyons filled with green. The quick drop felt like wind rushing up his face. He drove like a madman, the tires screeching at every turn. He used up the entire road. He was nervous. Would Tina leave him? He drove faster. When he was almost to Deer Creek, on another mesa top, with the washboard of the Burr Trail beneath him, he stopped. He opened the box and pulled out the revolver. He shoved a clip in. He reached under the dash, behind the instruments and along the steering shaft. He wrapped duct tape around the shaft and the gun so it was hidden there. He hoped that it wouldn't rattle. He practiced reaching for it a couple of times and felt good about it. He took the remaining clips of ammo, wrapped them in duct tape, and shoved them into the springs of the seat. He got out of the truck with the shotgun, hefted it, and aimed at a blooming yucca. He had never fired a gun before, except for a 22 with the old man. It was late afternoon and he was in the shade of a looming canyon wall. He stood there as quietly as the dust on the road. He smelled the sage and the far off water of Deer Creek. He heard movement in the brush and the ticking of the engine cooling down. A few seconds later he saw the jacks. Two, now three and four of them, venturing out, wary, but hungry in the late afternoon. He filled the slide with cartridges, slipped off the safety, and walked quickly but quietly around the truck to the edge of the brush. The jack hopped and skittered twenty feet away and then stopped, tense, only his whiskers moving. Beto aimed the shotgun, his finger slowly pulling the trigger, the jack perfectly in his sight, enlarged so he could see the veins in the jack's ears, its nose twitching and heart pumping, and then he swung the barrel around quickly. The jack exploded behind a clump of sage, the top of the yucca plant blown off. He liked the sound of the gun echoing off the canyon walls, so loud his ears were ringing, and he liked the feel of the gun against his shoulder with no padding. The recoil had slammed into his shoulder so that he had to place his feet wide. He felt as if he had really shot a gun. He walked back to the cab, opened the seat out and placed the shotgun behind it, wrapping the rifle in an old t-shirt he found back there. Then he got in and started the engine, surprised at how quickly the sun was going down today.

Seventeen

Beto came off the top of the mesa without shifting into second; the tires slid but didn't break. The road was steep, almost too steep for gravel, but all he wanted to see was the cottonwood next to the creek, the rope, and Tina. He saw the white Chevy. It didn't register. Campers, he thought; he would deal with that situation when he pulled in. He was halfway across the bridge when he focused on the car. "What the hell," he muttered, as he turned and stopped fast next to the old man's truck. Looking at the truck, he wondered when he would tell the Buchanans, stop in and tell them. He'd crossed the road to their house twice, speeding by each time, looking up towards the barn for Buchanan driving the other truck. He didn't move his hands from the wheel as he stared into the cab and then the bed, the spare tire against the back, the burlap bag filled with chains, a crescent wrench, hatchet and tire iron lumped into the center of the rim, sandstone dust layered in the metal valleys of the pickup bed. He would have liked just to stare into that truck for a long time, to put every crease and rust mark, the dust on the dash, the crack in the windshield into his memory and hold it so that it wasn't just the red on a cloud or the pink of his fingernails. He would have liked that in the setting sun and on into the night, but he couldn't; they were approaching.

Ray had moved first, had moved to break the spell, or he and Cecilia would have stood as if rooted, their mouths searching for water. He didn't look back at her, the muscles in his neck too tight to turn, perhaps, or was it the window? He couldn't take his eyes off the broken windshield reflecting the last of the sun like a rubber mallet on a bare fender. Cecilia didn't want to move; she felt a resistance to air in the flickering shadows of the cottonwood tree. She watched Ray take five steps as if he were fording an icy stream, his arms barely swinging, his shoulders bent heavy so that he looked thick and squat, his white t-shirted back a blot in her vision, and then she felt herself move, willing her hands first to release the sides of her legs.

Beto pulled at the door handle, then had to lunge at the tight door with his shoulder to open it. He hopped out quickly. He stared at them for a second and then turned to open the seat and find the shotgun. "What are you doing here?" he shouted, his hand resting on the rolled-down window of the door.

They stopped, and neither could say a word. Ray was in the sun, dark and thick in the low sun. Cecilia flickered at the edge of the cottonwood. Perhaps they stopped because of his voice; they felt like intruders, stumbling upon an odd picnic beside a quiet creek, their own hands empty, no cooler, no blanket. Ray couldn't speak, even though he had seen this before. He had buddies who had come out of the 'Nam jungle, yet this was his friend for life, a kid from Silver Lake. Where were the words that he could use? If Beto saw him, did he recognize his brother, or were this man's eyes in someone else's head? Cecilia saw the scratches on Beto's face and arms, the welt on his forehead, and she saw hands searching for pink beads.

The man at the country store in Boulder had told them exactly where they could find Beto and Tina: "Deer Creek crossing, under Molly's Nipple." How could he know, she had wondered, and then driving away from the store she had moved against the door because it had stopped feeling like a honeymoon. She had wanted to turn around then and go back to the gas station to call her mother, and tell her "momma, I'm married. Of course he's wonderful. We're having a great time, be back in a week or so." But Ray had been staring straight ahead, pushing the Chevy hard, tight in his seat. She had wondered if there were any secrets here, and then they were dipping down into Deer Creek and she had seen the red truck. She had had to will herself to move then as well, to open the door, to follow Ray. She felt the weirdness, spiky and bristling, before she took in the scattered camp gear and the remains of the huge fire. She hadn't yet seen the rope hanging from the Cottonwood tree when his voice, as quiet as the ticking of the engine, called for her.

"Ray, I'm gonna kill him. *Voy a chingar* that motherfucker," she heard Tina scream as she approached the tree. He was holding her face and body against his chest, but she wasn't crying; she was talking quickly, her voice a low scream. It wasn't the Tina of the black leather mini at the Rosary, but then again, it was. Ray was comforting her, rubbing her wrists so that Cecilia could see where the rope had been, the long fingers, his sidelong glance back at her that contained a certain discomfort beyond the rope, the long fingers. She rubbed her hands, her own shorter fingers, felt for the absent ring, and then she knew.

"Look what he did to me. He beat the holy hell out of me. You got a gun? I have to protect myself; he's gonna kill me. The fucker's crazy—*pelado*; he's been tanked up the whole time."

"Don't worry," Ray had said. "He's not going to touch you if we're here."

Tina stared long and hard at Cecilia as if she hadn't heard a word he said. "Who is this?"

Ray stepped back a foot, looking at Cecilia. "Cecilia, my wife."

Tina had snorted, dropped her hands away from Ray and combed her hair with her fingers. "The hell you say," she said at Ceci.

The two women had stared at one another, and then Tina had turned back to Ray. But Cecilia wouldn't look at Ray. He'd have to come to her. She'd wait, and then he'd better tell her what he had to say. Tina wouldn't shut up, and then she didn't talk to Cecilia anymore except to ask her for shampoo, soap, and a towel.

When Tina left to bathe upstream past the bridge, Cecilia thought about that man in the country store, how she'd like to tell him that there were things he didn't know, that there were secrets in this place, but that all you had to do was wait around long enough. They didn't sit down, and she didn't know how to judge time on sandstone walls. She could've learned by the time Beto's truck finally came.

Ray was angry. He was thinking of how he would have liked a gun in his hand, better an Uzi, to take out the front windows of that tired gas station and country store. The guy had asked him, without hesitation, if he was buying a case of beer or two to take along. That was the bullshit right there. Where did this paddy fuckhead come off telling him about his friend. But then he knew it wasn't that; he should have told Cecilia. He'd sat on it the whole way out, and then driving on that country road, the Burr Trail, he had known he should do it then, but he couldn't talk, and she was sitting away from him on the other side of the car. And then Beto had gone and done this, not that he hadn't wanted to tie Tina to a tree himself sometimes. He saw her when they crossed the bridge, and right then he had wanted to drive past the turnout and pull over to talk to Cecilia, to tell her. He didn't want to get caught hiding things from her, not this way, with Tina screaming and hanging on him. He watched an hour go by on the sandstone cliffs before realizing that Tina hadn't come back and he didn't give a good goddamn. He could have talked to Cecilia then, and now this asshole was here, and who was the asshole here anyhow?

I can't believe Ray drove the Chevy out here, Beto thought to himself as he stood at the door and stared at Ray and Cecilia. He'd noticed the rope, loose as he crossed the bridge. He wasn't worried. Of course they had let her go. I'll just have to wait until later to find her, he told himself. If Tina were smart, she'd follow his tire tracks, cut through to Deer Creek Ranch, and find the bunkhouse. A line shack was all it was, really, that's all, and she was smart. Why'd Ray bring a girl out here, he asked himself.

"Beto, Tina's not here. Come on over here and tell us about it." Ray turned to look at the strong voice that had stopped the flickering of shadows under the cottonwood. When he looked back at Beto he saw him staring into the cab of his truck.

Beto used a hand to shade his eyes as he answered back. "I know you let her go, but that isn't going to make a damn bit of difference. I'll find her."

"I don't think it matters," Cecilia responded quickly.

"Of course it matters. What are you talking about? Ray, what is this?" He looked at Ray as if just by looking at him the voice in the shadows would go away, but Ray wasn't looking back at him; he had turned to watch Cecilia. "It matters, don't you understand? She can't leave without me. She'd be lost without me. She's my woman. She can't leave me. Don't you see? Ray, she doesn't want you anymore. You've wasted your time coming out here. You can't have her back, you got that? She's mine now. She loves me. We're gonna get married and we've got our whole life planned out." Beto was shouting now, but he didn't notice. He saw that they still weren't moving, but that they looked relaxed somehow. It didn't make sense. Then he heard the cicadas, goddamn noisy bastards, as if all they had to do in the world was click their wings or their legs or whatever it was, and the noise, together with the calm quiet of Ray and the girl, just infuriated him. He couldn't think about it a second longer. He had to get rid of one problem at a time. He reached in through the window and pulled out the shotgun in one quick motion. "One at a time," he muttered as he walked around the truck and the ten feet over to the edge of the creek. "One at a time," he repeated as he pumped a shell in, heard it lodge, and started shooting and pumping, shooting and pumping until all he could hear was the hoarse throb of wind in his ears and the click of the hammer. Click, click, but he knew it wasn't the cicadas anymore, and then Ray was there at his side gently taking the gun from his hands.

"Here, let me carry that for you," Ray said, and Cecilia

appeared on his other side to gather his arm into the crook of hers. "Let's go sit down in the shade, brother," Ray continued, and then Beto found himself sitting on one of the large roots with his back against the cottonwood staring up into the leaves.

"So what's going on with you two, huh?" he asked them, as if nothing had happened.

Ray blew the air out of his cheeks, got up and went to the cooler. He pulled out three beers, opened one and handed it to Cecilia, opened another and passed it over to Beto, then sat down. He didn't open his; he set it between his legs and tapped on it with his fingers. Ray started talking first, hesitant, and then Cecilia, so that they were looking at each other, each waiting for the other to finish so they could jump in.

"That was when we got married," Ray finished, and then he opened up the beer he'd been tapping and leaned his head back.

Beto chuckled, rubbing his face with both hands so the chuckling was even more tired than it sounded. "Hey," he said, still rubbing his face. "I was talking trash back there." He looked over at Cecilia. It was dark now, and the quiet that came with the night in the canyons settled over them. He wished they'd say something about the way he had acted, let him go, but they didn't mention it, didn't say "that's okay; don't worry about it." Neither one of them brought it up. He'd said he was sorry, hadn't he? The least Ray could do was say something about it, dress him down, kick the shit out of him even. That was what he'd do; he'd tell 'em. Nobody got off the hook easy around Beto, but then they'd gotten themselves into it, hadn't they? He hadn't asked them for their help, so why should he feel sorry? Who asked them anyhow?

"Don't you think we ought to be moving, Ray?" Cecilia asked somberly. "We found him."

"Where you going? You can't leave now. Lookit, I got bags. You can spend the night here." Beto felt his gut, like a spike, a railroad spike in there, and his head started to throb again. He touched the bandage. That Cecilia was alright; she'd patched him up nice.

"Yeah, you're right. We got to get going, Beto. This is some sticky shit we're all in. You're going to be okay. You've been made a fall guy, brother. No one'll blame you."

Cecilia spoke up, "I don't think you're in trouble, Beto, unless something happens to your grandmother. You know what I mean?"

"No. I don't know what you're talking about. Whattaya mean, a fall guy?" Why'd they want to leave, go back so soon? They'd come to see him, not Tina, hadn't they? "You just got here. What's the rush to get back?" Beto continued. They're confused, he thought; lookit them looking at each other.

"Hey, Cecilia, got another beer there?" Beto asked. They're confused; think they've got to get back, he told himself. Dolores'll last another day. He chuckled. That rest home would be wishing he was coming back, just to get her off their backs.

"Just the one sixer, Beto," Cecilia answered.

"Oh well, hey, no problem. I'll take you guys up on the mesa in the moonlight; it's beautiful, man."

"Beto."

Damn, Ray could be serious. Beto shifted his gaze over to Ray, let the lids rest low, the breath release heavy as he wished for a cigarette.

"Beto, we got to go."

"Damnit! What's your damn hurry, Ray?" He was up and on his feet, one foot planted in front of the other, sweat already forming and growing icy up his back. Ray was up just as quick, short and thick and close, his face up in Beto's.

"What's going on, brother? What's happening up there?" He pointed at Beto's head and then they were inches apart, hands clenching, so close each could hear the other's heart, smell the beer sweat.

Ray didn't let up. "You know the story. I been waiting to hear what you're going to do about it and all you can think of is a moonlight walk. Well I'm putting it to you straight. You gonna leave your old lady in that rathole?"

"No, Ray," he answered, but his voice seemed to come from a far away place because he was thinking of the old man. The vision confused him for a moment, and then he felt clearer, even if he wasn't able to hear his own voice. "I'm going back. I gotta find Tina first." Beto wasn't shouting anymore. He had found this voice that sounded like his and he had found his hands. They were comfortable, flexing, and he took a step back.

"The fuck with Tina," Ray said, stepping forward.

"Leave her out of this, Ray. She's needs to go back too."

Ray stopped moving, and said, "You got her, man. I don't want her. When you wake up you'll see what she's doing to you."

It wasn't quiet now. There was the hum of the hunter in the air, and the moon had swollen boisterously from the top of the mesa behind them so that the leaves of the cottonwood could turn their curled edges flat and receive the silver paint they cared nothing about.

"Why're you so pissed off, Ray?"

"Forget it. You know where to find me." Ray turned and then stopped. He let his voice uncurl slowly. "Honey, give them to him."

Cecilia came over to Beto, reached for his hand, held it briefly, and then rolled the beads into his palm. He heard the clicking, remembered the cicadas across the creek, Guttierez and the bottles of pickled pigs' feet, the bonfire, the owl in the windshield, the BB gun in the corner of the kitchen, the walker.

"You took them away from her?"

"They weren't hers," Cecilia replied softly.

"But I gave them to her. She needs them."

Cecilia turned and started to walk over to Ray. She stopped, speaking over her shoulder. "That's not what she needs, Beto." She reached for Ray's hand and they started off to the car.

"Ray, take them. I don't want the goddamn beads," Beto shouted, but they didn't stop. He saw the interior light go on, and two faces appeared over the dash. The engine growled once, then twice.

Beto ran over to the driver's window and held on to the frame tightly. "What're you gonna do, Ray?" He was bent over, holding on to the car, willing it to stop. Ray gunned the engine once more.

"Talk to the cops."

"Don't do it, Ray. Talk to him, Ceci."

Ray put the Chevy in reverse, letting it back up and turn slowly. Beto walked at his side. Ray braked and put it into drive, turning the wheels as he inched forward in the sand.

"Ray, don't do it. I don't want you hurt, man. Wait for me at the shop." He was walking faster now; they were almost to the road.

"Yeah, you know where to find me." Then the '58 was up on the road and on the bridge, and Beto could hear the old wooden beams groaning and splintering as if the bridge were a cocoon, the butterfly breaking out of its long sleep, and then there were only the three taillights under each white wing disappearing up the hill.

Beto stood there for a long time, long enough to see his shadow in the dirt. He rubbed his face and walked out onto the bridge where he looked over the side into the water coming out of the galvanized pipe and dropping into the creek. He watched the water for a long time, until finally, clicking his lips and touching the rosary in his pocket, he left the bridge. He started walking fast, but by the time he had reached the mesa behind Molly's he was running so that he took the sloping sandstone at a dead run and a grunt. He ran for half an hour, slipping once, skinning himself, bruising his palms.

He ran without looking; he knew the route well. He stopped about fifty yards away to look for smoke; he thought he might see it this time. If he didn't see it, maybe the old man was okay, awake now, thirsty. He took a big drink out of the waterhole, saw the tadpoles and miniature horseshoe crabs scuttering through the clear water, the dense stand of cattails at the other side where the sand had collected. He crawled through the entrance of the cave, surprised at how black it was inside. "It's me," he muttered. He heard a high pitched squealing, the flap of wings, and felt them brushing by him and out the entrance, but he didn't lower his head and he didn't try to swat at them. The air was musty. He skirted around the fire pit on all fours, felt for the rocks, but came up with the old man's leg. He let go with a start and then replaced his hand, letting it crawl up to the old man's chest and then his face. He spoke for a while, rubbing the old man's face. He put the pink beads over the old man's head, and then moved them to his hands. He wondered if he should leave the belt buckle and then decided against it, thinking the old man had wanted him to have it, that there was a good reason for keeping it. He looked around the cave, surprised that he could see the drawings in the darkness, almost as if they were illuminated.

"I got to go now, ol' man," he said softly, crooning. "I wonder if you really did know her. I think you would have liked her." He leaned back a moment, and then bent over and kissed the old man on the lips. He picked the rosary up off the old man's hands and replaced the Giants cap, patted him above the knee, and then he crawled out into the moonlight, the smoky moonlight at the top of the mesa.

Eighteen

Tina leaned back into the torn seat of the pickup. She was calm, very calm. She noticed the young cowboy checking out her legs and her chest. She stretched so that he could get a better view of her inner thighs, and then she leaned back to pull at her hair. She'd taken her bra off when she'd heard his truck approaching, and now the truck was rolling and bumping and this idiot cowboy had a big stupid look on his face. Move the characters around, she thought, let them fantasize. It was too easy. She thought of Ray and his new girl, how they had let her run off for a bath. Ray was too easy to figure, holding and comforting her, the redhead ready for confrontation, about that close to crying. What was she doing with an old lowrider anyway? Sweet looking girl. And x-ray Ray—that was what she'd called him, 'bout that quick and varied—he didn't know what he was going to do. Yet he would try; she could tell. But what could he do? Good thing he'd brought the babe with him; she couldn't have planned it better.

"Where'd you say your car broke down?"

It can talk, she thought, even with that ridiculous hat poking over his face, the brim bent down so hard and far in the front he had to look out the sides of his eyes to see anything. I wonder how lonely these cowboys really are, she asked herself. "That's some hat you got," she said, looking at him until he flushed.

"Yeah, you like it? Shit, it's just mah work hat. Got a real fine Stetson at home. That's Tropic. Got me a nice little spread near the Green River. Only working this Deer Creek Ranch 'til I get cash in the bank. You know what I mean?"

"You married?"

He flushed deeper this time. She took the opportunity to stare out the window.

"Well, no. No, I ain't. Nope."

Tina smiled. He was lying. Good, that'll make him all the easier to deal with. Get a man to lie and he'd be covering his tracks before he made them.

"How far to your place?"

"Line shack? Well, like I was telling you, it's not my place. . ."

"Uh hum," she interjected loudly, fixing her eyes on him again.

"There it is, right there. I know it's not much to look at, but it's in the shade. By the way, you didn't say what was the matter with your car. I'm good with my hands. We'll just let you rest up a spell and then head back. Get your car running again."

"You got anything to drink?" she asked, her voice so low and sexy she thought she saw the brim of his hat straighten.

"You mean likker?" the cowboy said, dumbfounded, as he pulled up to stop.

"What do you think I mean?" Tina said, smoothly sarcastic.

"Well, yeah, I thought you meant that. I got some sippin' whiskey. No ice, tho'." The cowboy let what he must have thought was a wicked smile slide out from under that brim.

Tina didn't notice. She was anxious. There weren't any other vehicles here. Well, she'd figure something out. She'd probably have to screw him, after all, but she'd screwed in shacks worse than this one, even lived in worse. She got out of the truck, walked up to the shack, and let the screen door hang open for a minute.

She saw them all, some with dirt floors and no stove, unlike this one, and then she felt like rubbing her arms as if the rubbing would stop her from looking in on her five brothers and sisters, *mama* and *papa*, after they had crossed the river and come to live in the U.S.A. She rubbed her arms harder. She didn't want to feel this. There was even the identical smell of dust and urine and animals. She struggled to keep the feelings away. She tried to concentrate on the work in the fields, all of them together, or the canning factories, but all she could remember were those Sunday nights, when there had been money to shop, and one of them had been the lookout while the others fought and played, waiting for their *mama* and *papa* to return with the groceries and the Black Cows. Then they had been quiet, the threats and spankings forgotten as they watched the meticulous division of the Coke and the vanilla ice cream, each one with a glass and spoon. And she had carefully guided her favorite, Manolo—Manolito, she called him— to a corner where they could be alone, arms and legs close, as she taught him the precise spooning technique. She tried to walk away from the screen door and the line shack, but then there was the cowboy with the bottle leading her in by the shoulder, talking to her. She didn't hear him. She felt again the sleepy feeling after the glasses had been drained, the sides licked clean, the spoons sucked on, the pretend burps, and she and Manolito tucked in, feigning dreamtime, but waiting. Then they would tickle one another, but not making a sound, ardently keeping to the shadows, watching *mama* and *papa* with the leftover Coke and the bottle of Bacardi. She and Manolito would pretend they were asleep, wait for the er-ee, the er-ee of the metal bedsprings, before they would giggle.

She nonchalantly took the offered drink, turned and swallowed half the glass as she walked quickly outside, out of the line shack, away. Who was gone? She finished the glass, tasting now the creek water. Who was gone? Manolito, her favorite? He was the only one she saw anymore, and she hadn't seen him in a month. They had left together with the rich white lady because she had insisted. She was the one discovered. The bright one. The gifted wetback. Did Manolito miss them? She had taken him to her new life: all the books she could ever want, a big home, a car to use, her own room, and surfer boys to screw instead of *peons* in shacks. And then the husband. She had always liked screwing, as long as Manolito was still thére with her, but hadn't they missed the sound of metal bedsprings, giggling later as she made him cuddle with her so she could tell him about the latest er-ee? By the time she had left for college she'd destroyed that household, but that hadn't mattered because that, too, had been easy, and the offers had come in from everywhere for the exceptional *mojada*. She could have gone to Harvard, even, but Manolito wouldn't go, wouldn't leave the coast, so she talked him into moving with her to L.A. where she was a favorite, plenty of independent study time that she didn't need to maintain perfect grades. Was that pre-med she had been studying? She laughed to herself, then remembered how it was when Manolito had gone queer on her, and she had gone out looking for a man like Ray. The sun was going down, finally; her shadow was long. She wished for a refill, heard the tired swing of the screen, and held out her hand with the empty glass. "Get me another?" she asked, but not sweetly.

"Damn straight, babe."

So it's babe now, Tina thought. A long time ago. Had she changed? Had she ever really been different than this? "Oh Manolito," she whispered, and she started to cry so quietly she didn't know it until she tasted the salt on her lips. "Don't worry, I'm coming back. You and I. You miss me, don't you, baby? But don't worry; I'm coming back. We'll be together, and I'll take care of you. You and me, together; we always said that. You and me against the world."

She wiped her hand across her face. A couple more hours, at the most. She heard the screen door again and watched the cowboy go to the creek. Two more hours in this rathole.

Nineteen

You should have left an hour ago," Tina told herself. "Um-mm, but that last one was nice, and you needed it, didn't you, baby?" She reflected for a moment on young, horny, married cowboys. This one would have a hangover in the morning, but he'd lose it after his long horseback ride in. She looked for his keys, felt herself grow impatient and then nervous. "Fuck," she muttered. She stopped herself; she didn't want to wake him unless she had to. She saw his knife and pocketed it as she looked around the room. "Oh fuck," she whispered, elated with her intuition, "they're in his truck."

She walked out the wide-open screen door into a moon that was more than half full and almost high. The creek was shiny and noisy in the one spot that was cleared of trees, the sand as white and clean as a smile under that moon. It was so bright she couldn't help but fix her eyes there, away from the dark under the trees so that when she turned back to look at the truck, she had to wait a minute before she could see its dim outline. It was sandy here, too, under the oaks and cottonwoods, with few leaves as if the ground had been raked. It was slow going in the sand and she found herself looking down at her feet, but she was glad he hadn't parked next to the shack. When she reached the truck she stopped to breathe, her hand on the door handle. She didn't bother to check the ignition.

I'm a little high or worn out, she was thinking to herself as she turned the door handle down and started to pull and even when she was thrown against the door with a hand clamped down on her mouth. It was so quick she didn't react until it was too late, and then she only got her head banged against the side of the cab and her arm jerked up into the middle of her back. Tina knew who it was even before she thought of the cowboy, as she was thrown face down on the seat, her hands jerked back roughly to be tied. She tried to cry out then, but he shoved her face down hard into the seat so it muffled her voice and scratched her face up. He climbed in, keeping his hand heavy on her head, and then they were going, driving fast down the truck road without any lights on. He hadn't said a word.

They stopped about two hundred yards down the road. Beto pulled in behind his truck.

"Come on," he shouted, pulling her out and dragging her across the ground and into the cab of his pickup.

"You asshole," she said, as Beto started the truck.

"Fuck you too," he answered.

"I'm tied up," she snarled. He didn't answer. "And worn out," she added.

"Yeah, I noticed."

"You watched?" She was leaning over so close she could see the jaw muscles working and bones colliding. "Did you see the size of his cock? God, I'm sore."

He didn't so much as push her away as extend his arm against her until she was against the door. He held her there until they turned onto the Burr trail; then he shifted and put his arm back.

"Allright, let go of me. I can't insult your manhood, what precious, tiny little bit there is of it. Just take your goddamn hand off of me."

Beto wouldn't look at her. He shifted again, leaving his hand on the shifter this time, the vibration steady up his arm.

Twenty

About midway through Cedar Breaks, after Ray and Cecilia had passed the lava fields and the campgrounds had begun to appear on either side of the road in the flats between the meadow creeks, the rain came down heavy. It was as if they had parted a curtain, and before they could step back, the road had disappeared. Ray braked the Impala before he realized that it was just a summer storm on the top of the mountain, that they came and went in gusts, that a half mile down the road they would drive out of it. But Ray didn't know this; for where are the sudden rains in L.A. that slip off Silver Lake or descend from the observatory in Griffith Park? Thunderclouds at the fountain, a storm watch at the Cal Fed building, the Water and Power executives outside, like Elmer Gantry, with their hats turned upside down, secretaries checking their mascara. In L.A. Ray knew he had only to look outside to note that it would be dry or wet; surprises on the road came from other drivers, not the sudden rupture of cumuli. Perhaps he had been thinking too much; he couldn't decide what he needed and wanted to say to Cecilia. And the Chevy, being heavy, moved perfectly in the mountain air. They were on a flat stretch. He had reacted too quickly, he would tell her; there was no reason to brake, at least not that hard. They didn't have time to speak, but they looked at one another in that long moment when they were sliding broadside and the whole interior of the car was forever imprinted in their memory. One thin scrawny aspen, struggling to make itself known away from its group or family, a young tree, maybe glad for the sunshine but withering without its stronger cousins and brothers in the hard winds and storms, held the white '58 a foot back from Cecilia's door, the dent deep enough to lock it in place.

"Are you okay?" Ray slid across the seat and grabbed her to him.

"I'm fine. How 'bout you?" she responded, calmer than he.

"Oh baby, baby, baby," he said, rubbing her head harder than he realized. And Cecilia, happy for the break in their silence, laid her head heavy into his hands.

"Ray, I'm fine, okay? You sure you're alright?"

"Yeah. Yeah," he repeated, the sound beginning to collect in his chest.

"What happened?"

"Oh, I'm so stupid. I don't. . . . Are you sure you're okay? I don't know. What was I doing? I completely lost control. I'm an idiot."

"Ray, stop it. Ramón!" He turned off the engine.

"Ray, we're not hurt, and that's all that matters, baby."

He stopped rubbing the hair off her head, exhaled hard and held her tight. "I love you, Cecilia."

"I love you so much, Ray." They kissed. They kissed for a long time. If they had been at a drive-in, the movie could have ended and they wouldn't have known. The sweepers could have come to clean the popcorn and beer bottles, the second feature missed, the speaker hanging from the top of the window filling the car with static which they wouldn't have heard. When they finally noticed that the rain had gone and left them, they let go of each other, able now to see the meadow below them in the clear night of a passing storm.

"I'm so sorry. That was close," Ray said, craning his neck forward as if a sudden movement might propel them down the slope.

"Ray."

"No, wait a minute. I'm so," he paused a moment, "sorry that I didn't tell you about Tina. I hope you can forgive me, because I know it wasn't right. I don't know; I couldn't tell you. I wanted to, and I just don't know why I didn't. But I want you to forgive me because it's tearing my guts up, baby."

"It's alright. No, I mean it isn't, but I don't care now. Trust me, Ray, that's what I really want. You know? I want to feel good with you, like I don't have to worry about what I'm stepping in." She stopped for a moment, and then continued in the same serious tone. "One more thing: next time you want to tell me something, tell me before we get into the car." She started laughing then, kissing him on the neck, and then punching him in the stomach until he was laughing too, and grabbing at her hands.

It was three hours later, almost midnight, when Paul Johnson pulled the Chevy out with his dependable Dodge. He meant to ask the dark-skinned fellow if it had been a deer that caused the accident since they hadn't seemed drunk, but he was a quiet Mormon headed for Panguitch and a home-cooked meal. He wouldn't take the offered twenty dollars. "Shucks," he told his wife, "it but took ten minutes. They warn't hardly stuck. Lucky that little sapling was there, or they'd bin neck deep in Cross Creek." He thought about telling his wife that they were newlyweds, at least that was what he thought they were. Who else would be on Cedar Breaks in the middle of the night in a white t-shirt, the young lady without a coat, and asking about motels? But he didn't tell his wife, and he hadn't told them about the Shady Glen Motel either.

Twenty-One

Beto couldn't believe that she was still asleep. She had curled up in the corner, her hands still tied behind her back, and had fallen asleep a half hour out of Deer Creek. He had wanted to untie her so that she would be more comfortable, but he hadn't wanted to stop. He was at least two hours behind Ray. Passing Ray in order to arrive at the auto body shop first was the only thought he could concentrate on. He didn't wonder why he wasn't worried about Dolores even though he could feel the rosary in the pocket of his shorts on every fast turn. Just the pressure of the beads, like the old man's belt buckle, was enough to calm his fears for her. It was Ray and his new wife that had Beto pushing it.

He had taken the Zion Canyon route, figuring that it cut off fifty miles or more, and at this time of night it would be deserted all the way through Hurricane and St. George where he could connect with the interstate to Vegas. So how could she sleep? He was throwing the truck around, but then, she had always been able to sleep when she wanted to. He had gassed up in Panguitch, but now, twenty miles out of Mesquite on the Nevada border, he knew he would have to stop again.

How long had it been since he had slept? Last night with the old man, had he rested? He couldn't remember. His watch read 3:30 a.m. The speedometer needle was waving at 90; they'd be in Mesquite in ten minutes. He'd need some coffee.

Maybe it was the glare of fluorescents under the high white Mobil awning, or maybe it was the sudden lack of rushing air and engine rumble. Tina woke up quickly. The first thing she noticed was the empty cab, and then the casino attached to the gas station, more a coffee shop really, but lit up with people inside. It was noisy here, like the canning factories she had worked at. She saw the trucks in the huge parking lot, but didn't realize that the noise came from these trucks left running while the truckers had a cup of java inside. A truck pulled in on her left, surprising her, and then she saw Beto come out of the coffee shop. She noticed his skinny legs, longer in shorts and tennis shoes without socks, the dirty red tank top, and in his right hand the gleaming polish of styrofoam. Beto stopped. He wasn't looking in her direction; he was fending off an older lady, too pushy to be embarrassed in a mini-skirt with paunch showing, shoving a keno ticket at him off a tray. The gas station attendant and the trucker passed between her and Beto. Tina tried her door, remembering after she had bumped against it three times that it had been mangled shut from the impact with the cottonwood. The two men had stopped to talk, and Beto was still waving off the Keno lady. Tina scooted across the seat, but tied up, she couldn't open that door either. She backed up, lay down, and with her right foot lifted the handle, and kicked with the left. The door bounced against the gas pump, making a sound like a rock thrown at loose tin siding. She sat up and was almost out the door.

"Hi, honey, brought you some coffee," Beto said in a voice loud enough to be heard in the casino. He sat down at the edge of the seat, shoving her over roughly with his hip. The attendant and the trucker had stopped talking. They were staring at the truck.

"Come on. One buck to play Keno, mister; you look lucky. Loosen him up, sister."

Beto stared at the tiny Keno lady; he looked into every tight platinum curl on the top of her head, and his mouth hung open.

"Come on, baby, I never have any fun," he heard Tina say in a voice sweet enough to make him finally take his eyes off the wig in the passenger window and think about reaching in his pocket for a dollar to stop this nightmare. The trucker and the attendant were laughing about the hard sell as Beto switched the styrofoam cup from his right hand to his left, when Tina threw her head against his arm so that he seemed to still be watching the cup fall and tumble even after he felt the crud splash on his bare legs. He would have had a football-sized burn on both thighs if he hadn't followed his custom with coffee shop coffee: always add ice. As it was, he yelled and jumped back against the seat. Tina shrieked, "Help me! Get me outahere! He's kidnapped me." The Keno lady bumped her wig against the door frame and yelped. The trucker shouted, "Hey, what's goin' on?" And Beto pulled the rosary out of his pocket instead of the truck keys. He fumbled in his other pocket, unsure of whether he should shut Tina up and then drive away, or drive away with her screaming out the window. He knew Nevada was a crazy place. He remembered hearing stories of legendary parties here: carousing naked on the Strip in the back of a convertible Caddy with the top down, shooting up the local cathouse, falling into pools fully clothed. They were from L.A.; this should be passed off as the usual drunken fun, but the trucker was coming at him on his side of the pickup, the attendant was sprinting to the phone, the curious were piling up at the double-glass doors of the Mesquite Coffee Shop and Casino, and the Keno lady was adding volume to Tina's wide-open lungs. Beto pulled the keys out just as he felt the trucker wrap his big paw in the neck of his tank top. The keys dropped between his wet legs. He felt his door opening, and then he reached under the steering column and tore the pistol away. Duct tape was hanging off the barrel, but the trucker knew what it was, even gift-wrapped, and his eyes opened wide as he stumbled backwards and knocked over a display rack of oil cans, falling down with them in the process. Beto whipped the gun around to the other window. So this is what happens with a gun, he thought. Tina was the only one still yelling. He yanked her hard by the hair, the gun dangerously close in the same hand. He thought of the movies and wanted to hit her with the gun barrel, just a tap— no, a real savage hit so she would crumple. He wanted to hurt her, and then it felt as if his jaw were breaking.

He turned onto the main street of Mesquite and lit up the wheels in the direction of Utah. In the side mirror he could see people spilling out the double doors and pointing in his direction. He drove until he found a narrow road on his left where he turned, narrowly missing a row of mailboxes. He didn't have to hit the lights; they weren't on. Then he came at her, grabbing her by the throat and shaking,

"Why did you do that, Tina?" The question sounded stupid even as he spoke, but he had to say something.

"I hate you."

So that was the legendary flash of steel—he realized later— like a glint in the high sun, but there was no sun on this side street. A police car roared by, red lights looping around, illuminating the insides of second story bedroom windows. And it caught, as well, the too bright blade. If the cowboy hadn't bought a cheap one, one that shined so nice, or if Tina had gone in low instead of for the face in a wide high arc. . . . So that was what the flash looked like. It wasn't like the grimy shine of the BB gun in the corner of the kitchen, useless now against the cats around the goldfish pond. It wasn't the chrome grillwork and hub caps polished in Griffith Park on Saturday afternoons to the sounds of Willie Colon or Public Enemy. The blade didn't whistle as it flew through the air. It was red. Red before it spoke to him. Red as see-through plastic. Red from the reflection of sirens. And he only flinched because he thought she was going to scratch his eyes out with those long nails of hers. He flinched and moved his elbow out enough to hit her arm, enough to feel the shine slice at his shoulder, enough to see her eyes and fall on the wrist below it with two hands, until he heard the knife drop and he felt the sweat pouring down his left armpit. She went after him with her nails and fists, but he was still able to throw it out the window. He returned to her, falling over her. She tried to bite him. He felt more confused than he ever had. He thought of the sun on the creek under Molly's; he heard Dolores snoring as she watched TV; he saw the chain-link fence at St. Theresa's, the man he thought had come for him, and his mother in the kitchen. He repeated, over and over, his chin against her forehead, his body pressed down on her, his hands on her wrists, "don't worry; I won't leave you."

After they tired of pushing against each other in the truck, she felt the blood. It had grown sticky as it ran slowly down Beto's arm and onto her fingers. The cut wasn't deep, but he knew he had been sliced. He may not have cared, but the cut interested her. She made him switch on the door light. Tina didn't need to look at it long; she had the solution almost immediately. The panty-liners were the only semi-sterile cloth she had to dress the three-inch, perfectly straight line. Beto didn't speak. "You won't get a period, damn you," was all she said.

When he walked back from the corner after checking out the casino a half mile away, Tina was leaning into the corner, her eyes blank. She didn't look at his shoulder and the panty-liner held down with duct tape. It had been her idea, of course. She was the smart one. She could always come up with answers for anything. She liked problems. She could solve them and do most of the practical work as well. And if you couldn't decide which of her suggested routes you should take, she would tell you which one was best. Her opinion was rarely imperfect.

The street or road ended in a low dirt bank at the Interstate. Beto never slowed down. Then they were heading west again.

"The cops'll be looking for you."

"Yeah, thanks. You had to make that scene."

"Well, how would you feel, tied up and riding with a loco who's packing a gun."

"You never knew I had that gun."

"No, and if I had, I would have stabbed you in the dark."

"What?" Beto looked at her and the truck swerved a little.

"You're driving too fast, Beto. Slow down."

"I can't believe it."

"I don't see why not. What would you have done in my place?"

"I wouldn't have stabbed you."

"Oh, is that why you beat the hell out of me?"

"You were trying to kill me with the truck."

"I was trying to get away with my life, Beto. Sorry, you got in the way."

"Like the old man."

"I won't buy that. I'm very sorry about Sam. I don't think you saw what I saw. You might believe it, but no one else would."

"You ran him over." Beto's hands were gripping the wheel intensely.

Tina was calm, as if she were noting the gradual change of sky color.

"Wrong, Beto dear. If you recall, you were all over me. It was your hands that were on the steering wheel. If you had let me go, then. . . ." She stopped talking a moment. "But, I had this feeling that he didn't want me to leave."

"What?"

"That's right. And I can't explain it, but you can't blame me, and you know it, so just stop. The terrible thing is that it happened at all. I don't want to forget it, but don't start in on me. I can play the guilt game better than you anyway. Your foundation was well constructed by you-know-who."

"What's that supposed to mean?"

She didn't laugh, although she wanted to laugh her laugh, but it stopped inside somewhere. Tina fixed him with a bored look, a look that reveled in his slowness. "Maybe you'll never know, Beto."

He caught her expression, but he didn't need to see it; he could always feel it, and the feeling always hit him hard. It wasn't like an x-ray bombardment; it didn't creep in unseen. He kept the speedometer at a steady 65. The Interstate was empty. They passed a mining operation, the lights still on. Vegas came over the next rise. It twinkled like it was supposed to, but there was a haze resting on the tops of the highest casinos. They both noted a Nevada State trooper racing by in the other direction.

"Going after you."

"Us," Beto replied quickly.

"Maybe." She looked at Beto lazily, and then at the dirt still layered onto the top of the crumpled hood. She checked her side of the truck, the passenger door torn up from the cottonwood tree, and the rear window slider taped up with cardboard wheezing like an accordion. She knew that she must look like hell.

"We're gonna have to stop before the border, get a motel room."

"I'm not stopping, not with you." He stepped down harder on the gas, watched the needle push 75.

"We can't cross the state border, not looking like this." She leaned over and switched on the radio, dialing the AM channel until she found a local news station. Beto found himself listening intently to the Wall Street Report. Why hadn't he thought of the radio, he asked himself.

"They're looking for fruits and vegetables at the state border, that's all."

"You never know," she answered rudely.

The interstate turned into a freeway. They were passing auto wrecker yards on both sides. He slowed to 65, and then she started in again.

"What are you worried about? You want your old lady, don't you? So go get her. Leave me off at the airport. I'll arrive before you and set it up. Take her back. I don't care."

He was tired. He rubbed his hand hard over his face. Would it be that easy, he asked himself. Would he be better off without her? Better off without Tina, he repeated. He tried to listen to the business news that was still on the radio; instead he saw the house in Silver Lake, the bougainvillea over the front door, the lemon tree that wouldn't quit, the peeing Mexican boy fountain in the pond, the walker with its legs of chrome plating, and the picture in the breakfast nook. The Indian couple was still hiding the fuse box, but he couldn't remember the name of the artist. He had seen the original. He could remember the day clearly, at the museum in the Plaza de la Raza. He'd stopped off at Phillipe's for a french dip and three beers after he saw the exhibit. The Dodgers were playing and everyone was talking about Kirk Gibson, their new heavy hitter. He had watched an inning and a half from the long communal tables. It wasn't crowded at three in the afternoon. He had left without seeing Kirk Gibson at bat. Later that evening, he had told Dolores about the painting.

"There, you see, they're looking for us." Tina was animated. "Are you listening?"

"Huh?"

"The radio announcer said the kidnapper was heading for Utah, but had evaded the checkpoints. The kidnapper is armed and dangerous."

"What?" Beto said, more tired than ever now. "What did he say?"

Tina was really excited now. "They're looking for us, Beto. They don't have a license plate, but they think you're dangerous, which is the funniest thing I've ever heard. Of course you're dangerous—to yourself. You'd better just throw that gun out the window before you shoot your *huevos* off." She laughed that laugh reserved for herself only and hugged her arms to her sides. "What'd you bring that along for?" she asked after a moment.

"I didn't. I bought it in Escalante."

"Oh, that was bright."

Beto didn't say a word. He wondered if he had passed Ray. He wasn't sure.

Tina continued, animated. "We're getting off and going to a motel. I think we should buy another car."

"What?"

"We're not crossing the state border looking like this, *baboso*, so close your mouth; you're attracting flies. We're going to stop somewhere and get cleaned up. They'll be looking for us at the border. I know they will. I would, if I was a cop." She was enjoying herself. Her hands were moving and her eyes were wide and blinking like crazy. "Okay, forget buying another car. I'll drive. We'll clean up the truck. No, we'll leave it dirty like this. They'll think that we've been camping. That's it. Pull off at the next exit." Tina looked so clear and bright. She was changing his plan, but why did it sound so good? Besides, he didn't really have a plan of his own.

"No," he said tiredly.

"No?! Then what's your bright idea? To cross the border with your arm bandaged up and blood on your shirt? Come on; don't be so stupid."

"Ohhhhh," he exhaled. Where was Ray? He must have passed him. "I've got to tie you up," he said aloud.

"Forget it," she shouted, sitting up straighter. "You're not tying up anybody. We're in this together now. I want to get back."

He switched off the radio and the silence was complete. It was better to drive, he told himself. Better than what—think? They were out of Vegas now. He pulled off into the only gas station at the last stop before the state border. It was already too hot for this time of the morning; he felt the heat on the arm exposed to the wind and the open window. He was sweating. "Go on into the rest room and clean up," he said.

They had stopped amidst the last of the cheap casinos before the border. Maybe you could call it a town: two casinos like the one in Mesquite, one gas station, and a hamburger stand. But there was enough electricity here for two towns.

Beto got out of the truck. "Come on," he said, waving his hand at her.

Tina glared at him. "We're not stopping in a motel, are we? You're ignorant."

"Alright." He looked her over. She looked fine; no bra, he noticed, her hair combed back, her face clean in spite of everything. He tried to think. "You're driving across the border, Tina. I think that's a good idea."

"Oh, the light clicked on." She moved across the seat, stepped out of the truck, and kept on going. "We're stopping after we cross," she threw at him over her shoulder.

He felt foolish with the pistol tucked into the back of his shorts, but the attendant didn't know; neither did the lady who asked him if he wanted cream in his coffee. He felt harmless, yet he had a .38 prodding him in the ass. After Tina came out of the washroom he went in and washed his face, finger-combed his hair, and put on a long-sleeved shirt rolled up at the wrists. He couldn't decide on what he should do with the pistol once they started again. He put it in the glove compartment and then took it out again as Tina started to slow behind a car with a license plate that read "Z4CHERI." He finally stuck it between his back and the seat where it made him uncomfortable. Tina pulled in under the shade of the high tin roof. He read the sign about plants, etc. He could see the blond in the Z talking with the border guard or plant inspector or whatever he was. The man was past middle-aged, with an expanded gut dressed in unpressed green. His hat was shoved on a head that was a size larger than regulation. Beto could hear the girl laugh, and then they were pulling up. The man gave him a long look before he turned to Tina, his eyebrows arched up.

"Been out in the desert?" he drawled slyly, looking them over, and the truck too.

"Yeah, we've been camping for a week. I can hardly wait to get back," Tina responded sweetly.

"Looks like you been to hell and back." It was the longest sentence Beto had ever heard.

"Yeah, we had an accident in a creek bed. It took my husband six hours to get us out."

"Where was that? Camping, you said, right?"

Beto wanted to touch the pistol, but he couldn't move, and then the Highway Patrol pulled in. The officer waved at the inspector, yelled something, gave their truck the once-over and entered the one-room office. Beto couldn't take his eyes off him. The office was all windows. Coffee, he's going for coffee is all, he told himself. Then he heard Tina open the door and leap out.

"What are you doing?" he hissed. She ignored him. He watched as Tina and the man with the small hat walked around the truck, looked into the bed, leaned over to check the underbody. He could hear Tina's voice; it was high-pitched. He couldn't remember ever hearing her use that tone.

"So everything looks alright, officer?" she asked in that same tone that could sweeten day-old coffee. "I know we look a mess. We have to stop before we get into L.A., if I can talk some sense into this survival nut." She turned to Beto and smiled sarcastically.

"No problem," the inspector replied. "You aren't bringing in fruits or vegetables, and no wild vegetation that I can see." He backed off a moment, stood straight as if to wave them through, and then leaned in from the waist and addressed Beto. "You weren't in Utah by any chance, were you?"

Beto felt the sweat rolling down the sides of his chest. It was six a.m. They were in the shade, but it was hot, his mouth was dry, and he had to pee.

"Didn't get that far. We saw Lake Mead, though," Tina answered quickly. She, at least, wasn't having a problem speaking.

"Uh huh. Alright," he said, not taking his eyes off Beto. "You folks take care now."

Beto watched the officer move off out of the sides of his eyes, saw him lumber into the office and greet the highway patrolman drinking his coffee. Then they were in the sun and ten miles down the road before he made Tina pull off at the exit named Zzyyxx. As he stood off from the truck he realized that his hands were shaking. He let go of the zipper and just pulled it out from the underside of his shorts. He stood there for a long time, like at Dodger Stadium, he thought, waiting behind an old man who would be leaning, one-handed, against the tiled pisswalls.

Twenty-Two

You hungry, honey?" Ray asked.

Cecilia answered without lifting her head off of his chest. "Do we have to go?" She hugged him tighter.

"I think so," he said, but he didn't move.

"We'll see about that." She giggled unseductively as she slithered on top of him.

Ray snorted. "Again?"

Almost two hours later his watch read 11:30, but he'd never changed it from L.A. time. They were seated in the Cedar City Pancake House. The plates had been cleared and Ray was sipping his coffee.

"You were hungry."

"Yep, and I feel great," Cecilia answered as she stretched. She was happy. A beautiful day and an even better last night. God, had she really been that horny, she wondered. They could live here, get out of L.A., drive up to Cedar Breaks whenever, daily, nightly. She laughed.

"What's so funny?"

"Nothing, Ray. I love you."

He didn't answer; he just smiled.

Cecilia felt like hugging herself here in the restaurant. She didn't care what people would think. She felt like telling them all how good she felt, telling them she was pregnant. She wondered if she was.

"Whattaya think?" he asked, still smiling, but more serious now.

"I don't know. I hate to leave."

"It's nice here," he agreed.

They were quiet for a moment and then Ray spoke again. He wasn't smiling. "What about Beto?"

"Good question. I don't know. You think he's left?" She put her hands on the table and folded them together, as if she were praying.

"You know, I couldn't tell you. I don't know if I ever could figure him out." He was looking past her now so that the glare of the windows made her shadowy, and he found himself thinking of the cats. Nobody had fed them in three days. He was worried about his cats. He saw himself on the island, Beto there with him. Beto would ignore them for weeks and then show up with peanut butter sandwiches. "They love it," he'd say. Beto would laugh and try to rub the cats while Ray would watch, smoke his joint, and touch the can of cat food in his pocket. That was Beto, he thought.

"Well, we better go, Cecilia," he said finally.

She looked up dreamily. "Okay."

Twenty-Three

Tina and Beto stopped at 9:30 a.m. The sign said, "air conditioning, cable TV, free coffee." It was a courtyard motel in Baker, paint peeling, screens rusty and torn, an elm, maybe, in the front, and a nice little grandma of a lady who gave him the end unit. Cash up front. He needed rest. The room was at the back like she had promised, in the short part of the U, Baker desert behind it and not much else. They took their bags in, into identical heat. The air conditioner was a window unit with a pan beneath it, the pan rusting. The air conditioner needed to be plugged in, which he did. It blew hot air. He checked the dials, felt the air, still hot, but left it running. Tina was already in the shower.

The furniture was standard issue: a framed Remington out of a calendar hung over the bed, one kitchen chair with no arms, two nightstands, and a TV on the dresser. He looked for a place to hide the pistol and finally shoved it between the mattresses. He sat on the bed. She was still showering. He'd only lay down for a second.

He woke up suddenly, but he didn't move. He was frightened, wondering where he was in the dark, and then he saw the blinds shut tight and Tina sleeping next to him. He looked at his watch and shook it, thinking it must have stopped. Hadn't Tina just showered and now it was his turn? He got up and went to the window, stretching the venetians apart with the fingers of one hand. It was sundown. He felt a chilling breeze. The air conditioner wasn't hot anymore. He was drenched with sweat turning cold, his head felt fuzzy, and the rusting pan under the window was half-filled with water. Beto went back to the bed, sitting softly on it. He turned to look at Tina; she was naked. Was she ever shy? He continued to look at her, imagining that her breasts were so warm they were melting down the sides of her chest. The large brown nipples were erect from the air conditioner, he thought. He studied them. Her breasts were round and warm-looking, like kittens curled up asleep. His gaze wandered over her. He saw her toes, her legs spread comfortably so her thighs didn't touch. He looked at her pussy, the scant hair, and bent over farther so he could see the crinkled brown edges of her lips. He noticed that her belly was moving slowly with her breath. He slipped out of his shorts. It was painful. He didn't want to touch his prick or let it rub or slide against anything. Hadn't they done it this way many times? He sat looking away from her, then turned. She wouldn't mind, would she? She had never cared before, had said it was like waking up in a dream. It wouldn't matter, would it? They were going to L.A.; he might never see her again. He moved slowly, not wanting to brush against anything. He straddled her. She awoke as he tried gently to spread her legs.

Tina had smiled for a moment as he sucked a nipple into his mouth. She bucked when her eyes opened and she came fully awake, but the mattress was like a large dent, a *hamaca*, a cradle that held her, so that when she bucked, he fell flat on her.

"*Cochon*," she said. It wasn't a yell, but it was angry. "Get off of me, pig." She grabbed him near the ears, catching one, but he had her around the shoulders. He was hanging on by her shoulders and his hips were moving and he was on her belly when he came. He didn't stop humping; he was sliding in the semen and sweat and it felt too good. His ear was burning and that felt good too, and she was swearing at him in Spanish, but he didn't mind. He was a *cochino* and a *marano capon*; or worse.

"You stink. You're a filthy boy," she said, pulling his head up by the ears, but he wouldn't open his eyes. "Beto, what's the matter with you? I don't feel this way about you anymore."

She was silent then, waiting, but he didn't move. He rested his head on a breast and gently fondled the other. He didn't want to move. He remembered climbing the tree in the field next to Dolores's house. It was a tall dusty evergreen. He was about ten years old and he had nailed slats of wood, 2-by-4's, making a ladder about ten feet high up to the first branches. He had climbed the tree a million times. He knew this tree, the bark, the sap on his hands, the nails driven through the milled wood and into the springy fir, nails bent over from reckless hammering. On his way up he would stop, perched on tennis shoes—they were black and high-topped then—holding the 2-by-4 at his hands, hugging the tree with his body. And he would look out over the lot, the yellow weeds and tunnels he had made in his golden field. The field was an apartment now, but Beto didn't think of that. Instead he saw himself, after surveying his earth, climbing higher to where he would be alone and hidden, pulling himself up on the last rung when it came away. And then there was only the wind rushing by his ears, the sun spiralling crazily, spiny needles, a bee, the horrified look on his grandmother's face and her crying, a tile missing on the roof, the weeds slapping at him, the ground and his breath like a spurt of water from a drinking fountain. He started. Tina's hand was on his head, and the air conditoner beat on. He tried to move. Tina held him down.

"Relax, baby boy," she soothed, and pushed a tit into his mouth. He felt her legs move so that he was between them, and then her fingers caressing him until he was hard enough for her to pull him in.

When he awoke again, he was shivering. He got up and went into the shower. The water came out cold, but he held his head under it and pissed at the drain. The water turned warm, then hot; he adjusted it, breathing through the water pouring over his head. He read his watch. Nine p.m. He unwrapped the bar of Spring Bouquet soap and used the stuff on his hair and body. He left the bloody panty liner on the drain, clogging it up. He grabbed the bath mat by mistake. He didn't care. It was hot again and Tina had fallen back asleep. He locked the door and walked through the courtyard to the street and the Burger King. Beto ordered two Whoppers with cheese, two large orders of fries, a chocolate malt, Pepsi, and an iced tea. He was alone in the restaurant, the main business going past the drive-through window.

When he unlocked the door, she was awake. He could see her eyes in the dark. "You hungry?" he asked.

"Yeah," Tina answered, walking into the bathroom and closing the door. He heard the shower running.

Twenty-Four

Ray and Cecilia had driven past Vegas and Baker during the worst part of the day. All the windows were rolled down. What else could they do? It was late afternoon; Barstow was coming up, and Ray wanted to stop.

"What a nightmare. What day is it?" Cecilia asked.

"It's only been three days." Ray tried to laugh.

"Three days? It feels like three years. I gotta call my mother."

"Give her my regards." They both laughed.

Has it really been three days?, Cecilia wondered. No, this is the third day. I can't believe I haven't called her, she admonished herself. I hope she's not sick with worry.

Cecilia made the call, but she didn't have enough change. She slammed down the phone and practically ran back to the table.

"Ray, give me your change."

He ordered two Millers after she ran off, but he waited before he drank his. He watched the bubbles rise. Funny thing about bubbles in beer, he thought, they come from the same spots in the glass. He rubbed the sides of the long-necked bottle, wiping away the condensation. Then she was next to him, sticking the beer into her mouth.

"Hey, cheers," she said. "Momma's fine. She was worried before, but now she's planning suicide."

"Oh yeah?"

"She wanted to know who you were. When I told her she got very silent. Then she hoped we would be happy and that's all." Cecilia drank the rest of her bottle down and looked at Ray.

"Come on, am I drinking alone?" she teased.

"No," he said, and took a drink. "Is there a problem with your mother?"

"You mean, didn't she want me to marry a Mexican?" Cecilia started to laugh, then choked, coughing until Ray had beaten on her back and she had taken another large pull on the bottle.

"Order another, baby," she said, sputtering.

"Cecilia, this is not funny."

"Yes it is. It was even funnier when I told her you weren't really

a Mexican." Cecilia looked at him slyly and laughed some more.
"Why'd you tell her that?" Ray asked with a hint of anger.
Cecilia got very serious. "You aren't, are you?"
"Come on." Ray's face was reddening. His mouth went tight.
"I thought you were a *pachuco.* That's what I told momma. She
thinks that's a South American country."
"Cecilia, I want to tell you. . . ."
"That you're proud to be a father."
"What?" He was still angry, but there was confusion mixed in.
Besides, he couldn't figure out Cecilia's mood. Hadn't she left
worried? And now, well, now she was full of life.
"I'm going to have your baby. Aren't you happy?" She threw
her arms around his neck and kissed him more than once. He
spilled his beer.
"What?" he asked again. "How do you know?"
"I just know, Ramón. I just know."
He hugged her back and kissed her. He called her *cariña* and
mi amor. He figured she was crazy.
"He's a Mexican, you know."
"Not only a Mexican, Ray, and momma will love her."
"Her?"
"You've got a daughter. Maybe she can marry a white boy." She
started to laugh again, hugging him. The next round came, and
then another. Ray let her be happy. In fact, he was feeling pretty
good himself, though he didn't believe a word of it.

Twenty-Five

Beto sat on the bed and ripped open the bag of burgers and fries. He opened packet after packet of ketchup and spread them first on the opened Whopper, and then on the fries he'd spilled out. He opened salt and poured it over everything, and then added pepper. Tina came out and dressed in clean clothes. He admired her legs, clean and strong-looking; she never had to shave them. She tied a man's shirt above her belly button. He decided that she looked very good. He wondered if she were angry with him. He felt worn out, as if nothing much mattered, but he also felt embarrassed. He drank some of the malt, drinking until he could taste the chemicals under his tongue.

"It's after ten, three more hours to L.A.," he said.

"So what?" Tina answered.

"I want to stop and pick up Dolores first."

"What does it matter, one more day?"

"It matters."

"Alright, we'll go there first."

"There's no problem?"

"No. Why should there be?" She tasted her burger, opened it, and put more ketchup inside. She ate as if she were very hungry.

Beto wondered where Ray was. He wondered why Tina was so easy now. Maybe he could ask her for help. "You know what I can't figure out, Tina?"

"What's that?" Ketchup ran down from the side of her mouth. She rescued it gracefully with her pinkie.

"How am I going to explain the burial?"

"What's to explain? She's in the ground."

"Dolores?"

"You played a joke, or something like that. Hey, they'll be so happy to see her. Everyone thinks you're crazy anyway. Don't worry about it." She was eating her fries now, one at a time, and drinking the Pepsi.

It sounded sensible, but he wasn't so sure. Well, they had to get going. "Are you ready?" he asked.

"Okay, okay. You're in such a goddamn rush. Fuckin' A." She

gathered her bag, and he made sure to turn off the air conditioner and grab the gun.

They passed Barstow at 10:30. Beto pushed it, worried about Ray. He was sure Ray was in Monrovia at least by now. When he could, he drove at 80. Tina was chatty. He felt a little lighthearted himself. It was all working out for the best.

"You mean we just drive up and grab Dolores. No problem?"

"Yeah, I'm gonna be so glad to get back."

"We just go pick her up?"

"Come on in. Earth to Beto. ZZZ ZZZ, did you feel the rays? You get it yet? We go pick her up if I say so. The girl's buried, and that's all that matters. It's cool, very cool."

"You mean the young girl."

"Lay off of the junk food, Bozo. Where have you been?"

"You mean the hooker in the coffin?"

"Yeah."

He didn't feel her mood shift.

Tina sat up straight and leaned in on him. "What about the hooker?" she asked.

Beto didn't think anything of it. They were having a great time, and he loved her when she was like this. "What are we going to do with her?" he asked, and then he felt the mood change as surely as if they'd had a blow out.

Tina made him stop at the next gas station with a phone booth, but he wouldn't tell her any more about the dead girl. He really didn't know, and Ray was his man.

Twenty-Six

They weren't in Monrovia. They were cruisin', going 60 over the grapevine with a six pack of Miller between them, half gone. Cecilia was singing to an oldies station on the radio as they were descending into Riverside. Ray was hugging her. He even joined her in a few tunes, but it didn't ruin the song. The windows were down; it was hot, noisy, and she was next to him.

"Honey?" Cecilia began.

"Yes," Ray replied, exaggerating the word.

"Where we going for our real honeymoon?"

He looked at her, thinking she was beautiful. "Open another one," he answered, afraid to lose the feeling.

"You got that lovin' feelin'," she sang as she handed him another.

"Bakersfield," he replied, and they both laughed so loud they couldn't hear the truck passing them.

"I love Bakersfield," she said.

"And I love you. God bless, I love you." He hung his head out the window and shouted it to the wind. Cecilia laughed and spilled beer on his crotch.

"Oh my god, the lights of the city," Ray said as Riverside appeared.

"No more stars," Cecilia replied, mumbling sadly. She stared at the town of Riverside and thought of all the families tucked in and unaware of their Impala driving by, headed for L.A. Would anyone care that they were on their honeymoon? What if they stopped and knocked on a door? She saw a man answering the door in a hurriedly tied bathrobe, a woman asking in the background, "who is it, honey?" "Newlyweds, dear. They're on their honeymoon. Can you fix up the spare room?"

"No more stars and no more storms," Ray said, interrupting her thoughts.

"I won't drink to that," Cecilia said wistfully.

"There's no more to drink, so there. You drank it all."

"I did. You're drunk and you're nuts."

"I'm drunk and nuts and horny for you."

"Ray, we're almost home. We're less than an hour away. And we have to get back," she said, looking at the lights of Riverside once more before they came off the grapevine and connected with the freeway to L.A. "Besides, Beto may be waiting for us."

Beto was only thirty miles behind them now, stopped at a phone booth, listening to Tina.

Twenty-Seven

Beto insisted on listening in, but it didn't really help. Why hadn't Dolores taught him to speak Spanish? He heard "*sí*" a number of times; "*padrino*," and "*abuela*" he understood, and of course, there were a lot of swear words he knew, but she was talking fast and hardly breathing.

"Alright," Tina swore at him as she hurried from the phone booth, dragging him behind her. "They're taking Dolores home. Then we'll go get the girl."

"Where's the girl?" he asked.

"Give it up, Beto. I'm sure Ray knows. Why else would he have dragged out to Utah? To see you? Christ, I should have figured it out," Tina said angrily, staring straight ahead.

Beto accelerated back onto Highway 15, talking as if he hadn't heard her. "Who's the *padrino*?"

"What the fuck does it matter to you?" Tina answered.

"Godfather. That sounds a little patented, doesn't it?"

"Just drive, Beto. Speed it up; concentrate on one thing." She was hot, agitated, and being this way, she couldn't let him off the hook.

"You know, you've really disappointed me, Beto. I thought we had an understanding, but it seems that you're too stupid," she said, shouting the word.

He was shocked. Hadn't they made love? They were together again; maybe she didn't realize it. He wasn't stupid. They were together again; he would take care of her. He touched the pistol.

He passed three trucks, imagining that they were a convoy, their cab windows black but friendly, heading home with a dog on the front seat. He had heard that some truckers take a little dog with them, that some even take their women. He couldn't see into the trucks, but he waved anyway. One of the drivers probably had a little dog with him, petting it, going home.

"What are you doing?" Tina asked sarcastically as she turned around to look out the back.

"I'm waving at the truckers."

"Slow down," she shrieked. "Pull in front of the trucks."

"Why?" Beto shrieked back, but he pulled in front of the convoy. The lights of the lead truck filled up the pickup cab. Beto could count the hairs on his wrist in the light. He noticed the diesel was right on him. He sped up.

"Don't speed, you idiot. There's a Highway Patrol following us."

"Damn you, Tina. You scared the hell out of me." He pounded on the dash, hitting it hard enough that the green glow in the dash fluttered. "And don't call me an idiot." He emphasized the "me," drew it out, then pointed across the seat at her. Only part of his hand appeared in the light on the other side of the shadow created by the cardboard still taped to the broken back window.

"I didn't kill the girl," he said loudly, pointing a white finger at her.

"Neither did I," Tina shouted back.

"Then who did?"

"It's none of your damn business."

He tried to reach her, but she backed into the corner away from him. The pickup swerved. The diesel driver honked and flicked his lights, and the highway became a wide path of light.

"Tell me, or I'll pull over. I'll pull over right here and tell the man. I'll stop and I'll wave him down," Beto threatened. Tina was nervous; he could see it in her eyes.

"Relax," she said.

He heard her fear, moved his hand back to the wheel, and shouted, "Speak, damn you!" He sped up until the lights of the diesel were twin pinpoints in the mirror. It became dark again in the pickup.

"She was a nice young girl, and yes, she was a prostitute. She died by strangulation. Something went wrong."

"That's nice, Tina. You were involved in that. She was murdered."

"I wasn't there," she said, anger pummeling her voice like the highbeams of trucks.

"But you set it up." Beto was still yelling. He felt his back straighten against the seat, but it didn't help, his fingers twisting at the wheel.

"She was one of my girls, yes, but I didn't turn her, Beto. That wasn't my game."

"You led her to them, to the scumbags."

"It was part of the business. Some of them didn't want to be maids or *cuidaniños* for middle-class white assholes like you," she screamed at him.

"I'm not middle-class, and I'm not white, you—you slut."
Middle class, white, he thought. That bitch. Dolores speaks Spanish, she makes beans every week. How could she refer to him this
way? "My grandmother's Mexican and so am I," he shouted.
"She's Spanish. Ask her and she'll tell you. She hates Mexicans. She hated me and look what she got—a white boy who'd throw
her away. Yeah, you white boy. *Bolillo*," she swore at him. "You
don't even understand me and you think you should. You think we
should all be happy once we're here. You probably call it 'El Norte,'
don't you? Nice *Mexicanas*. Well, they want to get ahead too, or is
that impossible for your white middle-class mind to understand?
And some of them have to fuck you to do it."

"You let her die." He tried to gain his advantage back.

"It isn't right when the dark skins screw to get ahead, is it? It's
'getting down' with them, isn't it, Robert Reynolds? You don't even
know what it's like in my country. You don't even know what it's like
in East L.A. And yet you want me to tell you that it's a better life for
them here, as if you knew anything. But you don't know. We gotta
get out of it one way or the other, and it isn't pretty. And I help them;
yes, I do."

"Even murder." He shouted his way in.

"I didn't murder her. What if it was one of you, one of your kind
that did her in? Do you hear me? I would still be the bad one, right,
because I could have told her that it wasn't the right thing to do. I
told her what she was getting herself into, but that didn't stop her
so I helped her, and I'm not going to leave her now. I'm not going to
let her family know what happened to her. She's not going to be a
disgrace, and her family will never know what became of her if I can
help it." She came across the seat and grabbed his arm so that he
had to turn and look at her. "I'm not going to leave her like your
mother left you." She threw his arm at him.

"My mother, my mother," he repeated before he went limp. He
remembered his mother. Was that her? He was in a garage playing,
a woman calling to him from the open garage door, her face in the
shadow of the sun behind her. But he was busy, busy playing with
his trucks. He ignored her, and she left. After she had left, he felt
himself stumbling to where she had been, crawling on his hands
and knees. He saw the garage floor sloped at a crazy angle. He
couldn't pull himself up; he was sliding back, the concrete, rough,
tearing into his knees and fingers. He felt himself crawling, on his
stomach. He was little, tiny, crawling on the steep concrete. He

could smell the tar of thousands of cooling engines; his chin and nose were black with it. If he could only reach the edge where the light was spilling over, if he could only call her back. "Mommy."

"Beto, Beto. What's the matter?" Tina touched his arm. Was she nice again? He thought he could feel it. He started to cry, and then sob until he was choking and the snot was running off his lip.

"What's the matter with you? Oh baby boy. I'm sorry," she whispered in his ear. "Pull off at this exit."

Twenty-Eight

Where did she come from?" Beto asked.

Tina was driving. She had gassed up the truck; it was better this way. "The D.F.," Tina answered quietly. It sounded like "day effe," but he knew that she meant Mexico City.

"How old was she?"

"She was twenty-two. She wasn't married. She came from a large family."

Wasn't married. Wasn't a mother. Wouldn't be one. They were in Pomona now. Pomona was where Dolores had grown up. The mothers. Thursdays at St. Teresa's when the mothers would come and cook hot dogs. A dime apiece, and cartons of milk for a nickel. She was there, always there on Thursdays, no matter what he said, all the way through his eighth grade year. And she had looked like all the other mothers, hadn't she? Plump and short, her dark hair curly, a simple dress, and flat shoes. She could pass as his mother. She had always looked younger than her age, but this was a neighborhood where mothers still looked like mothers. He looked, and he could see her as if he were still on the playground, the cracked and patched asphalt, the open doors of the cafeteria with the mothers at the long cafeteria tables, the kettle of dogs cooking behind them, milk, cartons of paper straws opened, the cigar box, closed now, that would hold the change and iou's to remind other mothers to send in an extra fifteen cents next week because Thursdays were a tradition at St Teresa's, the hot dog tradition, and no one wanted her kids to go without.

"How did she come to you?" Beto asked after a long silence.

Tina drove fast, but she was nervous. She wasn't a good driver. Driving made her nervous, but she was very correct: she signalled long before she turned, she used the seat belts, and she never tailgated. They were in the San Gabriel Valley now. It was crowded on the road even at this hour. She swore at the Mexican drivers for going too slow. She knew they were Mexicans long before he did. Why? He knew the cars they drove and the things they hung from their mirrors. He lived in L.A. too, but she was quicker than he was.

"Her aunt sent her to me. I had given the aunt a good job taking care of a house and two babies the year before. She came from a large family, like I told you before. They needed to get rid of another mouth."

Another mouth, too many kids. But he had never gone hungry on Thursdays at St. Teresa's. He would see Dolores, always talking, always with the other mothers because she wasn't standoffish and she was sure that they liked her.

When it was time for the hot dogs, the bell would ring and the kids would all get in line, laughing and shoving until the line got close to the tables, and then a solemn silence would cover the five kids closest to the hot dogs, even though the mothers were jolly and sweet and wanted to do everything for them, like mothers always did whenever they helped out at school. Solemnness hit those five as if they were approaching an altar, as solemn and holy an occasion as their first communion. The kettle was a ciborium gleaming with yellow fat, the paper Safeway napkins were soft as linen, the buns smelled of frankincense, and nothing the mothers could do or say would break those kids. When it was his turn at the table, he too was sanctified. He was so holy, he could have prayed. His prayer was always that she wouldn't say the same thing she had said for eight years of Thursdays. "There's my son. Doesn't he look nice? Did you wash your hands?" she would ask in the sweetest of voices. "You should comb your hair," she would cluck, and the mothers would respond with a hum that mimicked the bubbling of the kettle. "Here, I have a comb in my purse," she would actually say, and then bend over to look for it. She would hold up the holy line, the procession, and he could feel their eyes accusing him; he could hear the stamping of feet, the muttering of the sixth graders. Even those in a trance next to him receiving the carton of milk and the straw were moving their eyelids. He would spread his hands in an act of supplication. "No, Dolores," he would say, "I don't need it." And then the mothers would look at him oddly because he didn't call her "*mama*," or "mommy," or "mom" even, but he never did. His Poppa always called her "Dolores," so that's what he called her. So why did he hate Thursdays? Why did he go to the end of the playground and sit on that hard cracked asphalt—even though there was room on a bench with his buddies—and put his

195 Ricardo Means Ybarra

back up against the cyclone fence so that the little edges of metal would dig in, when the last thing she always said to him was "mi'jito," in the sweetest of forgiving and understanding voices, as if it were a private language that they used. He could've answered her once, once in eight years of Thursdays; once he could have called her "mama," or "grandmother," or even "abuelita."

"I find them jobs and a place to live," Tina continued. "I can't deny that I make good money, but I work hard. I take care of them; they're my family."

"So what about the hooking?" Beto asked.

"That shows what you know, what a white boy you really are." Tina's eyes flashed. She passed a car and returned to a middle lane, turning the blinker off. She was nervous with her driving, but not when she spoke. "And you don't like women. It's very clear to me, Beto."

"That's not true," he tried to say, thinking of Dolores. It was true that he had rarely called her "grandmother" or "abuelita," never when he was younger. Maybe because in those days he adored his grandfather, Poppa, his short, fat, bald Poppa from Wisconsin. Poppa called her "Dolores." Poppa yelled at her. Poppa came home, drank his gin with tonic and lime, smoked his cigarettes, took his shirt off, read the paper, waited for dinner, and argued with Dolores. But it wasn't his Poppa that caused it. Poppa had never needed to go to the sanitarium or Rancho Tecate for a health cure. Beto remembered Ensenada. How for one week every year, after they had dropped Dolores off at Rancho Tecate, they would stay in the same cheap motel, and his Poppa would sit in a chair in the door and get drunk from a giant bottle of Oso Negro Gin. And he'd talk to everyone who passed, even though he couldn't speak any Spanish except for "callete loco "and "callete el burro," which Beto knew wasn't good Spanish because Dolores had told him so. He liked being with his Poppa, walking to the liquor store, Poppa's head shining in the light, and the light glinting off his glasses as he smacked his lips and sucked on his highball and talked with everyone in the store. Poppa would give him pesos for firecrackers or whatever he wanted, and then they would walk back to the motel room and sit down, and he would light the firecrackers with a cigarette, and they would laugh when it would scare hell out of someone. There were always women there, he remembered, who would talk to his Poppa in low voices, but he would laugh and always say, "not tonight, honey," and invite them over for a drink.

Sometimes by the third or fourth day the women would stop by for a drink and laugh with them both, and some of them would give him *pesos*, and some gave him Chiclets. They did the same things every trip. He would swim in the pool that had too much chlorine and the sharp sides. In the afternoon, when his Poppa would get up, they would walk through town and stop at the same curio shops they had seen a million times until they came to the same café that the fishermen used. It was always empty at that hour, and Poppa would drink cup after cup of coffee with cream while Beto ate french toast. Then he would go play on the beach, not returning to the motel until almost sundown when he'd always find his Poppa in the chair in the doorway in a very good mood with ice swirling in the glass. One morning Poppa would get up early with him, and they would go and have coffee and french toast with too much sugar, and he'd know they were going back to Tecate to pick up Dolores. Poppa wouldn't talk during the entire drive to L.A., but she would. He couldn't remember if he had been happy that she was back; he only remembered that he had had to sit in the back seat.

"It is so," Tina continued, interrupting his thoughts. "I know you; you have no understanding. I hear you talk, your attitude, the way you treat your grandmother. And then what? When it comes to us, you think it's okay for us to fuck our employers for the privilege of the job."

"Come on, that's rare," he said softly.

"Rare? You mean it rarely happened, or was it a rare afternoon when it didn't? What you really mean is why should anyone care? They're just little fucking machines."

"Come on, you're really laboring it."

"Yes it was labor, but better to get paid for it. Or do you call it love?" She drew the last word out, each syllable laced with contempt.

"I think it's bullshit, and you're shitting yourself. The girl was killed, Tina. What are the benefits? Where were you? She was your family, wasn't she?" He watched her now instead of the traffic. He could tell that she was angry. She waited a long time to answer.

"I made a mistake, Beto. Believe me, because I grieve for her every day, like I will for Sam. Oh yeah, look away. You don't believe me. You don't think I would care. You don't know anything about me because I never let you in. You see, I could tell that you wouldn't like it, not only my business, but me. I wouldn't tell you about me because I knew you would run, and you see I was crazy about you, enough that. . . ." Tina's voice cracked, but she didn't cry; she caught herself. He knew she was looking at him, but he couldn't turn from the window. She continued, "—that all you see is an exterior, that I'm smart and fun to be with, but I need to be loved too. And I can love, Beto, and I can be hurt from love. I have a brother who's dying, he's the most. . . . I love him so much. I wanted you to care. Maybe you could've, but I didn't want to take the chance. I was hard on you. I apologize. Beto, look at me please."

He turned and his eyes were sad. He felt very sad for all that he now realized he had lost.

"I'm sorry for how I've treated you," Tina added. "I hope you can forgive me sometime later. And I worry about you. I know you've lost a mother and it hurts you, and I don't know what to do about it. Maybe it's the hurt that makes you run. Maybe that's why you hate Dolores."

"I don't hate Dolores. She just—she just drives me crazy."

"Crazy enough to leave her."

"It was your idea," he said, almost whining, wanting her to believe him.

"But you wanted it. It was all you ever talked about, getting away from her. You were too easy. You wanted it." She had spoken quietly, and now in the silence, her gentle voice reverberated louder in his ears than the wheezing of the cardboard in the kicked-out window.

They passed Cal State L.A., came over a rise and saw the downtown buildings. There, a red light at the top; there, two floors lit up; Cal Fed, Arco, Cadillac, City Hall, the lights constant, yet distant, their message flowing on without interruption, without guidance.

"Why are you coming back?" Tina asked in the same tone of voice.

"The old man." He was still looking at the lights; he couldn't take his eyes off them. Now they were passing the Water and Power building. Every light was lit; he could see every office on every floor.

"What does Sam have to do with her?" She sounded surprised, but he didn't hear it.

"The old man was in love with her."

"What? When did they meet?" Her voice went high on the question. They were making the sharp exit onto the Hollywood Freeway. He saw ramps everywhere. The Harbor, Pasadena, Hollywood, smooth concrete filled with red lights.

"The night I hit my head on the tree. They were there, together."

"Oh," Tina said, and they were off the freeway, facing Echo Park Lake.

Twenty-Nine

Are we home, finally?"

"Yes, honey. It's not much, but it looks great, doesn't it?" Ray turned the engine off, but left the lights on so he could see to unlock the sliding doors of the garage. Cecilia watched him. She turned around to look behind her. It sounded so noisy here. The Hughes Market was lit up, but there were no cars in the lot. Ray came back to the Chevy and shut off the headlights.

"Ray, what's that noise?"

"I don't hear anything." He looked around. "It's just the city, I guess. I don't know. Come on, let's go in." They walked in together. Cecilia waited inside the door until Ray had crossed to the light switch. She hugged herself and smiled. Ray was closing the sliding door and locking it when the phone rang.

"Who could that be, Ray?"

"I don't know," he said, his voice sounding annoyed. "Just let it ring. It's probably a wrong number." They both stood there listening to the ring, looking towards the room with the phone. Neither moved, and then it stopped.

"Jesus, who would be calling? What time is it anyway?"

Ray looked at his watch. "Two in the morning," he answered, but he didn't move towards the room, and he didn't take his eyes off the room even when she came against his body.

"Well, should we go to bed?" she asked, looking at him with sleepy eyes. The phone started ringing again. They both jumped.

"Goddamnit," he said, his eyes flickering, but still he didn't move. He was hoping that the ringing would stop and that would be it.

"It might be Beto. You want me to get it, honey?" Cecilia asked nervously.

"No, no. I'll get it." This time he moved quickly. Cecilia waited until she heard him say hello in a plain voice. Then she walked to his side and looked into his face.

"Who is this?" he asked loudly into the phone. "I don't know what you're talking about," he said roughly.

Cecilia reached for his free hand, but he didn't respond. She noticed the heavy accent in his voice. It was the same accent he had used with Beto under the tree in Utah. She was scared. "Ray, what is it?" she whispered.

"I said, who is this, *ese*?" It sounded as if he were hissing.

"I don't know what fuckin' bitch you're referring to." His hand formed a fist, opening and closing.

"You don't listen well, *ese*. I tol' you I don' know a fuckin' thing. *Comprende, pendejo*?"

Cecilia grew more concerned. She could see that the cords in his neck were twisting like wrought iron. Who was he talking to? She tried to grab his hand, but all that helped was to breathe.

"Fuck Beto. Tha's right, and fuck you too. *Te voy a chingar*, motherfucker. Yeah man, I know. I live here."

Cecilia started to rub his back. She put her face against it, holding on to his arms.

"I have only one thing to say, motherfucker. Listen to me well. You fuck me up and there's goin' to be blood, bad blood." He slammed the phone down without waiting for a reply.

"Motherfucker," he shouted, ripping at the calendar until he had it off the wall, and then he tossed St. Teresa as if she were a twenty pound wrench.

"Motherfucker," he whispered, his back turned to Cecilia.

"Ray, what is it?" He didn't answer.

"Ramón, for chrissakes, tell me." She grabbed him by the shoulders and spun him around. He looked so scary to her she almost let him go.

"Ray, Ray."

And then he was hugging her without speaking, and she had to look into his eyes first to see if she knew him. He was there, she decided, but his edges, his edges were too smooth so that the light reflected off of them.

"Goddamn that bitch. That fool," he swore. "The *marielitos* have her, not the Heights," he added.

"Who? Dolores? The *marielitos*?" she questioned urgently.

"You remember I told you who the *marielitos* are?"

Cecilia looked perplexed. "The Cubans, baby, the prisoners." He didn't need to tell her again the story of the Cuban prisoners. He didn't need to tell her again that these *marielitos* were bad, ruthless mothers. She didn't need to be convinced. She had heard the phone call.

"You're not going, Ray. She's his grandmother. Let him deal with it." She hated Beto. She felt the hate in her jaws like a large dog shaking a cat by the neck. She could have passed out. He didn't answer. "I'm going with you," she shouted at him.

"No, you're not," he said simply. He continued to strap a knife to his leg. He went to the closet and pulled on his army coat.

"Yes I am."

"I said no."

She ran to him, jumping on his back. She threw an arm around his neck, choking him. He had to fall on the bed, fall hard on top of her, listen to the air between her lovely shoulders gasp out before he could pull her arm away. He kissed her. She was sobbing.

"Come on, let's go," he said finally.

Cecilia let him drag her to the bench where he picked up a foot-long metal bar with a leather handle. She didn't ask; he'd already told her the knife was for dogs. He promised her he wouldn't use it.

She sat next to him on the ride over to Beto's grandmother's house. They had decided it would be much safer than the garage, and besides, as soon as Ray had Dolores, he would return here, to Dolores's house. Ray let her in and walked through the rooms quickly. She watched him drive off, then ran to the phone to call Father Reilly.

* * *

Later, when she and Ray would reminisce over the events, what she remembered most was how excited she had been when she heard the key in the door. "Ray's coming back for me," she whispered. She'd just hung up the phone, not more than ten minutes earlier. She raced across the living room floor on her toes just like in the ballet.

"Well, look who we have here, Zavelito," the man with the Sinatra hat said after she'd shouted "Ray!"

Zavelito was not wearing a suit like the other man. Zavelito was not small, and Zavelito did not have a nice hair cut.

"*Nohay problema*, eh Zavelito? *Cómo te dije? Es un regalo, una perla. Zavelito, echa la vieja a su cama. Nohay problema*, eh Zavalito?"

She couldn't remember if the big one had answered the little one, the little one with the pink shirt, the good suit, the hat, and a face so pitted she didn't notice his moustache.

Zavelito carried a bundle like a normal person carries a grocery bag of bread and toilet paper. Cecilia could see that it was an old woman. She recognized Dolores as the big man carried the old lady past her and up the stairs to the bedroom. Cecilia could never remember what happened next. Did she turn and run? Did they corner her in the kitchen? Didn't she kick and fight?

* * *

"There, she's fine. Sleeping like a little grey-haired baby."

"Honey baby," Beto said, rubbing Dolores' head and kissing her forehead. "How come she's not waking up?" he asked Tina. He was worried. Dolores could never sleep through this much noise.

"They gave her a sedative. She's fine. She's breathing. She probably hasn't slept this well in twenty years." Tina patted his back. "Would you put that thing away, Beto? You're going to hurt yourself."

Beto realized he was waving the pistol around. "As soon as I check out the house," he answered.

"That's my man," she called out after him.

He walked into the kitchen first and waited. It always annoyed him how long it took for the fluorescent lights to come on. They flickered enough to drive him crazy. In the flicker he saw the BB gun in the corner, the fountain beyond the breakfast nook windows, the two *peons* guarding the electrical box, and the walker laying on its side. When the lights came on for good, he reached down and picked the walker up. He couldn't remember leaving it this way, but then he decided that it was nothing. Besides, Tina was yelling at him to hurry.

"I'll drive," he said as they walked down the long steps to the street.

"Have it your way. You're the boss," Tina answered sarcastically.

When they were on Glendale Boulevard he looked at his watch. "It's almost four."

"Perfect timing," she responded. Tina seemed calm, Beto thought. Why not? She had nothing to worry about from here on in unless he didn't go to the Lake. He could drive to the police station. He could drive away. He was in the clear with Dolores back at home, wasn't he? And besides, he didn't know what the fuck he was going to do at the Lake. If he drove away with Tina now, would she stay with him? He took the back streets behind the Pioneer market, past the Burrito King. He wasn't hungry, but he couldn't think. He pulled in at the Burrito King.

"What're you doing?" She looked at him as if he were crazy.

"I got to make a call."

He was three feet away, his back turned, when she told him, "Forget it, Beto. He's already there by this time. Ray's meeting us at the Lake. I know he has the girl."

Beto stopped walking. He smelled the *tomatillos* and *cilantro*, *chile verde* and grease, then he entered the phone booth. He dialed and listened to the phone ring. He knew she was right. She was always right and sure of herself. He replaced the phone and thought about Ray and Cecilia. He thought about Tina's brother and Tina, the old man and Dolores. He remembered how he couldn't see the smoke no matter how much he searched. The smoke had just vanished. Maybe the old man is still alive, he told himself, touching the bucking horse on the buckle, rubbing his finger across the raised profile; then he returned to the pickup and headed across Sunset for the Lake.

* * *

Ray walked across the bridge slowly, stopping in the middle to check his watch. Odd that he had never noticed it before, how quiet it was on the island; yet on the bridge he could hear the cars on the Boulevard, TV's around the lake, and even a guy talking to his girl in some apartment.

He squatted at the entrance to the reed cave. How long had it been since they could crawl through? Their old cave. He relaxed, one leg more bent than the other. He opened the can of cat food and placed it carefully in the cave. Then they came, three of them. They didn't purr, and he didn't try to touch them. He dug a hand into the wide pocket of his army jacket and pulled out a thin joint. He lit it, but he didn't drag deep. He stared at the glowing end. The island seemed larger, as if the lake was low. He worried about the ducks and the fish and the kids who came here with their daddies to rent boats and paddle around the lake. He smelled the marijuana, the glow at the end circling, dying out until he blew on it. Am I an old *vato*?, he asked himself. He pushed his fingers through his thick brush of black hair back to the neck until he reached the chain. He followed the chain around until he found her, warm and flat. She soothed his fingers even though she was almost rubbed smooth.

She would never leave him, not her, his *Virgen de Guadalupe.* But would she protect him? He muttered to himself as he looked at the cats finishing up, "they won't talk to me," and stood up. He wished that Cecilia were here to calm him, and then he touched the medallion again and bent over to retrieve the can. He looked out over the lake in the direction of the boathouse. He could see the boathouse and the small rental boats bumping under the over-hang, clearly in the lights. He saw the Mercedes pull up, and another car, an American car. Reinforcements, he thought. He watched for the doors to swing open, waited for men with uzis and shotguns, but it was quiet, and then he heard the truck. "Good for you, brother," he said quietly, walking quickly to the bridge, stopping only to throw the cold joint into the water.

* * *

Cecilia would remember the trip over, that the windows were smoked, and that she had been sitting between the big one and the little one. They were quiet until they parked under the light in front of the boathouse at the Lake. She didn't remember hearing the crumpled pickup park in the dark under the trees.

* * *

"What am I going to do, Tina? You got all the answers. What?"
"Stay close to me. Hold my arm, and whatever you do, don't show that gun. All they want is the girl. You understand?"
Beto nodded his head. He was sweating, and he had a hard time opening the door. They got out together, but she had to put her arm in his hand.

* * *

"Let's walk over to the lighthouse, hey kids?" the little man with a hat spoke at them. "Zavelito," he called, and Beto saw the heavy for the first time. Seeing him didn't make Beto feel any better, even with the pistol against his back.
"Juanita," the little man called out. "*Estás bien? Estás bien calma?*"
"I'm fine, Richard," Tina answered as they walked the fifty feet to the boathouse under palm and elm trees, moving in and out of the shadows.

"Is that the *padrino*?" Beto croaked.

"You got it, baby," Tina answered.

They stood facing each other about ten feet apart. The little man looked even smaller with his legs spread, but it didn't help make Beto feel any better, not with him rocking back and forth as if he had music in his hat and that confident smile pasted on his face, and his bag boy behind him. Beto felt sure that he could take them, that it would be just like the movies; he would drop on one knee and fire, roll over behind the palm tree to his left, and fire again. It would be that easy, and then Ray spoke up.

"Ray," Beto shouted, and Tina called out too. The *marielitos* turned to face Ray. The door of the American car opened and they all turned to see Father Reilly run down the hill at them screaming, "don't shoot!" Where'd he come from, Beto thought, and then he heard Cecilia shout out, "Ray!" and the night filled up with more than voices. He couldn't move. He heard the swish and the thunk of the metal bar, an automatic opened up from under Zavelito's coat and another from the Mercedes. He saw Cecilia running towards them, the big man pointing his gun at her, and the flying figure he knew could only be Ray knocking him over. There was the sound of sirens and moaning, and for the first time he wished that he could hear the cicadas. Tina was dragging him to the truck. She was right, he thought, as he allowed himself to be pulled away, even though he knew he shouldn't leave. He saw the man called Zavelito with a knife sticking out of his back, and Cecilia lying over the shadow in the grass that was Ray, and still he left. He drove like Tina, fast but correctly, up an alley, a half second before the first of the police arrived. He wondered if Kirk Gibson had helped out the team and who was playing at Club Candilejas. He hoped the good Doctor would remain in his office over the blind man's newsstand until Dolores was better. He prayed that Ray could help him fix his pickup. He'd call the Buchanans and tell them about the old man, but he wouldn't tell them about the smoke. He wouldn't tell anyone about smoke from a fire, or owls, or catching trout with your bare hands, unless he told Dolores, because the old man had been in love with her. But she'd have to wait before he told her about the old man. Dolores might have to wait a while since he was driving wherever Tina wanted to go.

"Stop here," Tina said, in the middle of the First Street Bridge. "This is as far as you go," she told him, and pushed him out the door.

He thought she was going to leave him there in the middle of the bridge and drive over to the East L.A. side, leave him in the middle so he would have to walk back towards Union Station and Olvera Street. But she didn't. She got out and started walking rapidly. She was walking into East L.A.

"Tina?" he called. "Don't leave me."

"Goodbye, Beto," she said, over her shoulder.

"Please don't leave me. I'll change," he yelled, running after her.

Tina stopped and looked at him full in the face. He stopped and looked back at his side of the city. She didn't say anything. She just stood there and looked at him until he couldn't think any more.

"Take this. I want you to have it," he said.

She looked at the rosary, swinging from his outstretched hand, pink like the fingernails of a young girl.

"No. It's not mine," she said.